D0065243

BLOOD MOON

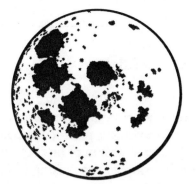

BLOOD MOON

HAL LINDSEY

WESTERN FRONT PUBLISHING
PALOS VERDES, CALIFORNIA

Library of Congress Cataloging-in-Publication Data

Lindsey, Hal, 1929–

ISBN 1-888848-07-3

Library of Congress Catalog Card Number:
96-060757

Western Front, Ltd.
416 Paseo del Mar
Palos Verdes, CA 90274

Cover design: Karen Ryan, Palos Verdes, CA
Book design and production: Publication Services, Redlands, CA
Printing: Banta Publishing, Menasha, WI
Manufactured in the United States of America

"And I will show wonders
   in the heavens and in the earth:
   blood and fire and pillars of smoke.
The sun shall be turned into darkness,
   and the moon into blood,
   before the coming of the great
   and awesome day of the Lord."
                              —JOEL 2:30-31 (NKJV)

Contents

Introduction

For more than a quarter of a century now, I have been writing books about the sad state of the human race, growing geo-political stratification, the degradation of planet Earth and what the Hebrew prophets have to say about the perilous times in which we live. All of my books are essentially chronicles of our times that have struck a chord with people all over the world and been translated into dozens of languages. While the titles and themes have all been different, my works have had one thing in common—they were all non-fiction.

So you might ask, "Hal, why have you now decided to venture into the medium of fiction? Why have you chosen to write a novel about what the Bible refers to as 'the last days' rather than another non-fiction book?"

It's a good question. First of all, let me say that my non-fiction writing days are not over. I have not given up that principal mission. I intend to write more books about current events and their relationship to the prophetic scenario. There is still a great deal of unexplored, uncharted territory, and I fully intend to continue to break new ground in the non-fiction realm for as long as the Lord allows.

What I have tried to do in my previous books is simply to illustrate how major prophetic events are being ful-filled before our very eyes. We see them unfolding on the front pages of our daily newspapers. We see them unfold-ing on the nightly news. And, occasionally, we see evi-dence of them unfolding more quietly in secret meetings in the world's major power centers. I have shied away, therefore, from date-setting and overly dogmatic analysis. Rather, I have drawn attention to events and trends that might be obscured by the secular media, and I have placed them in the context of prophetic progression.

Though I would have it no other way, there are short-comings to this approach. Despite the preponderance of evidence, some people remain skeptical that we are indeed living in the last days. They find it difficult to see the sensational predictions of the Bible being fulfilled in our rational modern world.

And what are some of those events?

- Somehow, the entire world will be seduced, terrified or shocked into accepting a global political leader and a worldwide religious system, initially ruled from Rome and later from Jerusalem.
- This charismatic world leader will hold the popula-tion spellbound, performing "miracles." He himself is raised from the dead, and he apparently solves most of the globe's most serious problems.
- Jerusalem will become the center of the world's

attention and a stumbling block for many nations.

- The Temple in Jerusalem will be rebuilt and the ancient sacrifice rituals of the Jews will be reinstituted.
- Millions of people will suddenly disappear from the face of the earth without explanation.
- A military alliance between Russia and several other nations now under the influence of Islam will result in a massive—but unsuccessful—invasion of Israel.
- Another invasion of the Middle East by a coalition of Asian nations—this one even bigger than the Russian-Muslim alliance—will also fail to win the big prize, Jerusalem.
- More than half the world's population will be killed through war, famine, disease and natural disasters.
- Believers will face unprecedented persecution.

No matter how great one's imagination may be, it's not surprising that there would be doubters. This is, after all, a lot to swallow—especially for those who are unfamiliar with the amazing, one hundred percent accuracy of Bible prophecy in history. So the purpose of a prophetic novel is to offer just one hypothetical scenario. That's my intent with *Blood Moon.*

Please don't misunderstand my intention. I am not suggesting this is the only way that such events can take place. Nor are the dates picked to indicate what I believe will be the timing of future prophecy. On the contrary, no one can predict with any accuracy exactly how the prophetic scenario will be fulfilled in minute detail. I seek only to offer one hypothetical approach.

This is not, however, simply a prophetic novel. It is also partly a historical novel. In some cases, I have taken facts that are known from biblical and extra-biblical sources and embellished them with imaginary conversations or dialogue based on fragmentary historical records. All of this was done to offer context to the prophetic events. They say that history repeats itself. If that is true—and I believe it is—then it is not far-fetched to believe that documented events of the past might have some correlation to the future. In fact, it would be far-fetched to believe otherwise.

In my non-fiction works, I have described how some of these "macro-events" might take place in our lifetime. But in the genre of fiction, I am able to tell the story through a series of "micro-events"—little stories about people struggling for survival and salvation through the most turbulent and tumultuous period in human history. The big story, then, is told through the eyes of these fictional characters.

Even in the context of a full-blown novel such as *Blood Moon*, it is difficult to include all of the relevant information one would like. I found myself occasionally disappointed at my inability to raise all of the important and persuasive data and still maintain a readable and fast-paced work of fiction. In fact, there is a lot more going on in our world today that would provide a backdrop to this novel if only it could be woven into the fabric in an unobtrusive and economical manner.

Rather than bite off more than I could chew (and more than readers could be expected to digest), I decided not to attempt to write a novel that would include all of the important prophetic events taking place in our world today. Instead, I chose to focus only on the major points.

Of course, there's much, much more going on every day that convinces me and millions of others around the world that we are on the brink of great upheaval and change in the world. The most important sign of all has been the return of the Jew to the land of Israel after thousands of years of dispersal. As people all over the world turn to astrologers, computer programs, witchcraft and Ouija boards for knowledge of the future, I believe this generation is overlooking the most authentic voice of all—the voice of the Hebrew prophets. They predicted long ago that certain events and trends would develop as man neared the end of history as we know it. Regional alliances would emerge. We would see signs in the heavens and in the earth.

I also wanted to use this book to show that not everything of significance that occurs in our world happens in the visible, natural realm. You will notice in *Blood Moon* that the action takes place both on earth and in heaven.

There is a war going on around us. It is a spiritual war, and the battlefields are both on earth and in heaven. Too many of us are simply not aware of this unseen conflict of which we are all a part. C.S. Lewis once wrote: "There are two equal and opposite errors into which our race can fall about the devils. One is to disbelieve in their existence. The other is to believe, and to feel an excessive and unhealthy interest in them. They themselves are equally pleased by both errors, and hail a materialist or magician with the same delight."

Lucifer is also called by the scriptures the Devil and Satan, the ruler of this world system and the prince of the power of the atmosphere. He is the most powerful creature God ever made. He is the real source, the constant source, of the persecutions of Christians that is now spreading around the world. God is restraining him now. But the Bible indicates there will come a time when that restraint on his power is removed. Then all hell will break loose on planet Earth.

He will make a creature of his own. His masterpiece is sometimes called the Antichrist. And the stage is virtually set for his appearance at any moment.

Another goal of the Devil is *to bring the world to accept supernaturalism* through the occult and false religions. Satan loves religion as long as it takes one away from the Truth about God. Though he also uses atheistic and humanistic philosophies to his advantage, Satan's ultimate goal is to bring about a religious world that believes in the supernatural so that it will accept and worship him through his global ruler, the Antichrist, whom he will personally indwell.

If we are indeed living in the last days of God's prophetic program of history, which I am convinced we are, then we must expect and prepare for a growing and accelerating scenario of catastrophic events. Do not be afraid of these times. Some of the things you read in this novel may alarm you. But, as I have often said, I would rather be alive right now than at any time in history, even if I could make the choice. We are the generation that is going to hear the Son of God shout, "Come up here!" Then, without experiencing death, we will have eternal, glorified bodies exactly like His.

I want this book to be a blessing for all who read it. I hope it opens your eyes to the amazing truth of biblical prophecy and how it is being fulfilled all around us.

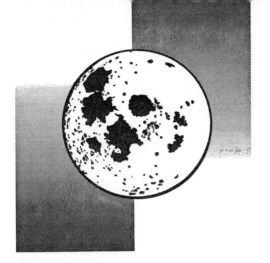

CHAPTER 1

Isaac and Ishmael: The Everlasting Enmity

The scorching desert sun had not yet completely set, but the man was already in a deep sleep.

Even though he was now 85 years old, Abram was a remarkable specimen of a man. He had just enough silver mixed in with his curly raven black hair to give him a distinguished appearance and hint of his hard won wisdom. His handsome, finely chiseled face appeared troubled as he slept. His muscular body twitched as if he were having a disturbing dream.

His recent physical exploits would have been an amazing accomplishment for a conditioned warrior in his twenties. Only days earlier, he and 318 of his clansmen, whom he had carefully trained as fighters, returned from routing an invading army of several hundred thousand soldiers. The powerful king of Elam (later known as Persia) had assembled the combined might of the kings of Goiim, Shinar (Babylon) and Ellasar. They invaded the wealthy cities of the then lush Jordan valley—including the beautiful, but notoriously decadent, twin cities of Sodom and Gomorrah.

This northern confederacy made only one big mistake. They took captive, along with everything of value, a man named Lot and his family. Lot just happened to be Abram's nephew.

Abram cared nothing about the Jordan valley cities or their wealth. But he was very touchy about someone harming a member of his family.

In the mission to rescue his nephew Lot, Abram made military history. By the use of courage and sheer audacity, in the execution of near perfect hit-and-run night attacks, he caused the opposing armies to believe there were thousands of soldiers coming after them. They finally panicked, forsook military discipline, broke ranks and ran for their lives. They left behind all their loot, including Lot and family.

When Abram returned to the Jordan valley with all the recovered loot and captured people, he totally shocked the local rulers. He refused to take any of the booty for himself. Instead, he attributed his victory to a strange Deity whom they didn't know. He called Him, "the Most High God, Creator of the heavens and earth."

Though the locals thought Abram was strange, he became a legend of heroic proportions. They may not have liked him, but they left him alone.

Abram was indeed a physical phenomenon. In the course of this war, he raced hundreds of miles on horseback. He led daring attacks that involved exhausting and furious hand-to-hand combat. His military tactics were nothing short of brilliant.

The natives of his adopted country came to believe that there just might be some truth to his constant claim that it was this supreme God he worshipped that strengthened and inspired him.

In spite of all this, Abram occasionally got depressed. Though he was still remarkably strong, he knew he was getting older. It took him longer to recover from the bruises, the saddle-soreness and the wounds of battle than when he was a young man. But Abram worried about his age for one basic reason—he wanted to be able to produce a son. More than anything else, he wanted to sire the son his God promised to give him.

His wife, Sarai, who was strikingly beautiful despite her age, understood his concern. She was just grateful her husband was home—safe and sound in their luxurious tent, attended by servants, guarded by loyal watchmen and well-stocked with food, gold and garments that would be the envy of any king in the world. Abram and Sarai were truly blessed. They were people of great faith who prayed to the creator of the universe with the same confidence a son or daughter would have talking to a loving father.

But despite all their good fortune, something was bothering Abram. It was a fitful sleep he was experiencing this early summer evening as a breeze blew the remnants of the daytime heat from his well-ventilated home.

Was it a dream or a vision he was having? All he knew for sure was he was getting another direct communication. God was talking—and Abram was giving his undivided attention. Then suddenly, God spoke unmistakably to him:

> *"Know of a surety that your descendants will be sojourners in a land that is not theirs, and will be slaves there, and they will be oppressed for four hundred years; but I will bring judgment on the nation which they serve, and afterward they will come out with great possessions. As for yourself, you shall go to your fathers in peace; you shall be buried in a good old age. And they shall come back here in the fourth generation; for the iniquity of the Amorites is not yet complete."*

What did it all mean? Abram awoke and pondered this strange message in the darkness of his tent. He went out to look at the stars, and instead he fell in to a trance-like state. He saw animals sacrificed, cut in two—each half laid opposite each other—creating a path between them. In the darkness, a smoking fire pot and a flaming torch passed slowly between the severed parts of the animals. He was familiar with this ceremony. In the culture of that time, this was the most solemn way for two people to make an unconditional covenant with each other. The two parties would join hands and walk between the sacrifices while repeating the particulars of the covenant. They would take an oath they would be cut in pieces—just as these animals—if they broke the covenant.

As the fire pot and flaming torch passed through, Abram heard the voice of God make a covenant with him and his descendants,

> *"To your descendants I give this land, from the river of Egypt to the great river, the river Euphrates, the land of the Kenites, the Kenizites, the Kadmonites, the Hittites, the Perizzites, the Rephraim, the Amorites, the Canaanites, the Girgashites and the Jebusites."*

As Abram thought about this vision, he suddenly realized a shocking thing. Only God passed between the sacrificed animals, and He alone made the covenant with him. Its fulfillment, therefore, depended only on God, not Abram or his descendants.

In spite of God's condescension to make this strongest possible pledge, the overwhelming odds caused his faith to stagger. He laughed to himself: "My descendants—hah! I have no children and I am 85 years old. My wife is 75. God must be joking. How am I to father a great nation when I can't even produce one son or daughter?"

But this was not some kind of an isolated revelation Abram had experienced—and he knew it. He knew this God had told him the same things several times before. As incredible as it seemed, the message was always the same: *"Look toward the heaven, and number the stars, if you are able to number them,"* Abram was commanded one clear summer night when the sky was bright with stars that seemed to be as numerous as the sands of the vast desert. *"So shall your descendants be,"* he was told.

Abram had learned a long time ago not to dismiss such

communications—no matter how self-serving they seemed to be and no matter how they mimicked the desires of his own heart. He shared what he had seen and heard with Sarai. He was rather embarrassed as he relayed every detail. He told her he didn't understand how the prophecy would be fulfilled. It was humanly impossible.

Sarai felt ashamed that she had not been able to birth a son for her husband—this loving, courageous and faithful man. She would do anything for him, but how could she be expected to bear a child at her age? If it had been impossible when she was young, how could it happen after menopause? The thought of Abram dying without leaving a blood heir had reduced her to tears more than once.

If Abram had died at this moment, Sarai thought, Eliezer, his steward from Damascus, would inherit all her husband had won in battle and accumulated through considerable enterprise. It was a fortune of which any man would be proud. Eliezer was a loyal subject whom Abram and Sarai treated like a son, but the thought of Abram's legacy being turned over to a former slave with no blood lineage to either of them made Sarai shudder.

For months she meditated sadly on the dilemma. "There must be a way," she thought. "Perhaps God is trying to tell me something through these visions Abram is having. Maybe there is something I am supposed to do to help fulfill God's promise."

Just then, one of Sarai's maidservants—Hagar, an Egyptian—walked into her mistress' chambers. She bore fresh fruit—tantalizing grapes, ripe bananas and bright red pomegranates from the Valley of Megiddo. Hagar's long curly black hair framed the silver tray on which she carried the food. How young and beautiful she is, thought Sarai. Indeed, she was. Hagar may have been a servant, but she had the appearance, bearing and grace of royalty—large dark, expressive eyes, olive skin and a perfectly proportioned, toned figure. She was discreet, but she had the legendary alluring ways of the women in Pharoah's royal court. Someone less beautiful than Sarai would have been extremely threatened by her.

"If only I had her youth and health," Sarai mused, "I could fulfill God's promise to Abram and make my husband's life complete."

"My lady," Hagar said softly, interrupting Sarai's daydream, "would you like some fruit?"

It did look delicious, Sarai thought. But her mind was elsewhere—not on food.

"No, thank you, Hagar. Perhaps you could take some to Abram."

As Hagar turned to leave, a thought came to Sarai. Hagar! Maybe God's will could be fulfilled through her. If I cannot serve as the vessel for Abram's son to be born, why not allow Hagar to be the surrogate? After all, it's the common custom of this culture we live in. At least Abram would have a true flesh-and-blood heir.

Sarai wrestled with the idea for days and sleepless nights. She told no one, at first. But finally, she could contain herself no longer.

"I may be unable to bear children," she thought, "but my husband is still capable of planting the seed that will bring him a son. I must give him this opportunity before it is too late."

That evening, as Abram and Sarai shared dinner together, she told him about her idea.

"The Lord has prevented me from bearing children," she said. "But there is no reason that I should deny you your rightful heir, my husband. Hagar is a strong, youthful and attractive woman. Maybe I can obtain children by her."

"What are you saying?" Abram asked.

"I am telling you to sleep with my maid. Impregnate her. And I will care for and raise her children as if they were our own."

Abram was shocked. He was a faithful husband and had never considered such a notion before. Although it was the common custom of the day in such a situation, he didn't think his God would approve. But, he had to admit, he couldn't see how God's promise of a son could possibly be fulfilled through Sarai. Maybe, he thought, God is speaking to Sarai and making a special exception. Perhaps this is part of his plan.

"I will consider your idea," Abram told Sarai. "But not this evening. Let us retire together now with no more talk." Abram and Sarai held each other tenderly like newlyweds through the night. Little did he realize it was the last night before their lives would be forever changed.

The next day, Abram decided to take Hagar as a wife. Not long after, the young woman conceived. When she realized she was pregnant, Hagar's attitude toward her mistress quickly changed. The formerly submissive maidservant now looked at Sarai with contempt. This did not sit well with Sarai. She realized she had made a mistake. No good could come of this bad decision.

"It's your fault," Sarai told Abram. "I gave you my maid, and now, because she has conceived your child, she looks down upon me. May the Lord hold you responsible for this!"

"Calm down, woman," said Abram. "This was your idea, remember?" "But Hagar is still your maidservant. She is under your authority. You will always be my beloved wife. Discipline Hagar as you see fit."

It didn't take Sarai long to do just that. She called for Hagar and scolded her harshly. She threatened her. She made it clear she was no longer welcome in their home. Hagar, feeling abandoned by both her mistress and her husband, fled into the desert.

Hagar had no idea where she was going. She vaguely remembered her journey from Egypt to Canaan. She headed in what she thought was the general direction of her homeland. All she knew was that she must escape the torment of Sarai. Hagar had not asked for this judgment. She felt victimized by her experience.

"Why," she thought, "couldn't I just have a husband of my own—someone who would love me for who I am?" She never felt so rejected, alone and abused in her life.

Hagar always imagined herself marrying a young man, someone close to her own age. She had seen the way the young men and boys looked at her admiringly and longingly since she was 13 years old. She had been certain she would be able to find a good husband—someone she could love and someone who would provide well for her and their children. She never imagined marrying someone else's husband—especially a man nearly 65 years her senior.

Now, pregnant, distraught and tired, she plodded on through the wilderness in search of sanctuary from her fate. She found a caravan trail which she hoped would lead her to Egypt. But she saw no one along the way. And she was fearful about this journey. What dangers would she face all alone out here in the wilderness? How cold would the nights be without proper shelter? What wild animals lurked about? Most of all, she was thirsty. In her haste to leave the domain of Abram and Sarai, she had packed very few provisions. She was unfamiliar with the surrounding terrain in the land of Canaan, and had no idea how scarce water was.

Finally, she found a small spring and refreshed herself. Later, as she rested by the brook, she caressed her growing abdomen and thought lovingly and anxiously about the child within. What would become of her baby? How could she provide for him or her? What kind of life could they as outcasts expect in Egypt? The questions distressed her, but she could hold up her head no longer. "I must get some sleep," she thought. The desert night was cold and windy, but Hagar's exhaustion was more powerful than her discomfort and fear of the night. The last image she remembered before closing her eyes and falling into unconsciousness was a blood-red full moon hovering just above the horizon.

When she awoke a few hours later, she was startled by

the presence of an imposing stranger before her. The sun had not yet risen, but light surrounded this figure. She had heard her masters in Canaan speak of angels, and she remembered discussion of them as a child back in Egypt. Now she was certain she was seeing one for the first time.

"Hagar, where have you come from and where are you going?" the figure demanded firmly but gently.

"I am fleeing from my mistress, Sarai," she explained, all the while suspecting this being knew far more than she was telling.

Then the angel told Hagar:

> *"Return to your mistress, apologize and submit to her," "You have an important role to play in great events you cannot begin to understand. But life will not be without rewards for you and your son. That's right, the child you carry is a son. God will greatly multiply your descendants—so much so that they cannot even be counted. The son you carry shall be called Ishmael* [God hears], *for God understands your troubles."*

Hagar felt a profound sense of relief to know that she was not alone—that God Himself was watching out for her and protecting her. The angel's words were so comforting that she even overlooked his somewhat troubling description of what her son would be like.

> *"He shall be a wild ass of a man,"* he said, *"his hand will be against every man and every man's hand against him; and he shall rule over all of his kinsmen, despite their opposition."*

Hagar was so thankful that God had provided a way

for her. She called out to the Lord in gratitude that He would care so much for a pregnant outcast servant girl like her.

"You are truly a God who sees me," she said in wonder. "Have I really seen God and remained alive after seeing Him?" she asked.

She had often heard Abram speak of his God, but now she had come to believe in Him for herself.

As soon as the sun rose, Hagar packed up her meager belongings and carefully retraced her steps on her way back to the home of Abram and Sarai. She was nervous about how she would be received, but confident it was the right thing to do because of her supernatural experience at the spring.

She saw Sarai first. Hagar approached her with her head bowed. She knelt before her mistress.

"Forgive me, my lady, for my haughty behavior," she begged. "I have returned to ask you for a second chance. I plead with you, for the sake of my son—Abram's son. Allow us to live in peace and harmony in the safety of Abram's tents."

"It will be as you say," agreed Sarai. "But I warn you, I will not tolerate any more insolence or arrogance in my household. You may stay. And Abram will have his son."

A few months later, Ishmael was born. He was a beautiful child—very strong, confident and energetic. In no time, he had the run of Abram's grand estate. He learned to bark orders at servants and run roughshod over other children his age. As Abram's only child, Ishmael was spoiled. There was nothing too good for him. By the time he was 12 years old, Ishmael had already concluded the world was at his feet.

But Ishmael was a little worried about his aging father. After a long period of silence, he was having visions—he said God was talking to him again. Is this what happens to you when you get old? Ishmael wondered. He loved his father dearly, but Abram appeared troubled lately. Was it the dreams again? For Ishmael, there was good cause for concern.

When Abram was 99 years old, the Lord appeared to him with a startling new revelation. Abram fell on his face when he heard God's commanding voice.

> *"I am God Almighty; walk before me and be mature. I will confirm my covenant between me and you and greatly increase your numbers. As for Me, this is my covenant with you. You shall be the father of a multitude of nations. No longer shall your name be Abram* [exalted father], *but your name shall be Abraham* [father of many nations]. *I will make you exceedingly fruitful; and I will make nations of you, and kings shall come forth from you. And I will establish my covenant between me and you and your descendants after you throughout their generations for an everlasting covenant, to be God to you and to your descendants after you. And I will give to you, and to your descendants after you, the land of your sojournings, all the land of Canaan, for an everlasting possession; and I will be their God."*

God continued to give Abraham instructions as to how he and his descendants should live and set themselves apart from the world. He also had another surprise for Abraham.

> *"As for Sarai your wife, you shall not call her name Sarai, but Sarah shall be her name. I will bless her, and moreover I will give you a son by her; I will bless her, and she shall be a mother of nations; kings of people shall come from her."*

Abraham, who earlier had fallen on his face in respect and reverence for God, now fell on his face in laughter. Abraham replied to God,

"Shall a child be born to a man who is 100 years old? Shall Sarah, who is 90 years old, bear a child?"

Abraham just couldn't understand how all this could happen. He truly loved his son Ishmael and wanted only the best for him. That's where his inheritance should go, thought Abraham.

"If only Ishmael might stand before You and receive your blessings, Lord," Abraham pleaded. But the Lord responded:

> *"No, but Sarah your wife shall bear you a son, and you shall call his name Isaac. I will establish my covenant with him as an everlasting covenant for his descendants after him. As for Ishmael, I have heard you; behold, I will bless him and make him fruitful and multiply him exceedingly; he shall be the father of 12 princes. But I will establish my covenant with Isaac, whom Sarah shall bear to you at this season next year."*

Abraham had learned to take these messages seriously. But if he still required confirmation, it came a few days later when three men visited him. Abraham was sitting at the door of his tent by the oaks of Mamre when they appeared. Abraham bowed until his head nearly touched the earth, for he knew these men were a manifestation of God Himself.

"Please, my Lord, make yourselves comfortable here in the shade of my oak trees," begged Abraham. "I will prepare some food for you and draw some water so you may refresh yourselves after your journey."

"Do as you suggest," said one of the three visitors dressed in robes of the finest linen. They appeared very serious. Whatever their mission was, it seemed to heavily burden them.

When they had all sat down to enjoy their meal, one of the men asked, "Where is Sarah your wife?"

"She is in the tent behind us," Abraham replied, knowing that his wife was straining to hear their conversation.

"I will be back in the spring, and Sarah your wife shall have a son," said the visitor.

"Sarah laughed quietly and wondered to herself, "After I have grown old, and my husband is old, shall I now have pleasure?"

"Why did Sarah laugh and say, 'Shall I indeed bear a child now that I am old?'" the man asked Abraham. "Is anything too difficult for the Lord? Just as I said, I will return to you next spring and Sarah will have a son.'"

Out of fear, Sarah cried out: "I did not laugh!"

"No, but you *did* laugh," the stranger corrected. Sarah was ashamed and lowered her head. He said, "because you did not believe my promise and laughed, you shall name your son, Isaac, which means, 'laughter'."

A year later, Sarah was laughing for a different reason—joy. At the age of 90, she did indeed give birth to a son, whom Abraham called Isaac, as he was instructed by the Lord. As promised, the three heavenly men returned, this time well-rested, upbeat and less preoccupied. It was a joyous time to be around the tents of Abraham.

"God has made laughter for me; everyone who hears will laugh over me," Sarah said. "Who would have said to Abraham that Sarah would suckle children? Yet I have borne him a son in his old age."

Isaac grew and was weaned from his mother's breast. On that day, Abraham held a great feast to celebrate. But all was not happiness and contentment in the tents of Abraham that day. Sarah caught Ishmael mocking her son Isaac. He was very jealous of this new half-brother. After all, he was the first-born. The rights of inheritance should be his. He became increasingly resentful and angry toward Isaac. Sarah saw in this a preview of the trouble to come. It was also a reminder of the hurtful mistake she had made by bringing Abraham and Hagar together.

"Cast out this slave woman with her son," Sarah told Abraham. "For the son of this slave woman shall not be heir with my son Isaac."

This suggestion made Abraham very sad. He truly loved Ishmael—sometimes even more than Isaac. He took his dilemma to the Lord in prayer. And God told him:

> *"Be not displeased because of the lad and because of your slave woman. Whatever Sarah says to you, do as she tells you, for only through Isaac shall*

*your descendants be named. But I will make a
nation of the son of the slave woman also, because
he is your offspring."*

Early the next morning, Abraham arose and packed
some supplies for Hagar and Ishmael before tearfully sending them away. The pair wandered in the wilderness until
their provisions and water were depleted. Believing the
end was near for both of them, Hagar hid Ishmael beneath
a bush and walked a good distance away.

"I don't want to see my child die," she thought. "Lord,"
she prayed, "why have you forsaken me and my son? You
promised if I returned to Abraham and Sarah and submit-
ted to them that you would make my son the father of a
great nation. Now we lie in the wilderness dying of thirst.
Was I imagining I heard your voice 13 years ago at the
brook? Or was that really you?"

Hagar began to weep. She heard her son, in the distance, sobbing, too. Just then, an angel called out to her.

"What troubles you, Hagar?" asked the voice. "Don't be
afraid. For God has heard the voice of your son. Stand up,
lift up your son and hold him fast with your hand; for I
will, indeed, make him a great nation."

When she opened her eyes, Hagar saw a well of water
where none had been before. She drank and gave Ishmael
some. As promised, mother and son prospered in the
wilderness of Paran in the Sinai. Ishmael became an
expert with the bow. He could hit a target from such a distance, his prey or enemies would not even be aware of his
presence. Later he took a wife from his mother's homeland of Egypt. Fulfilling God's promise, Ishmael lived to

the age of 137. He fathered 12 princes: Nebaioth, Kedar, Abdeel, Mibsam, Mishma, Dumah, Massa, Hadad, Tema, Jetur, Naphish and Kedemah. Ishmael's sons populated and ruled over lands stretching from Egypt to Babylon, thus he is considered the father of all the desert peoples of the Middle East. Their main center became known as the Arabian peninsula.

Isaac, meanwhile, fathered twins—Jacob and Esau. Isaac's lineage included such great men of the Bible as Joseph, Moses, Joshua, Gideon and David—all men of God who were able to claim Abraham's God-given Covenant, including the title deed to the relatively tiny land of Israel.

But Isaac and Ishmael never reconciled their differences. They never settled the blood feud that began in the tents of their father Abraham. Thus, the resentment between the descendants of Isaac and the descendants of Ishmael has carried down through the ages. Esau's descendants also joined with Ishmael's in this deadly feud for the past 40 centuries. Ishmael's people hate Isaac's people. Isaac's people distrust Ishmael's people. No ethnic conflict in the world can compare with this one in terms of duration and intensity of animosity.

◑

"Bull's-eye!" shouted Captain Isaac Barak, the young Israeli Defense Force (IDF) commando assigned to the top-secret testing facility at Palmahim.

"Mazeltov!" called out one of 35 rocket scientists and researchers in the underground base as they watched a simulation of an incoming warhead being shot down by the Jewish state's experimental new Arrow-5 anti-ballistic missile.

Applause filled the room. Every face wore a smile. This was a day of celebration. The Arrow project had begun back in the early 1990s. Now, in 2007, many of those involved in the program from the beginning were finally seeing their hard work pay off in concrete terms.

The test was a complete success. For the first time, Israelis had confidence they could shoot down incoming ballistic missiles fired from anywhere else in the Middle East. It wasn't so much the Arab or Iranian governments that caused concern for Israeli officials and citizens. Israel now had working peace agreements with every one of its immediate neighbors and a tri-lateral treaty with the United Nations and European Union that provided Israel special security arrangements. But it was the well-funded, well-armed Islamic fanatics sponsored by Iran who were now known to possess ballistic missile technology and have access to and possibly already have powerful thermonuclear warheads. This was the principal reason why this small, dedicated military group battled much opposition in order to maintain some vestige of the defense vigilance for which Israel in the past had become famous.

"Congratulations, Ariel," Jean-Claude DuMonde, U.N.-EU liaison to the anti-missile project, declared to the director-general of the Arrow mission. "This is a very sophisticated—though unneeded—system. I don't know why you folks insist on pursuing these plans, but you do deserve praise for making this system work where everyone else failed."

"Thank you, J.C.," said General Oved. "I appreciate your faint praise. I know your boss has been skeptical about this effort. But my interest, above all, is the defense of Israel. I don't care a whit about diplomacy. I care about the survival of the Jews. And, without offense to your boss, I think the Arrow 5 is the best hope we have for the long-term future. I certainly feel it's better than all these peace treaties. History teaches us that when push comes to shove, no one comes the aid of the Jews. Besides, the terrorists have warned that they will explode a nuclear device in the major cities of any nation that comes to the aid of Israel for any reason.

"Oh, Ariel," said DuMonde patronizingly. "Have a little faith in humankind. This is the 21st century. Wars and nationalism are a thing of the past. Israel's security is linked inextricably to the security of the rest of the world. But enough of that. I must get back to Jerusalem to make my report on your most impressive test today."

"O.K., J.C.," said Gen. Oved. "Drive safely, and make sure you spell my name right in the report to your boss."

DuMonde's "boss" was Juan Montez, secretary of international security for EU President and U.N. Secretary-General Gianfranco Carlo.

Carlo had recently become the most powerful man on earth. Carlo was born in Fiesole, a beautiful little town in the mountains of the northeastern suburbs of Florence. His family claimed royal ancestry dating back to the mysterious Etruscans who predated the Roman Empire. They were also very wealthy and powerful bankers connected to the Vatican economic empire. As a result, they virtually operated independently of the chaotic Italian government and were more than once protected from government investigation by the Popes themselves.

Gianfranco grew up a devout Catholic and even studied for the priesthood before receiving what he believed was a supernatural vision which directed him to build a career in international politics. Many believed the vision certainly was supernatural because from the moment he entered the political arena of the EU, he rose through the ranks like a meteor.

He volunteered to lead a peace negotiating mission for the EU to the seemingly unresolvable ethnic conflict in the Balkans.

It was after his stunning diplomatic success in the Balkans that he first took control of the EU. His diplomatic triumph was achieved in a few weeks. This contrasted sharply with the U.N.'s record of an 11-year peacekeeping effort that only resulted in an escalation of the ethnic and religious warfare that almost engulfed all of Europe. Carlo's skill in that dangerous regional conflict, as well as his successful negotiations with Russia on joining the EU, gave him global acclaim.

Gianfranco Carlo's greatest negotiating triumph, however, was bringing together the Muslim nations (excepting Iran) and Israel into a peace agreement that for the first time seemed to be working.

It was then that Carlo achieved his greatest political triumph. He single-handedly accomplished a feat most observers thought was impossible just two years earlier— the creation of the first true world government and new world order.

While there had been significant moves toward global

government for decades—beginning with the Treaty of Rome, the formation of the U.N., the creation of the World Court and the World Trade Organization—few really believed all of these agencies could come together with one centralized mechanism of authority.

Carlo flashed onto the world scene at just the right time and proclaimed that he had a divine vision that showed him just how to do it. His Mediterranean good looks, supreme self-confidence and mesmerizing personal charm, coupled with a mystical spiritual quality, seemed to cast a spell on everyone he met. He also had unparalleled (almost mystical) expertise in economics and military affairs. All of these gifts made him the ultimate negotiator with uncanny insight into people. There seemed to be no limit to his continuing rise to global popularity. And, most important of all, he had a moral and spiritual quality coupled with a boundless compassion for the underprivileged of the world that caused the small and the great to trust him as a leader. Many from various parts of the world even said there was a *"Messianic quality about him."*

The EU-U.N. system still represented a rather loose confederation. But once the United States signed on as a member a few years earlier, there was no longer any question about the ultimate success of this new world order. Though the United States was no longer a major world power since the catastrophic collapse of their economy due to their multi-trillion dollar national debt, they were still considered an important support for the real super-power—the Rome-based EU. Now the EU's central government base in Rome had unprecedented control over the world's political, economic and military agenda.

Everyone in Israel was now blindly trusting in the treaty which guaranteed Israel's security that was made in Rome (EUR) between Gianfranco Carlo and President Ben David. But General Oved didn't completely trust this new central authority to offer reliable protection for the state of Israel—no matter how binding it seemed to be. Oved had seen too many treaties guaranteeing Israel's security broken when war clouds appeared. So he and a small corps of other Israeli military men continued to press the Jewish state to rely only on its own initiative, and perhaps God's, to defend themselves against nuclear attack. After all, he often argued, by the time help was authorized by the bureaucratic EU-U.N., Tel Aviv would already be under a radioactive mushroom cloud.

The Arrow project was a good example of such initiative. The EU-U.N. authorities would have preferred that Israel simply drop the plan and all further testing on it. They alone wanted to be the guarantor of Israel's peace. All nationalist efforts at self defense were discouraged, not only in Israel but throughout the world. But General Oved knew better than to trust some foreign power—any foreign power—with the fate of the Jewish people.

Oved had been through more than a few small fights in his life. At 73, the stocky but fit professional military man had commanded troops in three great Middle East wars—the Six-Day War of 1967, the 1973 Yom Kippur War and the invasion of Lebanon. He was ordered to stand by in 1991 when Iraq's Saddam Hussein attacked his nation with Scud missiles. He watched quietly—but angrily—as the Jewish state made one territorial concession after another to its sworn enemies in the name of peace. Few had his understanding of the Muslim religion. He knew that the serious followers of Islam believed it was their sacred duty to Allah to drive out the infidels who had, in their view, invaded the heart of the Muslim world and taken over their third holiest site. To them, the very existence of the state of Israel was a blasphemy that must be destroyed.

The general was no politician. He never considered standing up publicly in opposition to moves he knew were dangerous to his country. Instead, he did what he could, as a military leader, to keep his nation and his troops prepared for the dangers he felt were certain to come.

One of his proudest accomplishments, besides the Arrow project, was his tutelage of Captain Isaac Barak, a promising young officer. Barak was not only expert in computers and missile technology, but an expert in military strategy and tactics. At 29 years old, Barak had not participated in any of Israel's wars. Yet, because of the lessons he learned from Oved, he too had become skeptical about this idea of relying on foreigners for protection. If Oved was the political and military inspiration behind the Arrow project, Barak provided the cutting edge of the latest technology.

Captain Barak was a born leader with tireless drive. Though he was brilliant in science and computers, he kept himself in the magnificent physical condition he had acquired during his rugged commando and airborne training. His strikingly handsome face didn't seem to fit his deadly fighting skills.

While there were dozens of scientists and technical staff on hand at the test firing, there was one person in the bunker who could have replaced any and perhaps all of them—Captain Isaac Barak. He understood every job and every facet of the project. And that's why he served as General Oved's right-hand aide. Oved didn't know how to turn on a computer. But with Barak around, he didn't need to.

"Good work, today, captain," General Oved told Barak after most of the technicians from Israel Aircraft Industries (IAI) and IDF observers had left. "I'm very proud of you for the hard work you have put into this project."

"Thank you, General Oved," said Barak. "You know none of this would be possible without your vision and persistence. I'm proud to be of assistance to you and for the work we are doing on behalf of our people."

"Isaac," the general continued in an uncertain tone of voice, "there's something else I wanted to discuss with you."

"Yes, General, what is it?"

"Well, I'm not quite sure how to put this. This afternoon, just as the test was commencing, I heard something unusual on my headset. It didn't sound like the voice of anyone on the control crew. The voice uttered just two words."

"Yes sir," said Barak, "You mean, 'Fear not'?"

"You heard it, too, then?" asked the general.

"Yes, General. I'm not certain who was responsible. I

asked a number of the techies, and none of them even heard the message. I don't know if it's part of some practical joke or what, sir."

"I, too, asked a few others about the message," said the general. "None of them heard it. But to me it was as clear a voice as I have ever heard in my life.

"There certainly was something unique about that voice," said Barak. "It was alarming, yet, somehow comforting."

"Yes," said the general, "I know what you mean. Captain, keep me apprised of anything you learn about that voice and its message. It just doesn't seem to be the sort of message a saboteur would say.

Also, first thing tomorrow, I would like a report from you on the progress on MIRACL. It would be nice to have two effective weapons in our arsenal."

"Yes sir," said Barak. "I will have a report on your desk in the morning. And I will continue to investigative this voice thing."

Barak was excited to hear of the general's continuing interest in MIRACL, an acronym for Mid-Infrared Advanced Chemical Laser, another defensive weapon designed originally in the 1990s as a means to shoot down Katyusha rockets terrorists were routinely firing on the Galilee region from southern Lebanon. MIRACL proved so effective on those slow-moving rockets that U.S. and Israeli researchers perfected it on faster-moving and smaller artillery shells. More recently, the laser weapon became a true descendant of the original "Star Wars" project. It was launched when it was proven effective against ballistic missiles in preliminary tests.

"The general is leaving no stone unturned," thought Barak. "He's serious about defending Israel against missile attacks. I often wonder if he knows something I don't know."

"Ishmael, you have a call from Damascus," said Nayaf Haddad, handing his friend the cellular phone.

"Yes, this is Ishmael Muhammad," he answered.

"Ishmael," a voice at the other end said, "I have news for you. The Jews have done it. Our intelligence reports here in the capital say they successfully shot down a live incoming missile today with the Arrow 5. I'm faxing you the full report as we speak."

Muhammad picked up the fax report as he listened to his officially unofficial intelligence briefing from the Syrian government. Officially, Syria was at peace with Israel. Years earlier, Israel had struck a land-for-peace deal in which they returned the Golan Heights captured from Syria in the Six-Day War. In return, Damascus promised a new era of cooperation and normalized relations. On the surface, all was working out as planned. There was trade between the former enemies. There were even some joint industrial projects. But it was an uneasy and unpopular peace for many in Syria. An ancient hatred just could not be quenched so easily. There were plenty of Syrians, including many in government and in the military, who longed for the good old days of wars of liberation and terrorist strikes against the "Zionist entity." One of those covert contacts was speaking to Ishmael Muhammad right now.

"This is nothing to worry about," Muhammad assured his informer as he pored over the fax report. "This so-called successful test took place under the most ideal conditions imaginable. When we fire our SATAN II, the Jews will not be sitting in their bunker in Palmahim waiting for it. It will not necessarily be a clear and sunny day. It will not necessarily be fired from a direction they expect. They will not even see the missile coming because of stealth technology built into it. They cannot shoot down what they do not see nor expect. Do I need to say any more?"

"No, Ishmael," said the source in Damascus, "you have said quite enough. We shouldn't stay on the phone too long. I hope you are 100 percent correct in your analysis—and, knowing you, you probably are. Salaam."

"Salaam, my friend," said Muhammad. "Tell our benefactors we will be ready for our own test shortly."

Ishmael Muhammad was 42 years old. Even though he was born in Syria, he was a pure blooded Arab from the Hashemite tribe of the Hejaz, the area of the holy cities of Mecca and Medina. Ishmael was most proud of the fact he was a direct descendant of the Great Prophet— Muhammad.

Ishmael was unusually tall and every inch a warrior. All the western intelligence agencies considered him to be the world's most brilliant and dangerous terrorist. He was viewed as far more dangerous than the legendary "Carlos the Jackal" of a few decades before. He was an honors graduate of the Patrice Lumumba University in Moscow. He received additional training in guerrilla warfare tactics from Cuba, Algeria and Bosnia. He studied nuclear science in Russia and ballistic missile technology in China and North Korea.

Born just two years before the Six-Day War, Muhammad grew up outside Damascus hating Israel. That hatred grew into an undisguised abhorrence of Jews. Sometime in his thirties he became a devout Islamic fundamentalist. It was this fanatical fundamentalist faith that enabled him to believe the wiping out of three million plus human beings in Tel Aviv with a thermonuclear warhead would bring supreme glory to Allah, and avenge the disgrace of five disastrous defeats at the hands of the Israeli Defense Forces.

In the last several years, Muhammad had put his technological know-how to use in the cause of murder and mayhem by designing suitcase size nuclear bombs. Now he had built the ultimate terrorist weapon—a medium-range ballistic missile armed with a five megaton thermonuclear warhead (stolen from the Russian arsenal by the Russian mafia) that would make Hiroshima look like a backyard barbecue. His funding had come from multiple sources—Iran, Sudan, Libya and Iraq. His technology, materials and supplies were provided by former Soviet republics in central Asia as well as Pakistan and North Korea.

"I have been following the progress of the Arrow project for 12 years," Muhammad told Haddad after disconnecting with his pipeline in Damascus. "I know that system as well as any of the Zionists. There is a fatal flaw in their design. I know its Achilles' heel. In the name of the Prophet, I am going to defeat these infidel swine and avenge the injustices of the last 4,000 years."

"Ishmael," said Haddad, "I am at your service. Just give me my marching orders."

"OK, Haddad," said Muhammad with a smile, "drive me home."

Haddad summoned two bodyguards to accompany them to the armor-plated Chevy Suburban that served as Muhammad's limousine. Haddad had picked it up on the black market. A few years earlier, it had been customized for Colombian drug dealers who had disappeared without a trace. Now it was in the service of someone who killed people much more quickly and efficiently than the Colombians ever imagined.

The entourage left their secret bunker in Lebanon's Bekaa Valley for the short ride to Muhammad's mountain-side retreat. Haddad was, among other things, an excellent driver. He had once served as the chauffeur for Yasser Arafat (before, as Haddad would say, he "sold out") and had been trained in evasive maneuvers. Muhammad sat in the front passenger seat while the two bodyguards, sporting AK-47s, sat in the back seat.

It was a clear day, with visibility for miles in the foothills. The Suburban slowly rounded the hill leading to Muhammad's hideaway. The road was a narrow, single lane, paved exclusively for the private use of Muhammad and his entourage by Iranians who first made their presence felt in Lebanon in the 1980s. Some still hoped to turn the once cosmopolitan pearl of the Mideast, with its heavy Christian influence, into a full-fledged Islamic republic. One thing they had brought with them from Iran was potholes.

"The Iranians have been good to me," thought Muhammad. "They have given me money, arms, training—even some plutonium. But they sure don't know how to pave roads."

The stretch ahead—the last half-mile before reaching home—was the most treacherous drive of all. The mountain jutted out in a way that required autos to drive precariously close to the edge. Below was a sheer drop of about 2,000 feet. There was no guardrail. Apparently, Iranians didn't believe in guardrails. Muhammad always held his breath going around that approaching curve. It was the only thing he didn't like about his mountainside home.

With the worst part of the curve about 10 yards in front of them, Haddad noticed something strange happening. He wasn't certain if the road was bumpier than usual or whether something else was wrong. The car was rumbling and shaking. With no more notice than that, Haddad and Muhammad watched in horror as the road immediately before them gave way. There was no way they could stop in time. They were doomed to plunge off the cliff.

But just as the braking, swerving auto reached the precipice, a large boulder—perhaps weighing 1,000 pounds—rolled down the hill from the left side and came to a halt in front of the vehicle. The Suburban smashed into the boulder, preventing the car from plummeting off the road.

Haddad, Muhammad and the two bodyguards emerged

from the wreckage. All were shaken up but no one was seriously injured. The Suburban's front end was severely damaged and the engine was steaming. Muhammad examined the rock. It could not have been more well-positioned to save their lives. Apparently the same earthquake that caused the road to give way jarred the boulder loose from the hill above.

"Praise Allah," said Haddad.

"Yes, praise him, indeed," said Muhammad.

But just then, the earth began shaking violently again. The four men realized the very earth they were so grateful to be standing on could break apart at a moment's notice. Instinct told them to drop to their knees and to hold onto the ground or anything they could grab.

The quaking was severe and seemed to last for minutes, though it was probably only seconds that seemed so frighteningly long. Just then, off to the left side of the vehicle—the same side from which the boulder had mysteriously plunged—a stranger appeared and called out to Muhammad and his colleagues.

"Come this way to safety," he commanded. "Come now!"

Without even thinking about it, Muhammad and the others ran toward the stranger and up the embankment from which the boulder had rolled. No sooner had they cleared off the road than it broke away, with the wreckage of the Suburban and the boulder falling 2,000 feet, along with a sizable piece of earth and pavement.

Within a second, it seemed, the quake aftershock stopped. Muhammad, Haddad and the bodyguards sat down on the hillside to collect themselves and gather their wits.

"Stranger," Muhammad offered, "thank you very much for saving our lives. You have done me, my friends and the entire Islamic world a great service today. How can we ever repay you?"

Muhammad looked over his shoulder for an answer that did not come. The others looked around, searching the vicinity for the Good Samaritan who had bravely and wisely led them to safety on the higher ground of the hillside. He was nowhere to be found.

"Where did he go?" asked Haddad.

"He couldn't have climbed all the way up the hill in such a short time," said the bodyguard named Gamel.

"He couldn't have gone in the other direction, either," said Hafez, the other bodyguard, gesturing toward the ravine below.

Muhammad just smiled. Then he got down on his knees, facing the east, and began to pray ecstatically.

"Praise Allah for delivering me from death by sending His angel, Jabril. Oh Allah, the only merciful and the compassionate God, you have surely saved me so that I may fulfill my Divine calling to slay the infidels and claim this world in the name of the Prophet," he began.

The others quickly joined him, face down, heads toward the east.

"Thank you, Allah, the one and only true God, for sending your angel, Jabril, to prevent us from plummeting to our premature deaths," continued Muhammad. "I am so honored that you considered my life worth sparing. This is the ultimate vindication of my vision. Now I am more certain than ever that my life here has been pre-ordained by your holy will. I pledge the rest of my days on earth will be spent fulfilling your sacred mission. We will do as the Holy Koran teaches: 'Fight and slay the infidels wherever ye find them, and seize them, beleaguer them, and lie in wait for them in every strategem of war.'

"More than 1,300 years ago, the Prophet wrote in the Sahih annals: 'The criminal Jews have brought destruction upon the Umma since the earliest times. Their leaders conspired to send the innocent of Canaan away from their homes. They repulsed the pleas of the Philistine widows and Moabite orphans and washed their fields in the blood of the Ammonite poor. Therefore, they shall not stand in the day of judgment, nor shall they prevail against the sure coming of Jihad. Allah shall pronounce retribution and the Umma shall observe with joy and gladness.' I thank you today for that promise, and I make myself available as the vessel to carry it out."

"Be assured that, with your help, I will do all in my power to avenge the many indignities heaped upon the Muslim peoples since ancient times. It is clear that Zionist policies today are little more than an extension of the imperialist tactics of the conqueror Joshua. Their theology is based on lies and deceptions from the beginning. We know from the word of the Holy Koran that it was Abraham's first son Ishmael who was promised the land of Canaan and your blessings for eternity—not his usurping brother Isaac. The Jews have distorted your holy word from the beginning. They have lied about their own heritage to glorify themselves as your chosen people. Surely the judgment of Allah is reserved for them until Palestine is transferred from Dar al Harb to Dar al Islam. Abraham's true son Ishmael, the one with whom you made your eternal covenant, shall now have his revenge."

They all finished praying with the ancient victory shout, "Allah akhbar—Allah is Great !"

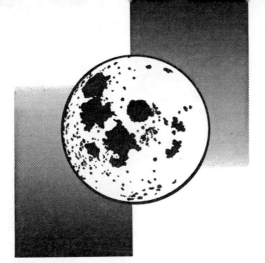

CHAPTER 2

Jeremiah's Lament

B aruch sat patiently next to his master. Quill in hand, he was prepared to make note of anything his tortured lord would utter. He had been sitting there for an eternity, it seemed. But perhaps it had only been a few hours since Jeremiah had spoken. Was he awake? Was he praying? Was he receiving some inspired message from heaven? Baruch did not know. All he knew was that, at a moment's notice, the prophet could arise and begin spontaneously orating. Baruch had better be ready to capture every precious word on the scroll. That was his job as loyal and devoted secretary to the world's most famous—and detested— seer.

It was not an easy job, but the only one Baruch had ever known. He had been with the prophet for nearly 20 years, most of Baruch's adult life. Jeremiah was terribly unpopular with the general public as well as the priests.

He told people things they didn't want to hear. Baruch merely faithfully recorded his master's words. But both of them often paid a price for the unpopularity of the message.

"Things could be worse, I suppose," thought Baruch. And they had been. Baruch had been with Jeremiah for many years—the last several spent roaming the countryside of Judah warning generally unreceptive audiences that the nation was forsaking God and risking grave judgment. More than once, the rural townspeople—including those in Jeremiah's own village of Anathoth—had tried to kill the prophet. But even when Jeremiah was not risking their lives prophesying, physical and verbal intimidation had been a way of life. Now, at least, there was a degree of stability and comfort associated with life in Jerusalem.

Jeremiah and Baruch shared a modest home a short walk from the Temple. For several months, anyway, life for the prophet and his scribe revolved around religious and political life in Jerusalem. The grueling days of extensive travel around the country by foot or on horseback were behind them for the time being. Best of all, Baruch didn't feel like he was a constant target of potential physical intimidation every day of his life.

Not that any of the threats ever really bothered Jeremiah himself; in fact, he thrived on them, thought Baruch. There were beatings. In one rural village, Jeremiah was locked in stocks. Both Baruch and Jeremiah were frequently pelted with stones. Instead of being silenced by such adversity, Jeremiah grew more assertive. He told the crowds that his admonitions were for their own good. He vociferously condemned their resistance to the truth as the greatest danger they faced. All that, of course, only served to inflame their passions against him.

Baruch's master was an unusual man. Jeremiah had resisted the call to be a Prophet when it came during his youth. But once he became convinced that was what God expected of his life, he plunged himself into his work self-lessly and without regard to his safety or well-being. For two men of profound faith in God, it had become a journey into the heart of Judah's darkness.

More than 600 years before the birth of Christ, the northern kingdom of the Jews was a frightful and unwelcome place for anyone bold enough to dare the nation toward repentance and faithful civility. Violent crime, religious idolatry, nature worship—even ritualistic human sacrifice—were rampant.

Baruch still had nightmares about their excursion to Topheth in the Valley of Ben-hinnom below the south side of Jerusalem's walls. There he and Jeremiah had witnessed a shocking and previously unimaginable scene. As they approached the village, they were repulsed by an unfamiliar and unidentifiable stench. Then they heard the wild cries—alternating between raucous laughter and frightening wails. A cloud of thick black smoke hung over the village. Nothing could have prepared Baruch and Jeremiah for the ghastly sight they discovered in Topheth. Of all people, the descendants of Abraham, Isaac and Jacob had built temples to the Canaanite god Baal and were bringing their screaming children to offer as burnt sacrifices. So many children were killed and burned at the site that their remains formed a *tell*—a large mound built up over months or, perhaps, years of such practices.

In the face of such abominations, Baruch reflected, Jeremiah's determination never wavered. He never gave any indication of fear. Instead, he confronted the pagan practices head-on. Baruch recorded in his scrolls what Jeremiah had said word for word:

> *"'Behold, days are coming,' declares the Lord, 'when this place will no longer be called Topheth or the Valley of Ben-hinnom, but rather the Valley of Slaughter. And I shall make void the counsel of Judah and Jerusalem in this place, and I shall cause them to fall by the sword before their enemies and by the hand of those who seek their life; and I shall give over their carcasses as food for the birds of the sky and the beasts of the earth. I shall make this city a desolation and an object of hissing; everyone who passes by it will be astonished and hiss because of all the disasters.'"*

Jeremiah was not one to mince words, no matter what the consequences might be, no matter how much personal danger it might mean for himself. He spoke from his heart and, Baruch was convinced, expressed messages God placed on it. No, it was not easy following the Prophet, but for a scribe as faithful as Baruch, there was no other way. He could not abandon his inspired and courageous spiritual leader.

Just then, Baruch was shaken from his daydream by the sound of Jeremiah clearing his throat as he sat up straight and began reciting part of his message to be delivered the next day at the Temple Gate.

"Thus says the Lord of hosts, the God of Israel, 'Amend your ways and your deeds, and I will let you dwell in this place. Do not trust in deceptive words, saying, 'This is the temple of the Lord, the temple of the Lord.' For if you truly amend your ways and your deeds, if you truly practice justice between a man and his neighbor, if you do not oppress the alien, the orphan, or the widow, and do not shed innocent blood in this place, nor walk after other gods to your own ruin, then I will let you dwell in this place, in the land that I gave to your fathers forever and ever. Behold, you are trusting in deceptive words to no avail. Will you steal, murder and commit adultery, and swear falsely, and offer sacrifices to Baal, and walk after other gods that you have not known, then come and stand before me in this house, which is called by My name, and say, 'We are delivered!'—that you may do all these abominations?'"

Jeremiah stopped and, again, rested his head on the table. Baruch knew there was no way to know how long this pause might last—a minute, an hour or more. Great patience was required of the scribe. When Jeremiah would awaken from one of his meditative trances, he did not even take notice of whether Baruch was sitting there, quill in hand. It was simply assumed. And somehow, Baruch always managed to be at the ready to take down every word of the Prophet, no matter the speed at which the message was delivered. This pause was a short one.

"Since the day that your fathers came out of the land of Egypt until this day, I have sent you all My servants the prophets, daily rising early and send-

ing them. Yet they did not listen to Me or incline their ear, but stiffened their neck; they did evil more than their fathers. And you shall speak all these words to them, but they will not listen to you; and you shall call to them, but they will not answer you. And you shall say to them, 'This is the nation that did not obey the voice of the Lord their God or accept correction; truth has perished and has been cut off from their mouth. Cut off your hair and cast it away, and take up a lamentation on the bare heights; for the Lord has rejected and forsaken the generation of His wrath. For the sons of Judah have done that which is evil in My sight,' declares the Lord, 'they have set their detestable things in the house which is called by My name, to defile it. And they have built the high places of Topheth, which is in the Valley of the son of Hinnom, to burn their sons and their daughters in the fire, which I did not command, and it did not come into My mind.'"

Jeremiah took a breath and relaxed. He looked at Baruch, signaling he was done dictating for now. He rose to pour himself a cup of water and asked Baruch if he was thirsty.

"Yes, Jeremiah. Thank you."

"We live in strange and fearful times, Baruch," said the prophet. "The world is changing rapidly. The Assyrian Empire is in decline. There is little besides Carchemish left of the great kingdom of Ashurbanipal now that Haran has fallen to Nabopolassar, who is leading Babylon into the breach. Our people understand nothing about what is to befall them. They look to the Egyptians to ensure their safety. This is a serious mistake. There is only one source of security for the Jews, and that is the Lord."

Jeremiah was only 45 years old, but he had the appearance of a man far more mature and wizened by age and stress. His hair was long, black and braided, his eyes deepset and dark. Flecks of white dotted his full beard. Baruch was several years younger, but his face, too, showed signs of wear and tear. They were both tired and looked it. But they were driven to work without ceasing by their firm belief that Jeremiah's prophecies were about to be fulfilled.

"Cyaxares of Media has made Babylon a more formidable foe for the Assyrians," offered Baruch. "Even an alliance with Egypt will not be enough to permit the Assyrians to recapture Nineveh and Haran. If Judah casts its lot with Egypt, the Babylonians will exact great revenge on the Jews."

"You're correct," said Jeremiah. "Egypt is an unreliable ally—and they are no match for Babylon. Not only is this dependence on the pharaoh a spiritual mistake, it is a strategic error as well. It will not work. God has shown me this."

Nevertheless, over the next few years, Egypt came to dominate the political landscape of Judah. Pharaoh Neco even chose Israel's leadership in the person of King Jehoiakim, who proved to be a curse. Israel was forced to pay a heavy price for "Egypt's protection." The former king, Jehoahaz, was taken prisoner as collateral to ensure the payments were forthcoming.

It was about this time that Jeremiah, moved by God's spirit, delivered his third temple speech on the occasion of one of the annual Jewish feasts. It was not an address that brought joy and comfort to the hearts of the priests and politicians.

Concerning the prophets:

"My heart is broken within me, all my bones shake; I am like a drunken man, like a man overcome by wine, because of the Lord and because of his holy words. For the land is full of adulterers; because of the curse the land mourns, and the pastures of the wilderness are dried up. Their course is evil, and their might is not right.

"Both prophet and priest are ungodly; even in my house I have found their wickedness, says the Lord. Therefore their way shall be to them like slippery paths in the darkness, into which they shall be driven and fall; for I will bring evil upon them in the year of their punishment, says the Lord. In the prophets of Samaria I saw an unsavory thing: they prophesied by Baal and led my people Israel astray. But in the prophets of Jerusalem I have seen a horrible thing: they commit adultery and walk in lies; they strengthen the hands of evildoers, so that no one turns from his wickedness; all of them have become like Sodom to me, and its inhabitants like Gomorrah."

Even as these fiery words were leaving Jeremiah's lips, a crowd was gathering around the New Gate. There were angry shouts of denial and rebuke. Priests and princes hastily assembled inside the Temple to figure out a way to restore order and control the violence provoked by Jeremiah's impassioned plea.

"Remember," said one of the religious leaders, "Uriah

once preached a similar message before he fled to Egypt for sanctuary. King Jehoiakim had him extradited and executed upon his return."

"That fate would be too good for Jeremiah," suggested one of the princes.

But the prophet was not without friends. There existed in Judah at this time, and throughout the 40 years of Jeremiah's ministry, a reform movement—a spiritual revival led by those who took the prophet's words to heart. Ahikam was one of the leaders of this movement—and a loyal friend of the prophet. After Jeremiah concluded his speech at the New Gate, Ahikam quickly hustled the prophet off to a secret hiding place.

"My friend," said Ahikam, "I know you must do what God puts on your heart. You must speak His words as He gives them to you. But I caution you not to be reckless. Your friends love you and want you to stay alive—to preach another day."

Jeremiah just smiled and nodded his head. Ahikam knew Jeremiah would not and could not modify his behavior or his spirited rhetoric. It was not in his makeup. So Jeremiah continued his thankless ministry of calling on the Jews for repentance, submission to the laws of Babylon and rejection of the false hope of Egypt. The new king, Zedekiah, didn't listen to Jeremiah. He began plotting rebellion against Babylon, which had taken into exile the king's son, other princes of Judah and many of the finest craftsman and artisans.

One night, as Jeremiah was sleeping in his home, he awoke to the sound of a knock on the door.

"Who could that be at this hour?" Jeremiah wondered. He thought for a moment: "Perhaps it is the Chaldeans here to take me away to Babylon, too."

When he opened the door, however, it was a handsome and confident stranger.

"Fear not, Jeremiah," he said. "I have a message for you from the Lord."

The stranger held out two baskets and asked, "What do you see?"

"I see two baskets of figs—one batch of very good figs and the other very bad—so bad they cannot be eaten," said Jeremiah.

The stranger turned and left as abruptly as he had come. And when he did, Jeremiah heard the voice of the Lord—a voice familiar to him for many years, even since his childhood.

> *"Like these good figs, so I will regard as good the exiles from Judah, whom I have sent away from this place to the land of the Chaldeans. I will set my eyes upon them for good, and I will bring them back to this land. I will build them up, and not tear them down; I will plant them, and not uproot them. I will give them a heart to know that I am the Lord; and they shall be my people and I will be their God, for they shall return to me with their whole heart. But thus says the Lord: Like the bad figs which are so bad they cannot be eaten, so will I treat Zedekiah the king of Judah, his princes, the remnant of Jerusalem who remain in this land, and those who dwell in the land of Egypt. I will make them a horror to all the kingdoms of the*

earth, to be a reproach, a byword, a taunt, and a curse in all the places where I shall drive them. And I will send sword, famine, and pestilence upon them until they shall be utterly destroyed from the land which I gave to them and their fathers."

In the intervening years, the military showdown between Egypt and Babylon intensified. Each time Egypt appeared to hold the upper hand, it meant greater persecution for Jeremiah, who was ridiculously characterized as a false prophet because of his staunch criticism of the pharaoh. Jeremiah never had confidence in Egypt as an ally for the Jews. Each time a leader of Israel would call for a pact with Egypt, Jeremiah would warn of God's judgment against it. Whenever Jews fled to Egypt for security, Jeremiah cautioned that a worse fate awaited them.

Jeremiah was not partial to Babylon, either. When Nebuchadnezzar, son of Nabopolassar, smashed the Egyptian army at Carchemish in 605 BC and returned to Israel as the conquering king of Babylon a year later, Jeremiah took the occasion to issue his great 70-year prophecy.

"This whole land shall become a ruin and a waste, and these nations shall serve the king of Babylon seventy years. Then after seventy years are completed, I will punish the king of Babylon and that nation, the land of the Chaldeans, for their iniquity, says the Lord, making the land an everlasting waste."

"You're mad," one of the chief priests told Jeremiah at the Temple one day. "No matter who is in power in

Jerusalem or which foreign entity is exerting influence on our lives, you insist on provoking them.

"No, false prophet!" retorted Jeremiah. "It is you who is mad. I merely show disrespect and enmity for mortal and temporal political leaders who mislead the people. You, on the other hand, demonstrate hostility to the living God, the creator of the universe, by ignoring His word and placing your faith in men."

"I have had enough of your insolence," said the priest. "Guards, seize this man!"

Jeremiah was hauled off, beaten and dropped into a pit. He was only semi-conscious when he splashed into a thick liquid substance. He couldn't see where he was because of the dark. But the overpowering stench convinced him he had been thrown into a sewage-filled cistern-pit dungeon. He had all he could do to keep his aching head out of the mire.

"How long will this last?" Jeremiah wondered. "I don't think I can stand the smell and the discomfort for another minute."

Yet, hours went by. There was no indication of any early release from this torment.

"Lord," Jeremiah wondered, "how much worse can Hell itself be than this fate? Give me the strength to endure."

Somehow, Jeremiah found the strength to last for several days—without food (though there was little chance he could have kept anything in his stomach under such conditions), water or sunlight. Finally Jeremiah, too weak to help himself, was dredged out of the pit and mercifully imprisoned in the guard house. After he was cleaned up and collected himself, Jeremiah thanked God for sparing his life and for removing him from the pit.

Shortly after Jeremiah had regained his strength, he received word that King Zedekiah wished to see him. He was taken to the third entrance of the Temple by guards who were dismissed by the king. The prophet, who had just been removed from the sewage-filled pit, and the king, in his regal attire and scented clothing, were alone together.

"I want to ask you a question, Jeremiah," said the king. "Please answer me honestly."

"If I do, will you put me to death?" asked the prophet. "And if I give you counsel, will you ignore it?"

"As the Lord lives, who made our souls, I will not put you to death or deliver you into the hands of these men who seek your life," swore the king.

"What is it then that you want to know?" asked Jeremiah.

"I want to know what I should do," said the king. "The Chaldeans are at our gates. The city is under siege. What insight can you give me?"

Jeremiah spoke confidently:

> *"Thus says the Lord, the God of hosts, the God of Israel, if you will surrender to the princes of the king of Babylon, then your life shall be spared, and this city shall not be burned with fire, and you and your house shall live," said Jeremiah confidently. "But if you do not surrender to the princes of the king of Babylon, then this city shall be given into the hand of the Chaldeans, and they shall burn it*

with fire, and you shall not escape from their hand."

"But I am afraid of the Jews who have deserted to the Chaldeans, lest I be handed over to them and they abuse me," explained Zedekiah.

Jeremiah responded:

"You shall not be given to them. Obey now the voice of the Lord in what I say to you, and it shall be well with you, and your life shall be spared. But if you refuse to surrender, this is the vision which the Lord has shown me: Behold, all the women left in the house of the king of Judah were being led out to the princes of the king of Babylon and were saying, 'Your trusted friends have deceived you and prevailed against you; now that your feet are sunk in the mire, they turn away from you.' All your wives and your sons shall be led out to the Chaldeans, and you yourself shall not escape from their hand, but shall be seized by the king of Babylon; and this city shall be burned with fire."

Zedekiah listened intently. His heart was troubled by what he heard. Clearly Jeremiah was giving him advice he did not wish to hear.

"Let no one know of these words and you shall not die," the king instructed Jeremiah. "If the princes hear that I have spoken to you and come to you and say to you, 'Tell us what you said to the king and what the king said to you; hide nothing from us and we will not put you to death,' then you shall say to them, 'I made a humble plea to the king that he would not send me back to the pit to die.'"

Indeed, when the princes came and asked Jeremiah about his meeting with the king, he told them exactly what Zedekiah had instructed him to say. But Zedekiah did not heed Jeremiah's advice. Shortly thereafter, Nebuchadnezzar's army made a breakthrough into Jerusalem and the city fell. When it did, Zedekiah did not surrender himself to the princes, but chose to flee instead.

The Chaldean army pursued the king and his guards and overtook them in the plains of Jericho. Zedekiah was taken to Nebuchadnezzar. His sons were executed in front of him. Then all of Judah's nobles were slain. Finally, he put out Zedekiah's eyes, bound him in chains and took him to Babylon as a trophy of war. The Chaldeans burned the king's house, broke down the walls of Jerusalem and carried into exile all of the remaining inhabitants of the city. Jeremiah, who had remained in the court of the guard until the city fell, was freed and released by the Babylonian king.

All was not tranquil, though, in the outlying areas of the new Babylonian Empire. The residents of Edom, Moab, Ammon, Tyre and Sidon continued to conspire against the Chaldeans. When the Ammonite king, Baalis, had the Babylon-appointed governor of Mizpah, Gedaliah, murdered, many of the Jews in the area feared for their lives.

"What should we do?" they asked Jeremiah, who came to counsel them in Jerusalem.

"Whatever you do," said Jeremiah, "you must remain in Israel. Do not flee to Egypt."

But the words did not calm their fears. They decided to

do just the opposite of what Jeremiah told them. Worse yet, they forced him and Baruch to accompany them on the trek to Egypt, a land where Jeremiah was already notorious as a troublemaker.

Nevertheless, Jeremiah continued his impassioned warnings in Egypt. Fearlessly he predicted a total conquest of the land by Nebuchadnezzar. In 568, Babylon fulfilled Jeremiah's prophecy and took over Egypt. In the village of Tahpanhas, Jews gathered to discuss their fate. Of course, they looked once again to Jeremiah for advice and insight.

"What will happen to us in exile?" one man asked.

"Yes, Jeremiah, tell us what you see for our futures," demanded another.

"I will tell you this," said the prophet. "You have sealed your own fate with your religious idolatry. The Lord warned you to reject these false gods and return to Him, but you didn't listen. Now you will pay the price for your sin."

"Nonsense," responded one woman angrily, "We enjoyed great prosperity while worshipping idols."

"Yes, that's true," said another man. "And when we heeded your warnings to stop, we often suffered."

Jeremiah responded:

"You are blind to God's will. Behold the storm of the Lord! Wrath has gone forth, a whirling tempest; it will burst upon the head of the wicked. The anger of the Lord will not turn back until He has executed and accomplished the intents of his mind. You will not understand what I am saying. But in the latter years, they will understand."

The crowd grew angrier and angrier as Jeremiah spoke.

"This false prophet is condemning us!" shouted one man. "Stone him! Kill him!"

The first blow to Jeremiah's head knocked him unconscious. He felt no pain after that. Later, his broken and bloodied body was collected by Baruch, Ahikam and a handful of other loyal friends and followers. That night, a blood red moon hung over the lands of Egypt and Israel.

❂

"Hmmm, 11 o'clock," thought Lt. Colonel Jeremy Armstrong as he simultaneously glanced at his Swiss Army watch, clutched the remote control unit and switched on the television. "Time for the news."

The special forces commander sat back in his easy chair for some relaxation. It had been a tough day. He was training his small elite unit in the techniques of desert warfare—or "peacekeeping," as they euphemistically called it these days. For the sake of authenticity, his United Nations troops were getting their survival training in the Mojave Desert.

"If you can survive the Mojave in July," thought Armstrong, "you're ready for anything." It was not unusual for temperatures to reach 122 degrees in the shade this time of year, with average temperatures hotter every year since 1996, when the global warming was officially declared. It reminded him of the heat he had experienced in Saudi Arabia, Kuwait and Iraq when he commanded forces there during the Persian Gulf War.

"Another terrorist bomb exploded in a school in Israel today with dozens of casualties...." Armstrong watched the chaotic scene on his screen and shook his head. "...The militant Sword of Allah claimed responsibility for the attack. Meanwhile, terror of a different kind back here in Southern California: Police in San Bernardino County say they have made a grisly discovery—a giant mound of earth and ash that is believed to be the site of dozens of ritualistic human sacrifices over the last five years.... " Armstrong's attention focused on the tube.

"Am I hearing right?" he asked himself. "What country am I living in? What's going on here?"

"...Investigators say most of the remains at the site appear to be those of children whose bodies were burned—in some cases, police believe—while they were still alive...."

Armstrong had seen and heard enough. He turned off the tube and grabbed a book he had been reading more and more lately. It was a family heirloom, though he was the only family member still alive. Several of them— including his Mom and sister—had vanished one day two years earlier along with several million others worldwide. Armstrong never did like the official explanations of those mass disappearances. Some officials suggested that space aliens had pulled off a mass abduction. After all, millions of individuals worldwide had previously claimed to have experienced a form of abduction. If that was plausible, certainly it was plausible that millions might be snatched away all at once. Others had a more spiritual explanation,

blaming it on "a harmonic convergence"—a natural function of the earth cleansing itself of the unwanted and
undesirable elements that were holding back progress.
New Age prophets had predicted such a phenomenon for
years.

"Cleansing my eye!" thought Armstrong. "The best people I ever knew disappeared that day—the best people all
over the world! What kind of cleansing action is that? If
the world was going to cleanse itself, the people who
would vanish would be the ones who blow up schools
and burn children alive. But they're still here—and
stronger and more plentiful than ever!"

As Armstrong saw it, the world was going to Hell in a
handbasket, and the worse things got, the more it made
him curious about lessons his Mom had tried to teach him
a long time ago. She had called it "the Rapture." She kept
sending him books by some nut named Hal Lindsey.
Armstrong had thought it was crazy. But he remembered
her telling him that one day Jesus was going to call up His
living saints into the clouds—"in a moment, in the twinkling of an eye," she would say. She warned young Jeremy
over and over again that he needed to accept Jesus into
his heart if he wanted to escape a horrible period of time
called the Tribulation that would last some seven years
until Jesus Christ came back to earth.

Well, the idea of getting swept up into the clouds
never had a particular appeal to Armstrong. He had
jumped out airplanes into the clouds and he wasn't too
crazy about that. He sure didn't like the idea of reversing
the process. So he never listened too intently about the

details of what it was his Mom wanted him to do. Now he wished he had, because the world was looking more and more like the kind of world his Mom had predicted for the time that would follow the "Rapture." He vaguely remembered that she had called it the "Tribulation." It was going to be a terrible time, she would say—unlike anything the world had ever seen.

It was reflections on those old teachings several months ago that had prompted Armstrong to dust off the Bible he found stashed away in his closet. He was reading it from cover to cover. One night he read:

> *"But realize this, that in the last days difficult times will come. For men will be lovers of self, lovers of money, boastful, arrogant, revilers, disobedient to parents, ungrateful, unholy, unloving, irreconcilable, malicious gossips, without self-control, brutal, haters of good, treacherous, reckless, conceited, lovers of pleasure rather than lovers of God; holding to a form of godliness, although they have denied its power; and avoid such men as these."*

"Boy," Armstrong thought, "that certainly sounds like the world of the 21st century."

Reading the Bible was an activity that was ridiculed everywhere in American society in the 21st century—even in church. The Bible was considered a relic of an earlier age that had more than any other source retarded man's evolution into a super-psychic species. Oh, sure, the modern theologians would pick and choose certain passages supporting their own viewpoint that man is the true center of the universe. But independent Bible study was a thing of the past. What Armstrong was doing tonight was considered illegal activity in this day and age. That's why so few could see what was so clear. And for a rebel, free spirit like Jeremy, it made the Bible attractive for the first time.

As Armstrong meditated on the implications of what he was learning, the phone rang.

"Hello."

"Jeremy?"

"Hey, Zeke!" It was Armstrong's best friend, Zeke Charlton—a childhood buddy who, like Jeremy, was a career military guy, one with big ambitions. "What's happening?"

"I'm getting promoted again," said Zeke, already a full colonel and bucking to be the youngest general in the Army.

"Oh, Zeke, you're making me look bad!"

"You don't need any help looking bad, my friend," joked Charlton.

"Seriously, what's up? What's going on? What are you going to be doing?" asked Armstrong.

"I'm being transferred from Fort Bragg to New York," Zeke explained.

"New York?" asked Armstrong. "What the heck is in New York?"

"What's in New York!" exclaimed Charlton in an exasperated tone. "The U.N. is in New York—and Rome still considers it a very important place."

"Well, what will you be doing at there?" asked Armstrong.

"I will be the secretary-general's personal military attaché," he said. "I will be advising him on all our capabilities, on regional hot spots and strategic deployment of peacekeepers."

"Wow," said Armstrong. "It sounds like a big job. Is this what you want?"

"Yeah, it's where the action is," said Zeke. "I'll be working closely with Carlo himself—or at least as close as you can get outside of E.U.R. in Rome. But I've already met him and we get along great."

Gianfranco Carlo was an impressive man all right, thought Jeremy. He was a genuine peacemaker with a proven track record. He didn't just talk about ending conflicts, he had a special gift that allowed him to actually accomplish something—every single time he entered the picture, it seemed. He was beguiling, charismatic and attractive. In many ways, he seemed to have the world at his feet. And even Jeremy had to admit, if any human being on the planet had the potential for turning things around, it was Carlo.

But there was also something about him that Jeremy instinctively did not trust. He couldn't even put his finger on it exactly. But just the thought of Carlo's supreme authority was enough to make Armstrong's skin crawl. A keen student of history, Jeremy could not find one man of history who hadn't been corrupted by such power. And no man had ever had as much power as Carlo.

"Well, Zeke, I wish you the best," said Armstrong. "I hope it all works out for you."

"Listen, Jeremy, I didn't call you for congratulations,"

said Zeke. "I called to see if you would join me in New York. I want you to come with me. I've got a great assignment for you."

Jeremy had no ties in Southern California. He was certain Zeke could pull the strings necessary to get him reassigned. But he had a sense of foreboding about going to the U.N. Headquarters. For one thing, Armstrong never liked the idea of being a U.N. soldier. He still had the old-fashioned idea that he was serving his country, not some amorphous idea like a world government. When he joined the Army, he remembered taking an oath to uphold the U.S. Constitution—not the U.N. Charter. Granted, he was already serving the U.N. in his current assignment. Everyone in the U.S. military was directly or indirectly since America's political leadership had given up on the idea of maintaining the national sovereignty that the nation's founders fought so hard to establish. Nevertheless, despite the realities of what he was doing in the military, Armstrong still resisted the direct control the U.N. would have over his life in a New York assignment. And he just wasn't comfortable with the idea of furthering the the agency's central control over the lives of people all over the world. And to top it all off, Jeremy hated New York City. After America's economic catastrophe, New York became a den of crime.

"Gee, I don't know, Zeke," said Armstrong. "I appreciate you thinking of me. I'm flattered by the offer. You know I would love working with you. But I'll need some time to think it over."

"Of course you do," said Charlton. "I will e-mail you the

details on your assignment, including all the many perks. I'll need an answer pretty soon, though. Carlo has big plans and he's moving very fast. There's no time to lose."

"I understand, Zeke," said Jeremy. "Don't worry about me holding you up. I'll let you know very soon."

"All right, man," concluded Charlton. "I've got to run. But think New York! I need you. It's very important stuff, Jeremy. Very important. And don't forget, Carlo is lavish with his gifts to those who distinguish themselves in his service."

"Good night, Zeke," said Jeremy.

"Good night, my friend," said Charlton. "I'll talk to you soon."

Jeremy was torn. He was always a curious person. And one part of him longed to go to New York just so he could get a better handle on what was really going on in the world—what Carlo was up to. On the other hand, he sensed that he wouldn't be pleased by what he found and he didn't want to be a part of something...well, for lack of a better word...evil.

"Oh, Lord, what I should do?" wondered Jeremy half aloud. "If You're really up there, like Mom and Sis said, I need You now. This world of ours just seems to be falling apart at the seams. I'm as confused about it as anyone else. But I don't want to be part of the evil I see coming. I never have. If You're really there, Lord, I need to know it. If You show me this, then I will serve You the rest of my life, which I don't think will be a long one."

Jeremy had been experimenting with prayer for the last several months as his exploration of the Bible became more serious. He hadn't seen any bright lights or writing in the sky or heard any voices, but he did feel a certain level of comfort in communing with the God described in the Bible, especially the one called Jesus Christ. He got the feeling—whether it was emotional or spiritual—that somebody was listening. He didn't believe he was alone anymore—a strange feeling given his circumstances.

You see, by conventional standards, Jeremy was alone. He had no family left, no wife, no girlfriend and only a handful of friends whom he found increasingly distrustful. Yet, for the first time in his life, perhaps, Armstrong felt like someone was watching out for him. In his earlier years, he was so daring and rebellious, he didn't think he needed anyone to look out for him. He had not yet become entirely convinced there was something super-natural about all this—but he decided he would continue the quest anyway.

As his interest in the Bible and spiritual issues increased, Armstrong had attended several different religious centers to see if they would help deepen his understanding. But they did not. In fact, he found the ministers were preaching messages in direct contradiction to what he was reading in the Bible. So he just kept secretly searching on his own.

Jeremy felt like a walk in the desert air would help clear his mind. The daytime heat was gone. It was a cool, comfortable evening. It was quiet and still outside his house in the officers' section of the base. There were no clouds, and since there were no city lights to hinder, he could see the sky full of stars. But the most striking sight was the moon. Jeremy didn't remember ever seeing a moon so full and bright, and he knew he had never seen one so blood red.

He walked about half a mile—slowly. Jeremy did some of his best thinking while walking. The profoundest thoughts and revelations seemed to come to him under such conditions.

"What's it all about, Lord?" he wondered. "Why am I here? Is there some purpose to my life for which I am not yet aware? Won't You please help me?" he asked. "I'm troubled by the state of this world. I want to know what I should do. I want to know what You would have me do."

Jeremy stopped for a moment. He had just read the passage in the Psalms that said, *"The heavens declare the glory of God and the earth shows forth His handiwork."* Jeremy took a deep breath and studied the beautiful sky. "Those untold millions of stars couldn't have just created themselves. And they certainly couldn't have kept themselves precisely in place on exactly timed orbits," Jeremy reflected. Then he thought of another verse he had read in the Psalms, *"The fool has said in his heart, 'There is no God.'"*

"If You're up there, Lord, if You're listening, please give me a sign."

Nothing. Jeremy wheeled and turned and headed back for his house. His thoughts turned to his Mom and his sister. "Where are they?" he wondered. "What really happened to them? What happened to all those others who disappeared at the same time—people of all walks of life from doctors to bankers to dishwashers and sanitation workers.

Some of the most dramatic disappearances, though, were the half-dozen airline captains who vanished from their cockpits without a trace. In some cases co-pilots were able to take control. In at least a couple of cases, however, the planes went down. There were some bloody messes on the highways, too, that day. Armstrong had read about cars cruising along at 65 miles an hour suddenly driverless. The horror stories were endless. But the news media, against every traditional practice with the greatest news event of history, downplayed the development—just as most of the world's governments did. No reason to create more panic than absolutely necessary, they apparently believed.

Armstrong found it amazing just how quickly people seemed to accept the inexplicable disappearance of millions of people worldwide on a single day at a single moment. Most would believe any official or semi-official explanation without question. The remaining population was eager to accept the worst about those who had left them. Of course, human nature being what it is, that reaction was understandable: No one would want to believe that they were left behind because of something they did or said or did not believe.

Jeremy was an exceptional case, however. He readily believed that his mother and sister were better than him. He always knew it. They were kinder, more giving, more spiritual and just...well, better than the average person. While Armstrong excelled at certain things—he had extraordinary abilities with athletics, mathematics, science and great physical endurance and courage—recently he had begun thinking of his life as a failure.

Sure, he had been decorated for valor in combat. He was one of the few who had been given the Congressional Medal of Honor. He was also a natural leader—especially in combat conditions. He understood weapons—from small arms to nuclear warheads and just about everything in between. But Mom and Carolyn, his sister...they were something special. Armstrong knew it and was proud of the kind of people they were.

Armstrong continued his walk back home, every once in a while looking up to scan the beautiful night sky. During one of those glances, Armstrong saw a shooting star completely traverse the horizon from east to west before plunging downward toward the earth. It was a spectacular sight—the best Armstrong had ever witnessed anywhere in the world.

"Wow," he said in an audible voice even though he was standing alone at the time. "Lord, are You trying to tell me something? Is this a sign that I should accept this opportunity in New York? Or should I be wary of it? Dear God, I appreciate the sign you have given me, but please help me to understand the meaning of it."

Armstrong waited and waited. No other meteors. No other visible signs. Was he imagining it? No. Was he projecting more into this natural phenomenon than was appropriate? Maybe, he thought. So, after staring up at the sky for 30 or more minutes, Armstrong retired for the evening back at his house.

About midnight, he was awakened by the phone. Armstrong reached for it instinctively in the dark.

"Hello," he greeted.

Nothing. No response.

"Hello?" he questioned a little louder.

He heard a small but authoritative voice say something. He wasn't quite sure what he heard at first.

"Excuse me?" he offered. "Is somebody there? Can you hear me?"

Nothing. He hung up. He thought about that small voice. What he heard sounded like something from the Bible. But what did it mean? Who was it on the other end? The thought of it all frightened even this 45-year-old combat veteran.

"I know what I heard," he thought. "I heard the words, 'I will return soon. Fear not'" Then he remembered a passage he had read in the Gospel of Matthew about Jesus' prediction of His Second Coming, *"For as the lightning comes from the east and flashes to the west, so also will the coming of the Son of Man be."* "Wow," thought Jeremy, "the meteor I saw tonight flashed across the entire sky from east to west. It truly was some kind of a sign. If this message was another sign—that Christ is returning soon—then I must make my life count for God."

The more Jeremy thought about it, the more he became convinced that this was no hoax. He heard what he heard. He saw what he saw. Was this the confirmation of the first sign? Was God telling him not to fear this assignment in New York?

Armstrong turned on the light. He dialed his old pal Zeke. He didn't worry about the fact that it was 3 o'clock in the morning in New York.

"Zeke?" Armstrong asked.

"Yeah, Jeremy?"

"Zeke, I'm in. Count on me for that assignment. It sounds good. Just tell me where to be and when and pull whatever strings you need to arrange my transfer."

"Great, Jeremy. It will be fun working with you again. I can't wait. However," he added dryly, "I could have waited another five hours to hear from you."

"Sorry about the time," said Armstrong. "I just decided and, oh, what the heck, you know me when I make a decision."

"Yeah, I know," said Charlton. "I know to get out of your way. I'll fill you in on the specifics in a few days."

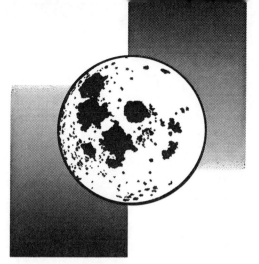

CHAPTER 3

From the Mouths of Genies

There, in the city of Mecca, standing before a strange and mysterious 50-foot cubic structure of gray stone and marble, Abdullah and Amina decided to name their son Muhammad.

Abdullah held up his baby son, just two weeks old. He smiled proudly. His wife, Amina, looked on with pride. They came to the Kabah, a strange and holy site in seventh-century pre-Islamic Arabia, to receive a blessing for their son. Inside the Kabah was the equally mysterious Jajar-ul-Aswad, the sacred black stone said to have fallen from heaven. Abdullah, Amina and their tribespeople believed the black stone had the power to take away one's sins. All you had to do was kiss it. Both of them did. They also placed the lips of the infant on the rock.

"This stone was a gift from the Angel Jabril in heaven to Adam," Abdullah told his baby son on a typically hot, dry day in the desert land of ancient Arabia. "God wanted us to have it so our sins could be forgiven after man was expelled from Paradise. The Kabah that surrounds the stone was built by Abraham and his son Ishmael at Allah's command."

Muhammad just gurgled. Amina smiled.

"He doesn't understand yet," Amina told her husband.

"You don't know that," said Abdullah. "I think we have a very unusual child here. I am certain Allah has a very special role for him to play."

Indeed, Muhammad was an unusual child. And unusual things seemed to happen all around him. Abdullah and Amina, members of the Quraysh tribe in Mecca, were affluent by the standards of the day. For instance, they could afford to hire servants to handle most of the mundane tasks of routine life in the bustling oasis city. They could also afford to hire a full-time caretaker for young Muhammad. A young Bedouin nurse named Halima was entrusted with this task.

"Care for my son, Halima," said Amina in handing over the boy. "Care for him as if he were your own boy. Treat him like a young prince. And bring him back to me when he is two years old." She was instructed to take the baby back with her to the desert where, long before petroleum-based industry and the automobile had made their impact, it was believed the air was healthier than in the city.

It was not unusual in those days in that culture for wealthy parents to place their young in the hands of nursemaids for the entirety of their early years. They didn't believe it was necessary for parents to bond emotionally with their young children. Since most adults do not clearly remember events or experiences prior to their fifth birthday, that period in human life was considered relatively unimportant to human development. So, why waste time with your baby?

Halima did as she was told. This was the way many young Bedouin girls and women helped to support their tribes and families. At 18 years of age, Halima's knowledge of child-rearing was limited to what she had learned from her mother, aunts and three older sisters. But she had been a good student, carefully observing the way her female relatives comforted, cleaned and suckled the babies. In no time at all, baby Muhammad was feeding at her youthful breast.

Halima grew attached to Muhammad, as might be expected of anyone in that situation. She would sing to him as he bathed. She would tickle him until he laughed so hard he could not breathe. She would pamper him and groom him like the prince his mother suggested he was. In many ways, Halima loved her little charge. But she also worried about him—especially as he reached the toddler stage.

By that time, Halima had married and birthed a son of her own. If anything, she had become more expert at raising children. Yet there was something deeply troubling about Muhammad. He was...different.

"He's a strange boy," Halima told her sister, Salma, who had three sons of her own. "Sometimes he seems to be in a world of his own—so deep in thought he cannot hear what I say to him. Other times he seems frightened by things he sees that are not visible to me. I am beginning to look forward to the day I can return him to his natural mother."

On Muhammad's second birthday, Halima wasted no time in doing just that—returning him to Amina. Halima had nursed the child until a few days earlier, when he was weaned. It was time for him return to his parents, she thought—not only for his sake but for hers as well. Muhammad's mother seemed truly happy to see her son. But, much to Halima's chagrin, the homecoming party was short-lived. Delighted with Muhammad's healthy look, Amina said, "Take the child with thee back again, for much do I fear for him the unwholesome air of Mecca." So, reluctantly, Halima returned to the desert with Muhammad in tow.

Soon, Halima became even more convinced that something was truly wrong with Muhammad. One day at mealtime, for instance, he suddenly bolted from his plate and ran screaming into the dark night. She followed him by listening to his panicked cries.

"They're after me," he yelled. "They're after me."

"Who is after you?" she queried after the exhausted child fell to the ground weeping uncontrollably.

"The two men in white garments," he said as he pointed into the night.

Halima looked around and saw nothing but darkness. Though she saw no one, she was frightened by an eerie, invisible presence she could not explain. Her husband suggested the boy had eaten some bad dates. But none of

the other children were affected. They just sat there quietly, puzzled by the behavior of their older playmate.

And this was no isolated incident. It was the kind of
thing that Halima had come to expect in caring for
Muhammad.

When Muhammad turned four years old, Halima's concerns only increased. He began telling his caregiver of regular visits he was having with angels or "jinnis," as they
were called in Arabic. This worried Halima gravely, for she
understood that there were both good jinnis and bad jinnis. She felt certain, because of the nature of the torment
Muhammad was experiencing, that these visitors were up
to no good with the youngster.

During one such "visitation," Muhammad sat on the
ground with his legs crossed and rocked back and forth
for hours—apparently unable to hear or see her. At other
times, he ran to and fro, carrying out orders from his
unseen companions. Halima referred to these episodes as
"fits," and, indeed, that was no exaggeration. It had been
two years since Muhammad had seen his parents. Halima
decided she would try once again to return him to Amina
and Abdullah.

Amina seemed surprised to see her son, but she smiled
slightly nonetheless. Halima was not smiling, however.

"You must take the child back now," Halima said out of
earshot of Muhammad. "I believe he is demon-possessed."

"Nonsense," said Amina. "Just look at him. He is healthier than ever. You are doing a wonderful job raising him.
The desert air is just what he needs. Besides that, my husband, Abdullah, has died and I am not prepared to handle

the boy now. Just keep him awhile longer. You will be greatly rewarded for the care you are giving him."

Disappointed by Amina's reaction, Halima returned to the desert again with Muhammad, determined to give the arrangement one more chance. The fits and visitations only increased in frequency and intensity. When Muhammad was five years old, he was walking in an open field with one of Halima's sons on a beautiful sunny day. Suddenly he fell to the ground in anguish complaining that two angels had cut open his belly in search of something. That was the end, as far as Halima was concerned. She could take it no longer. She took Muhammad back to Mecca. This time she wasn't taking no for an answer.

Muhammad barely had time to adjust to his new life with his natural mother before she, too, died of a mysterious illness, leaving Muhammad an orphan at the age of six.

He was entrusted to the care of his 70-year-old grandfather, Abdul al-Mut-Talib, and Amina's slave Umm Ayan. Muhammad continued to have visions, but his grandfather scarcely noticed. He had failing eyesight and his hearing was impaired. For all intents and purposes, Muhammad lived in a world of his own—a world of scary angels and very little human tenderness and compassion.

When Muhammad was 12, Al-Mut Talib died. So Muhammad moved once again—this time to live with his uncle, Abu Talib, who apprenticed him in the merchant trade by taking him on caravan runs carrying frankincense and silk north to Damascus and other cities. It was an adventurous life, and while the visitations didn't cease, they subsided.

The seventh century Middle East in general, and Arabia in particular, was a land divided ethnically as well as geographically. This was reflected in the different tribal gods, the diverse lifestyles and even distinct dialects. Politically, its western and southern coastal region, the Yemen, was basically stable. Its northern and central areas, on the other hand, were literally fields of battle on which warring desert tribes and family blood feuds took place.

The vast, largely desert region contained little to invite foreign invasion. Its national, political and religious disunity offered no threat to its militarily superior neighbors. Oil and its value were as yet unknown. But geographically, located between Asia, Africa and Europe, its strategic importance was incalculable. Even before the industrial revolution and the discovery of vast reserves of oil, economically the Middle East represented a bonanza because it included the main trading routes between three continents.

Topographically, its vast deserts offered relief only around the scattered wells and oases used as stops by various caravans. Many of these stops, in fact, became prosperous trading centers and towns. Some even became cities. One such place was Muhammad's birthplace of Mecca. In addition to its commercial importance, it thrived and grew mainly because it was home to the Kabah. The West, during this period, was represented by the Greco-Roman Empire of Byzantium, the East by Persia. The upper Euphrates and the Tigris formed the physical boundary between the two. The Arabs lay slightly to the south of, and in contact with, both empires.

In AD 115, Trajan, the warrior-emperor, had led the

Roman legions into this area, establishing the provinces of the Nabataeans in Northern Arabia, Arabia, Armenia, Assyria and Mesopotamia—at the time, the furthest eastern borders of the Roman Empire. On the plains of Mesopotamia in 363, the Roman Emperor Julian was mortally wounded in a desperate battle with the Persians. As a result, Rome lost five of its eastern provinces to the victorious Persians.

Fifty years after the fall of the Roman Empire, Justinian ascended the throne of Byzantium. On becoming emperor, he reluctantly engaged in another series of wars with Persia. To protect their open southern flanks, both Byzantium and Persia maintained a group of Arab satellite states.

The struggle between East and West—with the Middle East caught in the crossfire—had raged for centuries. The Arab peoples, tribal nomads separated by great expanses, with no central government, were often at each other's throats. Most of the tribes were idolaters. Each tribe had its own collection of gods. They worshipped holy rocks and trees that they believed were indwelt by spirit beings.

Of the 360 or more gods in their pagan theology, the four most important in the hierarchy were Uzza, Allat, Manat and Hubal. The first three were female and formed a tri-theistic relationship. On the other hand, Hubal was a male considered to be the Moon deity—a god that originated in ancient Babylon. Hubal was held to be the guardian of the Kabah. The chief of all the deities, however, was "Allah," who was worshipped as the supreme creator as well as the father of the tri-theistic female gods.

So Mecca, with the Kabah and its "sacred well," became the religious vortex of the Arab Middle East. From 100 BC, the Kabah and its sacred well were under the guardianship of a tribe known as the Beni Jurham. In the third century, they were driven out and replaced by an Ishmaelite tribe known as the Khuzaa. In AD 235, Fihr, the leader of another Ishmaelite tribe, the Quraysh, married the daughter of the Khuzaa chief. Then again, in about AD 420, Qusai, a descendant of Fihr, married the daughter of another Khuzaa chief of Mecca.

Although not a Khuzaa, Qusai made himself virtually indispensable to his father-in-law, who was guardian of the Kabah. Therefore, Qusai was given the sacred keys of the Kabah. When the Khuzaa chief died, Qusai claimed custody of the Kabah for the Quraysh. One of his first acts was to relegate the Khuzaa to a subordinate position. Qusai also ordered the building of a semi-permanent housing around the temple and restructured tribal social order. He instituted tribal council meetings, and a hall was built near the Kabah.

Qusai died in 455, leaving the sacred custody of the Kabah to his eldest sons Abdul Dar, Abid Menaf and Abdul Uzza. Jealousies arose between the descendants of Abdul Dar and Abid Menaf, resulting in divisions of family responsibilities Abdul Dar's heirs retained custody of the Kabah and the right to carry the tribal banner into war, while the descendants of Abid Menaf were given the menial responsibilities of caring for the Arab pilgrims who came to visit the shrine.

Of Menaf's sons, the most distinguished was Hashim.

While the eldest brother, Abid Shems, inherited the military and family leadership of the Quraysh, Hashim grew rich in the caravan trade. He also gained much popularity and fame in his lavish treatment of the pilgrims who came from all over Arabia.

By the time of his father's death, Hashim had not only inherited his father's credibility, but he had equaled his great grandfather's innovativeness. In the course of his commercial travels, Hashim married a woman named Selma, who gave birth to a son, Abdul al-Mut-Talib. Abdul had seven sons: Harith, Talib, Lahab, Jahal, Abbas, Hamza and Abdullah. Abdullah married Amina, who was a descendant of Qusai's brother Zuhra. It was this union that resulted in the birth of Muhammad, a man who would affect not only the fate of the Middle East but the entire world for the next 1,300 years.

When Muhammad was 25 years old, his uncle suggested that he go to work for a rich widow merchant in Mecca named Khadija. He was hired to accompany her merchant caravan to Syria, which he did several times. Although she was 40 years of age, widowed twice with three daughters, she was quite beautiful. She was undeniably attracted to the sensual young Muhammad. After only a brief courtship, they married. Together they had two sons, Abdullah and Qusim, both of whom died in childhood, and a daughter, Fatima.

Even as a young married man with the responsibilities of fatherhood, Muhammad continued to exhibit mystic tendencies. Because of Khadija's wealth, he could afford to retreat to the hills around Mecca for uninterrupted periods of religious meditation. But rather than inner peace, these excursions produced only spiritual anxiety.

He would retire to caves for seclusion and fasting. When he did, he was prone to dreams. In AD 610, on the occasion known as "The Night of Power," Muhammad received his mightiest revelation of all.

It was an unusually dark night. The moon was partly obscured by clouds that cast a blood-red haze over the heavenly body. While Muhammad meditated by himself in a cave in Mount Hira overlooking the Hejaz Valley in Arabia, a visitor appeared who later was described by Muhammad as "a gracious and mighty messenger, held in honor by the Lord of the Throne." The messenger identified himself to Muhammad as the angel "Jabril" or Gabriel.

"Proclaim!" commanded the apparition three times.

"What shall I proclaim?" asked Muhammad.

"Proclaim in the name of your Lord who created, created man from clots of blood! Proclaim! Your Lord who created the most bountiful one, who by the pen taught man what he did not know."

That fateful night, the religion of Islam was born, though Muslims might argue that the faith was merely about to be "re-established" by Muhammad. They see Islam as the first and true religion of the Middle East and Muhammad more as reformer and restorer than founder of a new religion. His mission, they say, was essentially to re-establish monotheism as it had originally been revealed to, but subsequently corrupted by, Jews and Christians.

This was no easy task. For despite traditions that hold Muhammad as the one author of the Koran, the prophet of Islam was quite illiterate. He relied not on the pen, but on his fiery oratory to captivate his audiences. When he returned to his tribe after "The Night of Power," his skills as a preacher were witnessed for the first time.

Prior to that evening, it was not unusual for Muhammad to regale companions sitting around a campfire with engaging stories and detailed theological treatises. But there was a different look in his eye after "The Night of Power." He was a changed man. No one around him doubted he had become "The Prophet." He gained his first 200 converts to his faith the very next day.

"Bism'illah ir-Rahman ir-Rahim," he told his friends and fellow caravan guides. "In the name of Allah the Merciful, the Compassionate, " he said, "I am here to proclaim his word, his truth. The sons of Ishmael have lost their way. They are like sheep who have wandered off the path of righteousness—off the Lord's trail. If we are to be redeemed as a people, we must obey Allah. I am here as his final and most important prophet to lead the way back onto the path of truth and righteousness. Follow me."

And follow him they did—like an army of the night. Their first destination? To secure a strategic base of operations that would help them spread the new Islamic faith throughout the Middle East and the world.

Pope John Paul III stepped back from the veranda at St. Peter's Basilica. Below, thousands of Sunday worshipers began streaming out after hearing the pontiff say Mass.

"God bless you all," he said in closing. "Be tolerant of one another."

This was the pope's most familiar catchphrase. Some snide critics had compared it unfavorably with one of Jesus' most memorable phrases: "Love one another." Somehow, "Be tolerant of one another," just didn't have the same ring to it. But most of what this pope had said and done in the last five years did indeed strike a winning chord—not just with Catholics, but with most people in the world. He was clearly one of the most popular popes ever, and a dramatic change from one of his predecessors, Carol Wojtyla of Poland.

While Pope John Paul II had tried to steer the Church back toward a more traditional role—standing firm against women priests, abortion, ordination of homosexuals, marriage by priests, etc.—this pope had a much more worldly view. Pope Pius XIII, his immediate predecessor, was only trying to hang on to the status quo. But John Paul III not only knocked down barriers to all of the previous rulings in his first year in the Vatican, he also moved quickly toward unification with mainstream Protestant churches.

There had been a mystical prophecy given the children of Fatima that predicted the second pope after John Paul II would be aligned with the Anti-Christ. John Paul II, who was probably a true believer, also predicted the same thing, along with a famous Jesuit author named Malachai Martin.

All of this present pope's radical opinions were well-known to the College of Cardinals long before they voted to make him pope. But even the conservative Italian delegation went along with the radical shift in Vatican personality and policy. Why? For one thing, he was Italian. And many of the Italian cardinals—even the most traditional—had vowed that there would not be another "foreigner" named to the papacy for a long, long time. "Foreigners," of course, meant any non-Italian. This is how Cardinal Marco Vesuviani, who was born on the steps of Mount Vesuvius near ancient Pompeii, became John Paul III.

Meanwhile, back on the veranda at the basilica, the pope continued to smile and wave until he was no longer visible to any part of the crowd below. Then his face quickly turned serious—almost dour.

"Get me Secretary-General Carlo," he snapped to one of his aides, who began dialing the European leader's number on a secure cellular phone. Within minutes the most powerful religious figure on the planet was talking to the most powerful political figure on the planet.

"Everything is in place," said the pope.

"Good," said Carlo. "It's time."

Perhaps no one else in the world could have deciphered their cryptic conversation. But the important thing was that *they* knew what they were talking about. They always seemed to know—even when their inner circles of top aides were baffled. It was as if the two of them shared some strange intuitive powers. Many observers had suggested they were, in many ways, a "team." But none could have imagined just how close this team was, nor the powerful spirit being that pulled them together.

Both agreed the three most important cities in the world were Rome, Jerusalem and New York. Therefore, they maintained homes and offices in all three locations.

While still an Italian cardinal, this pope had spent a great deal of time in Israel and felt increasingly and almost mystically drawn to the Jewish state. Carlo, a realist on the other hand, understood the geo-strategic importance of Jerusalem. That's why he spent so much time there. They played an almost equal role in negotiating and establishing the peace covenant in the Middle East that essentially made a smaller, lesser-armed Israel a virtual United Nations protectorate.

But because, as someone once observed, "Man does not live by bread alone," Carlo the materialist politician knew he needed a spiritual leader to usher in his new era of peace on earth. The pope was always there to help. But what they had up their sleeves this time was anyone's guess.

"I need to fly to Jerusalem tonight," the pontiff told Father Vittorio. "Make the necessary arrangements."

"Of course, your excellency," said Father Vittorio. "Is there anything else I should know?"

"I'll tell you exactly what you need to know, Vittorio," said the pope. "Sometimes too much knowledge is a dangerous thing."

"Yes, your excellency," said Father Vittorio.

With that, Vittorio ordered the pontiff's plane readied. He would arrive in Jerusalem by 6:30 p.m., and his ground staff there would be prepared to whisk him wherever he needed to go. Such an unplanned and unannounced itinerary would have been unheard of for his predecessors. But this is the way Pope John Paul III often traveled. He was the only pope in recent history who could actually conceal his whereabouts at times. And he liked having that ability.

Carlo, meanwhile, was already in Jerusalem. He was scheduled to make a major policy speech. Not only would it be broadcast live by UNN, the United Nations Network, but also by CNN. Vittorio guessed that the pope would probably make an appearance at the event—perhaps even say a few words himself.

While 20th century popes were always revered guests in any foreign nation, no matter what the dominant religion might be, the 21st century began like no other. Shortly after New Year's Day, there were signs in the heavens. They were spotted all over the earth—in nearly every country. As in Fatima, the sun would change shapes and dance across the sky. The sun would appear to have rings around it. It would pulsate.

Then, what seemed to be angels appeared in the sky. There were visions of the Virgin Mary. And there were messages for all those who observed. These were not sights witnessed only by a few hundred thousand people, mind you. Nearly everyone on earth saw some of it, either directly or on television. And one thing became clear to most of humanity after several weeks of these supernatural phenomena—the world was entering a new spiritual age. No longer was there any reason to evangelize or proselytize. No longer were differences between the religions considered significant. No longer was there reason to fear a central religious figure—like the pope.

In fact, the pope was the single biggest beneficiary of Fatima II. The messages people received from the angels in the sky frequently urged people to look to the pope for spiritual guidance—to believe in his infallibility. So persuasive was the show in the heavens that stone-cold atheists began professing faith in the pope afterwards.

But not everyone believed. Some felt the signs were part of a grand deception. A few of them were rebellious fundamentalist Christians or Orthodox Jews, but the most vocal were Islamic fundamentalists. Many mainstream Muslims accepted the signs, especially since they did not indicate that Christianity or Catholicism was the only true path. Most religionists took from the signs what they wanted to take—Hindus loved them, Buddhists loved them, New Agers loved them. Even most Jews accepted them. A new wave of universalism swept across the world, and nearly everyone it touched was intoxicated by the euphoria of love and peace that it seemed to bring with it.

It was this remarkable event that permitted—perhaps demanded—the pope to maintain a presence in Jerusalem. This pope was only too happy to accommodate.

"Israel is the country which, after Italy, I know best," he had said even before becoming pontiff. "Even the stones there are dear to me."

It was during those days, while still a cardinal, that the pope—or Marco Vesuviani in his pre-papal days—first met a very mystical Jew named Elijah Ben David, who had already become legendary among the Israelis. Ben David was born in Bethlehem but raised in the mystical city of Safed, which is perched high in the mountains above the northern area of the Sea of Galilee. For centuries, Safed has been the center of the mystical Jewish religious order called The Kabalah. They search the Hebrew Old

Testament for hidden, encoded messages—often using mathematics to find hidden patterns of communication under the normal meaning of the text.

Ben David was steeped in the knowledge of the Kabalah from infancy. But it was on Elijah's eighteenth birthday that he received a "divine visitation." He testified that God appeared to him in a brilliant, multi-colored light. In this visitation, God told him he was the predicted Anointed Prophet of which Moses and Isaiah spoke, who would lead Israel into the complete fulfillment of all that was promised to Abraham, and he would bring great blessing to all the nations. From that time onward, Ben David began to demonstrate a prophetic gift. He prophesied with great accuracy near future events involving not only Israel, but other nations as well. He also received a gift of seeing right into a person's mind, discerning his very thoughts and motives. Perhaps most amazing of all, he was miraculously enabled to speak almost every language in the world. Cardinal Marco became the intimate friend of Elijah Ben David, which served him well after becoming Pope. He also felt indebted to Ben David because he publicly predicted Cardinal Marco would become pope several years before it happened.

Because of this, the Jewish state immediately took to this pope. They believed he was a real friend. Even the orthodox Jews liked him, because they believed Ben David was the Jewish Messiah, and whatever he said was immediately accepted by them. They rolled out the red carpet for him whenever he visited—which, lately, was frequently. There was even talk about establishing a kind of second Vatican in Jerusalem.

The pope's plane touched down right on schedule. Only after he had deplaned did he give instructions to anyone on the ground.

"Take me to the university," he told his driver.

"Yes your excellency," said the chauffeur.

The university was where Carlo would be speaking in about an hour, thought Father Bonano, the pope's top Jerusalem attaché, who was seated next to the pontiff in the limousine.

"Should I call ahead with the usual security provisions?" asked Bonano.

"Don't bother," said the pope. "Nothing is going to go wrong tonight."

"But your excellency," interjected Bonano, "these are still dangerous times here in the Middle East. There are some people who reject you and Carlo. Some are violent people...."

"Please, Bonano," said the pope, "it's not necessary this time. But if it pleases you to have a small group of Israeli police officers meet us at the parking lot closest to the auditorium, I won't object. But absolutely no military people!"

"Yes, your excellency," said Bonano. "I understand."

Fabio Bonano, a meticulous career foreign service officer for the Vatican, picked up the phone and gave instructions to the Jerusalem police.

When the car arrived at the university, it passed through a small protest by perhaps 20 Islamic students carrying placards that read, "Carlo go home" and "Liberate all Palestine." The students wore *kaffiyeh* to cover their faces. Israeli security kept the protesters at least 100 yards from the entrance to the auditorium, where the pope was now arriving.

As soon as his limousine door opened, the pope was surrounded by Jerusalem police officers who had kept even the media away. They whisked the pope and his entourage into the relative safety of the auditorium's backstage dressing rooms.

"Let the secretary-general know I am here," the pope told Bonano.

"He already knows," proclaimed President Ben David as he walked in the door.

"Good," said the pope. "Is there somewhere just the three of us can talk?"

Bonano looked bewildered. He and the security team officers stared at each other. In about 30 minutes, Carlo was scheduled to begin his world address. Now the pope announces he wants to have an impromptu private meeting with the two most powerful political and religious figures on earth—next to himself—in an unfamiliar setting.

"May I suggest you talk with the secretary-general's staff," said the pope. "I am sure they have this place staked out well by now."

"Thank you, your excellency," said Bonano. "That is an excellent suggestion."

Within minutes, Bonano was back. Carlo had the same idea about a private meeting with the pope and Ben David, and already had a meeting room set up. They could see each other immediately. Bonano ushered the pope and Ben David into the adjacent room with two security officers in tow. The pope dismissed them as soon as he had seated himself alongside Ben David. Carlo entered the room a minute or two later.

"I hope I didn't keep you waiting, your excellencies," said Carlo, smiling broadly.

"Not at all, Gianfranco," said the pope. "So good to see you."

Ben David spoke more cryptically, "My people have waited centuries for you. I surely don't mind waiting a few minutes."

The three men embraced warmly.

"Now, there isn't much time for me to tell you what I have to say, my brothers," Carlo began. "When I finish my speech tonight, I am going to be mortally shot in the head."

The pope looked as shocked as one might expect he would be by such news.

"Gianfranco," he said, "I had a feeling things were leading up to this, but why?"

"Don't worry, my good friend," said Carlo, "you don't believe death is really the end, do you?"

"Of course not," said the pope, "but this world needs your leadership. And I need your friendship."

"And the world shall have it," said Carlo. "And you shall have it."

"What do you mean?" asked the pope.

"I am going to be led like a lamb to slaughter and I will be resurrected," explained Carlo. "God Almighty appeared to me in blazing light and assured me of this. In fact, He said that I would become as Him after being raised up from death."

The pope's eyes grew wide. He was surprised, but he never disbelieved anything Carlo said. He knew better. He looked over at Elijah Ben David and saw that he was not surprised by this revelation.

"It is true. I also foresaw this," Ben David said. "I am personally a little bewildered and saddened by this revelation. But I know there had to be a fulfillment of all the prophecies, both of the Bible's and mine."

"That's right," added Carlo. "Tonight is the night. One of those radicals from the Islamic Flame will shoot me. I will truly die. And I will be resurrected. My supernatural powers will be greatly increased. In fact, in my resurrection body, the Lord has promised I will have extrasensory powers of all kinds—my knowledge will be greatly increased. All things necessary to truly lead the world government will be given to me. We, the three of us, will be able to govern this world in a way that was never possible before."

"What will be my role in this incident?" the pope asked.

"I simply want you and Elijah to witness my resurrection and declare it what it shall be in truth—a miracle of God," said Carlo. "That's all. Both of you be there by my side after I am declared officially dead. I want you to witness everything together. It is so important that this not be misunderstood by anyone. We will never have another opportunity like this to unite humanity. OK, I must go now. I will see you on stage, my friend."

"Peace be with you, my friend," said the pope, a tear running from his eye.

"Shalom, my brother," Ben David said sadly. "We will see each other again."

Carlo left the room. The pope sat for a moment. Then Bonano and others entered.

"Holy Father, can I get you anything before you have to go on-stage?" asked Bonano.

"Yes," said the pope. "I need a glass of water *and a Bible.*"

Carlo's speech was, as everyone expected it to be, a masterpiece of encouragement and affirmation for those who believed man really was on the verge of leaping into a whole new dimension of spiritual consciousness.

"We are truly entering a New Age," Carlo told the group of mostly Arab and Jewish students, international media representatives and a large contingency of leaders flown in from around the world for what was billed as a historic address. "We are about to see just how far human potential can take us. Together, mankind—and wom-ankind—can conquer injustice; we can conquer disease; we can conquer prejudice; we can conquer ancient hatreds; we can conquer ignorance; we can conquer hunger; we can conquer violence; *and we shall!*

"What we need is unity. Never in the history of the world has there been a moment like this, when we have been so close to achieving real unity—real peace, real har-mony. With all mankind working together in one great new united world, there is no limit to what we can do. We are about to take a large evolutionary leap forward—a quantum leap toward a world we can't even imagine. Will you take this journey with me? Do you dare follow me?"

Every time Carlo punctuated his speech with one of his famous rhetorical questions, the audience roared its approval. He was a spellbinding orator, and tonight he was at his very best. Most of the audience had tears of joy in their eyes.

"The days of naysaying are over, my friends. There is nothing we cannot achieve together. We can explore the universe. We can build great new spacecraft to reach out into the heavens. We may even discover extra-terrestrial beings of immense power and intelligence. We can create machines to do all of our unpleasant chores. All we have to do is come together. Is this a ride you want to take with me? Are you ready to leave?

"There is a paradigm shift of colossal magnitude about to take place. Look for it. It will be as obvious as those signs in heaven were a few years ago. When you see it, you will recognize it. Trust the words I am telling you. There is nothing we cannot do together. Do you believe it? Am I telling you the truth?

"There are always going to be mockers and scoffers. There will always be doubters. Even when the heavens opened up and cleaned the earth of millions of them, more sprang up. They will always be with us. But we don't have to listen to them, do we? Don't you think it's time we stopped listening to these archaic Christians who retard any advancement with their false interpretations about a coming doomsday?

"I believe we're entering that special time, that true prophetic time, that holy time—that millennial kingdom which we will bring in. You will see the lion lie down with the lamb simply by meditating it into being. I really believe it. Do you believe it? Do you want to believe it?"

As Carlo spoke these words, he turned around and made eye contact with the Pope and President Ben David seated behind him. The Pope nodded in acknowledgment of the remarks and his tacit agreement with them.

"What will it take to get us there? Well, my friends, it's going to take positive thinking. It's going to take trust. It's going to take leadership. And it's going to take community. That's right, we need to start treating each other like we're all members of the same community—of one great family. Why? Because we are! The world is becoming one big global community.

"Now, as you know, every community has its problems, its disputes, its troubles. But a functioning community has a system for handling them. There is a hierarchy. There is order. And that's what this global community needs today more than anything. We need order and leadership. And I am prepared as never before to offer that to the world. Do you want it? Do you accept it?"

The hall erupted in a standing ovation that seemed to shake the very foundations of the building.

"Thank you. Thank you very much," concluded Carlo as he walked slowly off the stage while waving to the crowd.

Before he reached the stage left exit, a shot rang out that could be heard even over the raucous din of the thunderous applause. There was no mistaking the sound. All at once, there was chaos on stage. Carlo was down. A pool of blood was forming from a massive wound in his head. Security surrounded him and there was a scuffle taking place near the curtain. At least ten police officers and others were wresting a Glock 9mm automatic pistol from a man in a black and white *kaffiyeh*.

Security forces were streaming out on-stage from both sides. They surrounded the pope, who didn't look surprised by the scene. The audience, meanwhile, was gasping in horror, standing on their seats to get a better look at what was happening. They could vaguely hear the faint sound of sirens outside. An ambulance arrived, a stretcher was brought out for Carlo. No one in the audience or on-stage believed for a minute, however, that he would live. No one, of course, except Ben David and the pope.

The police now had completely subdued the killer. He was shackled and brought outside to be transported to the police station. Several cars accompanied him. A police helicopter flew overhead. There was always the possibility that his friends might try to ambush the police and break out their "hero." The police weren't taking any chances. They called for IDF backup all along the route.

Meanwhile, back on stage, the pope pushed aside his security people and strode toward the microphone. The wailing and the shouting were still too loud for anyone to be heard in the auditorium—even with a microphone. He motioned for people to sit down and asked for quiet.

"At a time like this, ladies and gentlemen, there is little else we mortals can do but pray," he said. "Please join me in a moment of silence for our beloved leader Gianfranco Carlo." Miraculously, there was silence in the auditorium. Thirty seconds later, the pope resumed.

"Gianfranco Carlo is my friend," he began. "Yes, he is the pre-eminent leader in the world today—a great hope to us all. But to me he is much more. He is my dearest friend. My heart goes out tonight to his wife and his entire family. Let us pray for the best. Let us pray for a miracle. We all saw what happened tonight. I know it doesn't look good. But I believe, in the spirit of Gianfranco Carlo, we should remain positive. We must not give up hope. Let us pray for a miracle.

"Heavenly father, are You still the God of miracles? If You are, we need one tonight. Will You deliver us from the evil of religious prejudice? Gianfranco Carlo envisioned Your kingdom coming to earth. Will you help us to bring Your kingdom to earth, Lord? Will You do it soon? *If You work a miracle and restore life to Your servant, Gianfranco Carlo, then we will know that we have been ordained to bring Your millennial kingdom on the earth now.* We will establish Your will on earth as it is in heaven. Amen.

"Brothers and sisters, this is a trying time. But remember, there was One who gave His life as an example of God's love and power 2,000 years ago. And many believe that He was raised up from death. Miracles happen. Believe. Believe with all your heart. Peace be with you all."

The message was heard not only in the 1,750-seat auditorium, but throughout the world. As soon as word of the assassination got out, every television station on the planet switched to live programming from the satellite feed. The pope's decision to wait several minutes before going to the microphone ensured that every word he spoke would be immortalized and broadcast live for billions.

After he was finished speaking, news media focus shifted to the hospital where Gianfranco Carlo had been taken. It was not good news. Carlo was alive, but barely. A 9 millimeter hollow-nosed bullet had entered an inch above Carlos' left eye and exited the back of his head. There was massive brain damage and great loss of blood. The brain wave monitor indicated he was virtually brain dead. Only a respirator was keeping him technically alive. The prognosis was that he was all but dead already. The doctors worked frantically over him anyway.

"It will take a miracle for him to make it," said Dr. Chaim Ginott, a brain surgeon who examined the wound. He would certainly have permanent brain damage even if he survived.

Meanwhile, over at police headquarters, authorities announced that the suspect in the assassination attempt was Mustafa Muhammad, a member of the notorious terrorist group called The Sword of Allah. He had been long sought by Interpol for terrorist activity. His brother, Ishmael Muhammad, the group's brilliant and ruthless leader, was still at large.

"I must be with Carlo at the hospital," the pope told Bonano, back at the auditorium.

"Do you think that's best right now, your holiness, with all the confusion?" asked Bonano, already knowing the answer he would get.

"Let's go," said the pope.

Bonano informed the police escort of the plan, and the pope was on his way to the limousine for the five-minute ride to the Hadassah Hospital. When they arrived, the scene was indeed chaotic. It looked like Parkland Memorial Hospital in Dallas must have looked back on November 22, 1963, after President Kennedy was shot. There was a sea of humanity around the place—mostly just people who were drawn there after watching the shooting on television. There was a lot of sobbing, and even wails of recrimination against Muslims.

"It's just like Rabin again!" shouted one lady. "How many times do we have to see this?"

Israelis seemed to be as touched by the attack on Carlo as they would be if he was one of their own—a Jew, an Israeli. In many ways, the Israelis were fonder of Carlo than any of their own leaders except for Prime Minister Ben David. He somehow rose above politics for them, and his close friendship with Ben David made him even more loved.

But it wasn't just Israelis who were mourning Carlo at the hospital. There were a large number of Muslims as well. The pope noted this as his limo slowly made its way through the throngs and close to the door of the hospital.

The pope, heavily escorted this time, made his way slowly through the door and down the hall to the intensive care unit. Reporters mobbed the police escort trying to get a word from the pontiff. But it was no use. Police just pushed them aside.

When the pope reached Carlo's room, he found Elijah Ben David in the hall waiting for him. He was informed that no visitors were allowed. The secretary-general's condition was extremely grave.

"I know," said the pope. "That's why I'm here. I wish to

administer last rites and I want only Prime Minister Ben David to be with me. Would you please clear the room."

The doctor agreed that this was an appropriate time for the last rites.

"Please clear the room," the doctor instructed. Nurses and orderlies scurried outside.

The pope and Ben David were now alone in the room. He looked at Ben David and then his friend in the bed. Cameras were flashing outside. The pope looked up, annoyed at the distraction. He walked to the window and closed the curtains. Now it was just Carlo and the pope and Ben David. He knelt beside Gianfranco and prayed aloud.

"I commit the spirit of Gianfranco Carlo into the hands of the Lord of this earth. Take him and use him to Your honor and glory. If You keep Your promise to resurrect him, I will follow You as never before. Amen."

As if on cue, the EKG whistled and the line on the screen went flat. Prime Minister Ben David opened the door and solemnly announced, "Gianfranco Carlo is dead!"

CHAPTER 4

The First Jihad

"Woooohh!" Jacob called to the horse pulling his makeshift plow. The horse stopped and Jacob wiped his brow. It was a hot day in Yathrib, the Hejaz city dominated by Jews like himself who brought with them from Israel the technological know-how of mechanized agriculture early in the seventh century. Sweat poured off Jacob's brow. He dabbed at it with his headdress. He could feel the desert sand sticking to his face. But that wasn't Jacob's principal irritation at the moment.

Jacob was concerned about something he saw in the distance. Far off at the eastern horizon a cloud of dust was rising dozens of feet into the air. Was it a windstorm? Jacob's 62-year-old eyes were beginning to fail him. He climbed on top of his plow for a better look. From that vantage point he determined that many riders were headed toward Yathrib. It was not the normal caravan of merchants bringing goods to sell in Yathrib. This was a much faster moving force of perhaps 200 men. Jacob feared it was an invasion by nomadic marauders. The force was about an hour away, Jacob judged. He hurried home to warn his family and friends.

"Trouble is coming," he told his wife, Rebekah, as he entered his stately stone home.

"What do you mean, Jacob?" she asked.

"An army of riders is heading this way fast," he said. "I can't imagine that they are coming to buy our produce. I fear the worst. We must warn the others."

Rebekah and Jacob quickly spread the news among the thousands of Jewish settlers who made up the majority of the population of the city of Yathrib.

"Be prepared!" shouted Jacob. "Trouble is headed our way."

"Retreat to your homes," warned Rebekah. "We must be on guard. Gather your families together."

All around Yathrib, Jews scurried behind prepared fortifications. They left their fields and their farming equipment. Merchants closed up their doors. Bustling open-air markets quickly shut down. The Jewish community resembled a ghost town within moments after the riders were first spotted.

While the Jews of Yathrib had not experienced invasion or persecution since their forebears arrived in the Hejaz, they retained the historical memory of what it was like to be driven out of their homeland by the Romans. Judaism was actually experiencing something of a revival in seventh-century Arabia. Hundreds of thousands—perhaps millions—of Jews had fled from Israel after Roman legions plundered the Jewish state in the first century. Rome renamed Jerusalem Aelia Capitolina and banished all Jews from the area. In the Diaspora, Jews fled to all parts of the known world, including Arabia, where they formed new settlements or joined existing Jewish-Arabian communities established at the time of release from captivity in Babylon.

Jews and Arabs mixed fairly easily during this pre-Islamic period. Jews from Israel and Arab converts lived everywhere throughout the Arabian peninsula—especially in Yathrib. Mainly farmers and artisans, the Jews led thriving communities—so much so, in fact, that Arabs emigrated from other parts of the Hejaz for the jobs, the markets and the commercial opportunities that were being created in places like Yathrib. Jacob was one of the spiritual and civic leaders of the Jewish population in Yathrib—a population which reached into the thousands.

Much to Jacob's relief, when the band of well-armed horsemen reached Yathrib, they did not draw their swords from their scabbards. Instead, they watered their horses and arranged a meeting between their leader and the leaders of the various communities within the city. Jacob was among those asked to join the discussion.

Sitting inside an elegant tent owned by an Arab prince just after sundown, about 20 farmers, clerics, artisans, politicians and shopkeepers listened with interest—if not apprehension—to the leader of the unexpected visitors. He was introduced by an enthusiastic and handsome young man named Moammar as "a great Prophet of Allah." His name was Muhammad.

"Greetings, my friends, in the name of Allah the merciful and compassionate," he began. "I am here to bring you great news and glad tidings. It is true that I speak to you as a Prophet of Allah. Our Lord has graciously revealed to me truths that have become obscured by the ravages of time—truths that our forefathers, including Abraham, Moses and Jesus, understood, but which we, the sons of Ishmael, have too often forgotten."

So far, Jacob thought, he liked what he was hearing. Here was a godly man—not a warrior. He evidently had come to preach to the heathens and idolaters in Yathrib. And the central tenet of this man's faith seemed to be that there was one God and one God only. Of course, it made Jacob a little bit uncomfortable that this man professed to be a prophet. Where was the evidence? he wondered. What was his track record? Jacob knew well the teachings of the Torah, the five books that Moses received from God. The fifth book, Deuteronomy, warned about the dangers of listening to self-proclaimed prophets. The test given for a prophet was specific—he must be one hundred percent accurate in specific predictions and his doctrine must agree with that taught by Moses.

Nevertheless, Jacob had little choice but to hear out this man and give him a chance to make his case. He was grateful that he seemed to be a man of peace and persuasion rather than a proponent of violence and force.

"I want to invite all of you—all the people of Yathrib—to follow me," Muhammad said. "Become converts to the original faith of our people. Worship Allah as he requires that we worship him, as the one true Lord of our lives. Put away your idols. They are an abomination in his sight. Get down on your hands and knees and thank Allah for all you have and all he has given you."

He was attractive, thought Jacob. He was persuasive and charismatic. This young man would undoubtedly go far preaching this message of monotheism in the polytheistic Arab world. But he wasn't going to make any headway with the Jews. Jacob's people never doubted that there was one God and one God only.

Muhammad talked for a long time. Jacob estimated it had been, at least, a two-hour message. It wasn't anything he deemed terribly controversial. He seemed to be talking mainly to the non-Jews, the polytheistic Arabs. He could not tell precisely how this new faith differed from Judaism—except that Muhammad paid homage to Jesus and Ishmael, of all people, in addition to the Hebrew prophets.

When Muhammad was finished, he urged all of those attending to pledge their support to Allah through him. He invited questions and discussion. The Arabs spoke first.

"You are indeed a Prophet," said a venerated old man named Nibatayah. "I have listened carefully to you and I accept everything you say. Just tell me how to follow you and I will be the first in line, my Lord."

There were shouts of approval by many in the tent. One after another, the Arab spokesmen rose to pledge their loyalty to Allah through his prophet Muhammad.

Finally, after everyone else had spoken, it was obvious to Jacob that several of the Arabs were looking to him to make a statement of some kind. Fearfully he rose.

"I appreciate much of what you have said tonight, my son," said Jacob. "My people have long accepted that there is only one God. Worshipping idols is an insult to our Lord—one of the gravest sins, an abomination, as you say. I am grateful that you are preaching the acceptance of Abraham and Moses to your people. But what of my people? What would you have us do differently? How does your creed compare with the Hebrew faith?"

Muhammad smiled broadly as if expecting the question. He was prepared for this one. His answer was hardly music to Jacob's ears, no matter how diplomatically Muhammad tried to phrase it.

"My brother," Muhammad began, "The Arab people of the desert have much to learn from the Jews. You have clung to the principles of your faith more steadfastly than have the Bedouin. Our people are completely lost—worshipping false gods and living in sin. But the Jews, too, are guilty of corruption. They have distorted their own history in an attempt to glorify themselves over Allah. For instance, I have heard your rabbis say that it was his son Isaac whom our father Abraham was about to sacrifice for Allah. This is not true. Allah has revealed to me that it was his favored first-born son Ishmael, the father of all desert peoples, whom Abraham was prepared to kill upon the instructions of the Lord. Therefore, I am not so much asking you to change your faith, my brother, as I am urging you to reform it. Allow me to correct the errors of the Jews so that we may all live as one family in the sight of our Lord."

Jacob sat quietly for a moment, just staring at

Muhammad. The audience was silent, anticipating a response.

"I cannot accept this," said Jacob. "I must first see the evidence that you are what you say you are—a prophet of God. I wish you well with your outreach to the Arab people here in Yathrib and throughout the Hejaz. But I can tell you as an elder statesman of the Hebrew community here that the Jews will not accept messages that contradict our holy book."

There were a few sighs and grumbles in the room, but mostly silence. The momentum and energy of a great and unifying revival meeting had been leached out in the span of a few seconds. The disappointment on Muhammad's face was palpable. But he refused to accept dissent. What happened in Mecca would not be repeated here in Yathrib.

"Let me suggest, my brother, that we cannot resolve all of our differences in one short evening," said Muhammad. "The spiritual errors that have been introduced into our faiths have developed over thousands of years. Can we agree, at least, to continue our dialogue so that we may peaceably—and in the spirit of brotherhood—reach consensus and agreement?"

Muhammad looked to Jacob, who nodded affirmatively. This acknowledgment was met with applause throughout the tent as the meeting spontaneously broke up on a positive note. One by one, those present departed the tent after bowing respectfully to Muhammad and thanking him for his message. Jacob did likewise.

After Jacob had left, Muhammad turned to his disciples

and said: "Once again, I see it is the Jews who are going to give us the most trouble."

Muhammad was referring to his experience in Mecca, from which his band of 200 had just fled. Actually, there it was a combination of Arab discontent with his zealous brand of anti-polytheism and Jewish rejection of his attempts to convert them that made him very unpopular—even in the city of his birth. A group of Meccans had even tried to kill him on his last day in the city—just ten days earlier.

Things were going to be much different in Yathrib, thought Muhammad. He had learned from his mistakes in Mecca. He would try gentle persuasion at first. And if that didn't work he would resort to ruthless coercion. Generally he was pleased with the way the meeting went. There was much more resistance in Mecca right from the start. Muhammad and his disciples would rise early the next day and resume their politicking full-time. His goal was nothing short of a takeover of the oasis city, with the intent of using Yathrib as the base for spreading his new Islamic creed and launching strategic attacks on Meccan caravans and armies.

The Arab population's enthusiasm for Muhammad did not ebb. Within a week, the Arab city fathers had decided to rename Yathrib in honor of Muhammad. The name was changed to Medina —"The City of the Prophet"—without the consultation of the Jewish community. But Muhammad was not writing off the Jews. In fact, for weeks he attempted to win them over. He met several times with Jacob and some of the Jewish holy men for what amounted to "negotiations." But no matter what he did, the Jews in Medina refused to acknowledge Muhammad as a genuine prophet.

In his early meetings with the Jews, he represented himself as only a teacher of the creed of Abraham. He suggested behind closed doors that what he was actually doing was introducing the Jewish faith to Arabs in a form that would be acceptable to them. When the Jews asked him about honoring the Sabbath, he adopted the Jewish practice as his own. When they asked him about their dietary laws, he adopted those, too, for followers of Islam. And, long before the practice of prayer facing Mecca became de rigeur in the Islamic world, Muhammad tried to appease the Jews of Medina by having his followers face Jerusalem during their worship periods.

No matter what Muhammad did in the weeks following his arrival in the city, however, the Jews refused to acknowledge him as anything but a false prophet.

"My dear son," explained Jacob toward the conclusion of one of the negotiating sessions, "we all wish you well in your attempts to convert the Arab world. But we Jews do not wish to be converted. We are content in our faith in the Lord. We believe we would dishonor our heavenly father and our ancestors by taking this new course that you suggest. But, at the same time, we mean you no harm. We do not wish to offend you or our neighbors. We seek only to live in peace with you and lead our own lives in harmony."

"I understand," is all Muhammad said in response. Jacob and the Jews hoped he meant it. But they weren't optimistic. Within days, the worst fears of the Medina Jews were realized.

Tensions between Arabs and Jews began to rise. It was evident in the marketplace, in the streets and even in the homes of some Arab converts to Judaism as some family members switched allegiances to Muhammad. Then, one day, Jacob saw Muhammad overseeing the training of battle troops in a section of the city far from the Jewish quarter. When Jacob inquired as to what the military training was all about, he was told that Muhammad feared an attack by Meccans still angry about this new Islamic creed.

But, as Jacob had feared, this army wasn't trained to fight Meccans—at least not yet. Muhammad's first target would be the Jewish tribe—the largest homogeneous community in the city. Without warning, the Islamic army attacked the Jews on the Sabbath and besieged the community. The Jews were not well-armed and resisted mainly by locking themselves in their homes and shops. When the futility of their resistance became apparent to some, they came out and surrendered. One by one, they were summarily executed upon orders of Muhammad.

Jacob and Rebekah were not among those who surrendered. Their home was relatively secure—fortified with bolted doors and heavy-shuttered windows. The Muslim army did not attempt a house-to-house round-up. Muhammad's strategy was to lay siege—to deny the Jews food and supplies, to wait them out; starve them out if necessary. Jacob and Rebekah were well-stocked with food and other provisions. They even took in half a dozen other Jews, including their son, David, and his wife, Rahab, who were not so well off. Cramped in small quarters, the Jews spent most of their waking hours praying for deliverance from their enemies. One evening, before the household retired for the night, they all prayed in unison:

> *"The Lord is my shepherd, I shall not want; he maketh me lie down in green pastures. He leadeth me beside still waters; he restoreth my soul. He leadeth me in paths of righteousness for his name's sake. Even though I walk through the valley of the shadow of death, I fear no evil; for thou art with me; thy rod and thy staff, they comfort me. Thou preparest a table before me in the presence of my enemies; thou anointest my head with oil, my cup overflows. Surely goodness and mercy shall follow me all the days of my life; and I shall dwell in the house of the Lord forever."*

When he was finished, by the light of one oil lamp, the group exchanged stories about the things they had heard during the daylight when they were bold enough to venture out of the house and meet with other Jews in the community.

"Jacob," said Teman, a young bridegroom who, along with his new wife, Esther, shared the home of Jacob and Rebekah, "something is happening with the Arabs. They are preoccupied with some crisis. Today, their attention was diverted from us as we scurried around the community for news and supplies."

"Yes," said David, "someone spotted an army approaching from the east. It may be the Meccans. They are as

angry with Muhammad as we are. Perhaps this is the miracle we have been praying for."

"Trust not in men for your deliverance, my children,"
said Jacob. "Trust only in the Lord. Pray that His will be
done. Our reward has never been here on earth. It is in
heaven. If we are true to our Father, we will be rewarded
for the trials of this lifetime. Our reward will be beyond
our imaginations and it will be eternal."

"Still, father," said David, "I don't want to die like this. If
we must go, I would prefer to die fighting, not hiding."

The next day, David and Teman ventured out at first
light. Just outside the Jewish community, they could see
the Muslim army digging a long trench. They had obviously begun even before the sun rose, probably working by
torchlight. They were exhausted and working in shifts. By
the end of the day, the trench, about 10 feet wide and 10
feet deep, nearly surrounded the city. Some time that
evening, it would be completed.

"Jacob," asked Teman later that evening, "what do you
suppose that trench is for? Will the Muslims hide themselves in there and surprise the Meccan army when they
arrive?"

"I don't believe so," said Jacob. "My guess is that it is
simply a device to hold off the attackers—to slow them
down and make their approach to Medina difficult."

By the next day, Jacob was proven right. Unable to get
beyond the trench, the Meccan army laid siege to Medina.
Without the trench, conceived by Muhammad, the
Meccans would have undoubtedly overrun the city in no
time. Nevertheless, the attack by the Meccans provided an

opportunity for the Jews held hostage in their own homes. The survivors feared certain death if they took no action. Their only option was to organize their own attack on the Muslim army, thus opening up a second front for Muhammad's forces to deal with.

Every able-bodied man, including Jacob, David and Teman, participated. If they had no swords or bows, they marched on the Muslims with clubs and stones. With most of Muhammad's forces holding off the Meccans, the Jewish attack presented a real crisis for the Muslims. However, just when "The Battle of the Trench" appeared to be turning against Muhammad, a severe sandstorm forced the Meccan army to retreat, thus permitting the Islamic army to turn all of its fury and vengeance on the Jews.

"Two religions may not dwell together on the Arabian Peninsula," Muhammad told his disciples. "It's time for the Jews to go."

The Muslim troops showed little mercy. As the Jewish fighters surrendered, they were put to death immediately, often in front of their wives and children. Hundreds were beheaded. Every Jewish man in Medina was either killed in battle or executed afterward. There was no escape for Jacob, David and Teman. They were killed together in the first counteroffensive by the Muslims after the retreat of the Meccans.

"Do not fear these who can only take your earthly life," Jacob said to David and Teman as they were about to be beheaded. "I will join you in the bosom of Abraham, our Father, in the presence of Jehovah."

When it was Jacob's turn, he looked with calm assurance and compassion at his wife, and children, and said, "Shalom, my beloved ones. Keep your faith."

"Hear O Israel, The Lord our God is one," were Jacob's last words. As for Rebekah and the other women and children, they were all sold into slavery. The spoils captured in the Jewish community were divided up by Muhammad between his supporters. But this was just the beginning.

In short order, the entire network of Jewish communities in northern Arabia was systematically slaughtered. First the Quraiza tribe was exterminated. Then Muhammad sent messengers to the Jewish community at the oasis of Khaibar "inviting" Usayr, their war chief, to visit Medina for peace negotiations. Not suspecting foul play, Usayr set off with 30 unarmed companions and a Muslim escort. On the way, the Muslims ambushed the defenseless delegation, killing all but one who managed to escape.

Muhammad explained such tactics by saying, "War is deception. Its only purpose is to win." Practiced Muhammad-style, war was more than deception. Even with the primitive weapons of the seventh century, it was truly a savage hell. The complete annihilation of the two Arabian-Jewish tribes, with every man, woman and child killed, remains, as one Israeli historian has written, "A tragedy for which no parallel can be found in Jewish history."

This is a lesson Israelis should remember in the last days. Muhammad's practices set the pattern for Muslim strategy and tactics for all time to follow.

As an example of the enormity of the brutality and

barbarity, after one Jewish town surrendered to the Muslims, 700 to 1,000 men were beheaded in one day while, as in Medina, all the women and children were sold into slavery. Elsewhere, as the attacks on the Jews continued, some managed to survive. The Muslims found a new use for these "infidels." They were permitted to maintain their land so long as they paid a 50 percent tribute for their "protection."

Thus the Jewish *dhimmi* system evolved. Tolerated between onslaughts, expulsions and pillages from the Arab Muslim conquest onward, the non-Muslim *dhimmi*—predominantly Jewish but Christian, too—provided the most important source of new revenue for Muslim imperialism.

Much of the wealth of the region, which had been concentrated in the hands of the enterprising Jews, was seized by the Muslims, transforming them from indigent immigrants to wealthy landowners and men of substance. This phenomenon only caused Muhammad's fame to spread faster and further than ever. Bedouins began flocking to his army by the thousands. They had practiced ambushing and pillaging caravans for centuries. The combination of doing these things in the name of a God who favored Arabs and blessed them for their "holy wars against the rich infidels" was irresistably intoxicating. Not surprisingly, there were great numbers of "converts" to Islam among the marauding Arab tribes. And since they were warriors from youth, they began Holy Wars, or Jihads, of conquest "to convert the infidels" almost immediately. Of course, they were well paid for their "missionary work" with the lands and wealth they captured and confiscated.

All this began in Medina—or Yathrib, as Jacob called it. The very first step for Muhammad in securing his economic base and strengthening his prestige in the Arab world was the seizure of the property of Jews at Medina. The betrayal of the Jews at Medina, the massacres of the Nadhir and Kainuka tribes and the dispossession of property by Muslims set up what was later termed *"the precedent of prey"*—a pattern that would be repeated again and again. The agrarian and merchant Jews lucky enough to escape death would be plundered and exploited by the nomadic Arabs. Muhammad and the precepts of Islam not only gave them an excuse for such oppression, they commanded it.

"Some Jews you slew and others you took captive," said Muhammad. "Allah made you masters of their land, their houses and their goods, and of yet another land on which you had never set foot before."

Ishmael Muhammad had never set foot in the land of Israel. Neither had his parents or grandparents. Nor had any of his ancestors been associated with the land when it was known briefly, thanks to foreign imperialism, as Palestine. Nevertheless, Muhammad felt certain it was his fate to "liberate" this land to restore the honor of Allah and Muhammad, his prophet.

His narrow and mystical escape from death on a

Lebanese cliff a few months earlier simply solidified his fervent conviction that he had a special role to play in re-establishing the primacy of Islam throughout the Middle East and, for that matter, the world. Now he thought he had hatched a plan to set off a chain of events that would lead to just such an eventuality.

"Nayaf," Muhammad called out to his trusted companion, "look at this."

Haddad walked over to the desk in Muhammad's well-appointed study high up in his retreat above the Bekaa Valley. He looked over some calculations that were meaningless to him.

"Yes, Ishmael, what is it?" asked Haddad.

"I've got it!" said Muhammad. "I've figured it out. I know exactly how to deliver a fatal blow to the Zionists. I know how to overcome the Arrow 5. It's time."

"What's your plan, Ishmael?" Haddad wanted to know.

"This is the key," he said holding up his diagrams and algebraic formulations. "I hold in my hands the key to unifying the Arab world against the Zionist dogs. The leadership of most of the Arab nations has gone soft. Some have fallen for the soothing phrases of Carlo. Others are content to lavish themselves in the lifestyles of oil wealth. Do you know why the Arabs lost to Israel in all of the modern wars?" Muhammad asked his friends.

"Because of American arms," said Haddad. "And because we Muslims had poor leadership, inferior weapons technology and stupidity."

"No," said Muhammad. "We lost because we wandered away from our religion and faith; we forgot about Allah.

And our enemy prevailed because it could combine faith and modern warfare. "I remember as a youngster watching the Israelis triumph in 1967, raising that hideous flag over Arab Jerusalem. I remember watching Gen. Shlomo Goren, the Zionist army chaplain, at the Temple Mount on June 7, a Torah under his arm and a shofar in his left hand. They were victorious because of the power of their faith— something we Arabs have forgotten. It was a wakeup call to many of us. Only then did many of us go back to the Koran and learn about the meaning of *jihad* and to use today the inspired military campaigns of the Prophet."

Muhammad worked himself up into a near frenzy. He could talk for hours when he got like this. Knowingly, his friend, Haddad, sat down for the lecture that was coming.

"Do you remember what our book says about these infidels? Do you remember what it says about how we are to battle them?" he asked rhetorically. "'Take neither Jews nor Christians for your friends with one another. Whosoever of you seeks their friendship shall become one of their number. Allah does not guide the wrongdoers.' Do you see what I mean? 'Allah does not guide wrongdoers.' Our people had lost their way! That's why we couldn't beat the enemy. Our leaders are soft. They don't read our book. They don't understand the words of the Prophet and the power behind those words."

Muhammad picked up his copy of the Koran, never far from his reach. He fumbled through the pages looking for something.

"The Prophet says, 'Ignominy shall be their portion'— meaning the Jews— 'wheresoever they are found....They have incurred anger from their Lord, and wretchedness is laid upon them...because they...disbelieve the revelations of Allah and slew the Prophets wrongfully...because they were rebellious and used to transgress."

He shuffled some more pages. "And listen to this, 'Though wilt find them' —the Jews—'the greediest of mankind.' And this: 'Evil is that for which they sell their souls....For disbelievers is a terrible doom.' The Prophet says that Allah has cursed the Jews for their disbelief. Don't you know that he cursed us even more for our disbelief? And what are we to do with the Jews? What does our book say is their fate?"

Muhammad turned more pages in the Koran: "'Taste ye'—the Jews—'the punishment of burning.' That is their fate. 'Those who disbelieve Our revelations, We shall expose them to the fire,' it says right here. 'As often as their skins are consumed We shall exchange them for fresh skins that they may taste the torment. Because of the wrongdoing of the Jews... And of their taking usury...and of their devouring people's wealth by false pretenses. We have prepared for those of them who disbelieve a painful doom.' And, with the help of Allah, that's just what I have been preparing for them. I have done it. The Arab leaders don't have the backbone to stand up—to use their power and to do Allah's will. The only thing that will force them to unite is if they are attacked."

"So you will launch an attack without the approval of Damascus?" Haddad asked.

"Our benefactors have commissioned us to refine their most advanced missile systems for them—to keep them a step ahead of the anti-missile capabilities of the Jews," said Muhammad. "But they don't have the stomach to use these weapons they way Allah intended them to be used. They will sit around and look at them—admire them. And the missiles will be obsolete before you know it. But we have the power!" he said pounding his fist on the desk for emphasis. "The weapon is in our hands. I have the launch codes. The time to act is now!"

"Where will you strike? And what do you believe will happen when you do?" asked Haddad.

"Tel Aviv will be our target," Muhammad said. "That's where the Jewish population is. I could not stand the thought of destroying Al Aqsa and the other holy sites in Jerusalem—even if it did mean destroying their capital. Some day we will walk into Jerusalem and claim it for ourselves. I don't want it reduced to a pile of radioactive rubble. Once we strike, we will inflict hundreds of thousands of civilian casualties. The Israeli command-and-control structure will be seriously impaired. The only thing left for the Israelis to do will be to resort to their Samson option—to go nuclear. They will want revenge. They will seek retribution. Their first target may well be Damascus or Tehran. They will blame Syria and Iran because the attack will come from territory theoretically controlled by them. Once that happens, there will be an all-out war, and a severely weakened Israel will fall into our hands because of our vastly superior numbers."

"Soon Israel will compromise even its nuclear option," suggested Haddad. "The Jews believe Carlo and the United Nations can protect them. Why not wait to strike until they give up their nuclear weapons?" he asked.

"Number one: if we wait, the Arab governments, in the name of a false peace, may also compromise their defense apparatus," explained Muhammad. "We may lose our warheads and our only chance to light this fuse. And second: if Israel does not have the means to respond because of its own defense compromises, we will lose perhaps our last chance for real Arab unity. Carlo is extremely dangerous. We must act before he assumes any more power and authority over Israeli and Arab defense policy."

Captain Isaac Barak and Gen. Ariel Oved were sharing a traditional Israeli breakfast of bread, olives and cheeses at a small restaurant just outside Palmahim. They were making small talk, inquiring about the health of their families and the weather, when Oved cleared his throat and put on a serious face.

"Captain," the general said, "I want you to promise me something."

"Yes, general," said Barak, "what is it?"

"I want you to hand-pick a half-dozen of your most trusted and skilled men and teach them all you can about the Arrow system," he began. "You cannot be awake 24 hours a day, seven days a week, 52 weeks a year to protect this nation. And, frankly, I don't trust anyone else to do it. I fear we are entering a very dangerous period in the history of our nation. The United Nations is usurping more and more responsibility for our defense. Arrow may be our last line of defense. I don't want it in the hands of anyone but Israelis."

"Well, general, I can do that, but it won't rid us of the U.N. staffers who look over our shoulders every day," said Barak.

"I understand, Isaac," he said. "But if we have our own people in the bunker all the time—people who are fully capable of taking control and doing what is necessary to defend our nation—then we will at least have a fighting chance to survive what I believe is an inevitable attack."

"Why do you believe such an attack is inevitable, general?" asked Barak.

"Do you remember that message we heard during the test a few months ago?" the general asked.

"Yes, of course," said Barak. "I checked it out thoroughly. I spent days investigating it. Apparently no one else heard anything except you and me."

"That's right," said the general. "Well, I don't know how to tell you this exactly. I've never been a particularly religious man. But I had another similar kind of experience recently. My doorbell rang. When I answered it, there was a man standing in the doorway. He was dressed in white. There was something strange about him, though I can't really say what it was. He was very handsome, tall. But perhaps he was a little too perfect looking. The thing I remember most about him, though, was his voice. It was the same voice I heard on the headset that day. I'm sure of that. Anyway, he stood in the doorway, not identifying himself in any way, and told me that Israel was facing grave danger. 'An attack is imminent,' he said. 'Only months away.

It will be the kind of attack that only you can repulse. Fear not,' he said. 'But be prepared.' The strangest part of it is that my house, as you know, is under constant guard and surveillance. Yet none of the guards saw anyone approach the house or leave. Even the video camera positioned at the doorway recorded nothing of the visitor. It was as if he was not there—or invisible."

Barak's normally olive-toned face turned ashen white as he listened to the general relate this story. He sat there for a moment in stunned silence.

"Do you think I'm crazy, Isaac?" the general asked. "Do you think I'm seeing things?"

"Not at all, general," said Barak. "I'm very grateful you told me this story. Because I had a very vivid dream in which a visitor, much as you described, gave me a similar message. I didn't take it too seriously because it was just a dream—or so I thought. What do you suppose this means? What's happening here?"

"At the risk of sounding nutty, I'll tell you what I think is happening: I think the God who gave this land to Abraham, Isaac and Jacob thousands of years ago is trying to tell us something of great importance. He made a promise to the Jews, and He intends to keep it—even if some of our leaders today have forgotten about it."

"What do you suppose we should do, general?"

"Well, as I suggested already, we need to be prepared— prepared to take matters into our own hands if necessary, prepared to defend our nation," the general said. "Secondly, my son, I think we need to pray. I think we should consult a rabbi as soon as possible. I know a man—a very learned teacher. You may want to come with me to see him. He will be better able than me to make sense of all this—I hope."

"I'm with you all the way, general," said Barak. "Just tell me where to be and when."

"Tomorrow, at noon, I already have an appointment with Rabbi Shlomo Goren," the general said. "He is orthodox and very knowledgeable about things like angels and what the Hebrew prophets foretold about the future. I think he will be quite fascinated by what we have to say. And if he doesn't have any advice for us—any insight—no one will."

The old man stared straight ahead, his gray beard flecked with black, the hint of a twinkle in his eye. There was just the trace of a smile upon his lips. Rabbi Goren was both alarmed by what he was hearing and encouraged. He believed as fervently as any man alive in the reality of angelic messengers. But right now he was thinking he had never been so close to a real-life encounter with one as this. After listening to Gen. Oved's story he sat quietly, contemplatively in the study of his synagogue in Jerusalem—a bemused look upon his face.

"So what do you think, rabbi?" asked the general.

The rabbi raised his hand gently as if to signal his mind was still working on the problem. Finally, after a few minutes of silence, he spoke.

"I think you know very well what you have encountered," he said. "I have never experienced anything as dramatic as this. I both envy you and pity you. You have a grave responsibility. I believe God is using you for a very important mission. I know you do not take that lightly—and you shouldn't."

"What does it mean, though?" asked the general almost impatiently. "How should we respond?"

"Again, I think you know exactly what you are supposed to do," the rabbi said. "Is there really any doubt in your mind?"

The general paused. He looked at young Barak, then back at the rabbi.

"No, there is no doubt in my mind about what we are supposed to do," he said.

"Well, then, how can I be of help?" the rabbi asked.

"You already have been, rabbi," the general said. "But I do have some more questions for you—questions that may or may not be relevant to the situation in which we find ourselves. Do you have more time?" Gen. Oved asked glancing at his watch.

"Yes, my son," the rabbi said. "I can say with certainty that I have nothing more urgent, nor compelling, nor important than the matters at hand. I am at your disposal for as long as you care to listen to this old man."

"Rabbi, I remember when I was a youngster going through my religious training—I remember hearing about the prophets and what they had to say about the coming of Messiah," the general recalled haltingly, almost timidly. "Do you think—is it possible that we may be nearing that time? Tell me what signs we should be looking for."

"You ask very good questions," the rabbi said, "very insightful questions. Let me tell you about two prophecies that you should be concerned with. The first is in the Book of Zechariah, chapter 14." He picked up his book and read:

> *"Behold, a day of the Lord is coming, when the spoil taken from you will be divided in the midst of you. For I will gather all the nations against Jerusalem to battle, and the city shall be taken and the houses plundered and the women ravished; half of the city shall go into exile, but the rest of the people shall not be cut off from the city. Then the Lord will go forth and fight against those nations as when he fights on a day of battle. On that day his feet shall stand on the Mount of Olives which lies before Jerusalem on the east; and the Mount of Olives shall be split in two from east to west by a very wide valley; so that one half of the Mount shall withdraw northward, and the other half southward. And the valley of my mountains shall be stopped up, for the valley of the mountains shall touch the side of it; and you shall flee as you fled from the earthquake in the days of Uzziah king of Judah. Then the Lord you God will come, and all the holy ones with him."*

"I don't see any signs of all the nations of the world coming to attack us," said the general. "So perhaps I am wrong in my feeling that we are somehow on the edge of a precipice."

"No, you are not mistaken," the rabbi said. "The attack is indeed coming, even though you see no sign of it yet .

Here— let me show you where it will come from first."

The rabbi flipped through the pages of his Bible and turned to Ezekiel 38. He read:

> *"Son of man, set you face toward Gog, of the land of Magog, the chief prince of Meshech and Tubal, and prophesy against him and say, Thus says the Lord God: Behold I am against you, O Gog, chief prince of Meshech and Tubal; and I will turn you about, and put hooks into your jaws, and I will bring you forth, and all your army, horses and horsemen, all of them clothed in full armor, a great company, all of them with buckler and shield, wielding swords; Persia, Cush and Put are with them, all of them with shield and helmet; Gomer and all his hordes; Beth-togarmah from the uttermost parts of the north with all his hordes—many peoples are with you. Be ready and keep ready, you and all the hosts that are assembled about you, and be a guard for them."*

The rabbi closed the book and looked into the general's eyes.

"Does this have any meaning for you?" the rabbi asked.

"Well," the general began, "it sounds like the attack will be coming from the extreme north. Of course, that can only mean Russia—the one nation that is due north of Israel."

"You are very perceptive, general," the rabbi said. "That is indeed who will lead the assault against Israel."

"But, I must say to you, rabbi, I don't see any signs of this attack being imminent," said the general. "I fear an attack is coming from elsewhere. Could I be right?"

The rabbi thought for a moment.

"You could be right," he replied. "We are not to understand God's timing—at least not his precise timing. Perhaps you are being warned of another fateful event—a prelude, perhaps."

After a moment or two of silence, the rabbi asked: "Do you have any more questions?"

"No, Rabbi Goren, you have been most generous with your time already," said Gen. Oved. "But I hope you will allow me to call you from time to time as questions do arise."

"Yes, of course," he said. "In fact, if you do not call me, I will call you. I want to be kept abreast of all developments. I insist!"

Two months later, Gen. Oved and Captain Barak had their team assembled and trained. They now felt confident, with a 24-hour-a-day shift at Palmahim, that they could intercept any incoming missiles on a moment's notice—without help from U.N. forces or authorization from official channels. This was something of a rogue operation—and Oved and Barak kept the mission secret from all but their hand-picked corps of elite technical wizards—and, of course, the rabbi.

Gen. Oved and Captain Barak, both early risers, were in the bunker every morning—except the Sabbath—by sunrise. Oved and Barak had become quite observant since their meeting with Rabbi Goren. They even attended services together. Isaac Barak was becoming like a son to Oved. He grew to admire Barak's skill in training young men in complicated technical procedures and his cool head even more in the last eight weeks.

"This is a very special young man," thought the general.

It was pitch black in the Bekaa Valley below Ishmael Muhammad's hideaway at midnight.

"It's time to go," Muhammad told his comrades as they got into his new bullet-proof Mercedes Benz. "I miss that Chevy," Muhammad said as six men squeezed into the five-passenger car.

They drove down the winding hill, past the spot in the road where they had nearly lost their lives months earlier, and into the valley. Then there were a few turns before they reached the side of another mountain.

"This is where we get out and walk," Muhammad told them. Not even Nayaf Haddad, Muhammad's most trusted aide, knew where they were going. They walked for more than a mile in total darkness, broken only by their flashlights.

"This is a poppy field," Muhammad told his cohorts. "Our friends make heroin from these flowers and sell it to the American dogs for hard cash. Without this money, and Allah's blessing, we could never have performed the miracle I am about to show you."

Even Muhammad seemed lost for a moment or two. He shined his flashlight up and down the side of the mountain searching for something.

"Oh, here it is," he said. It was an entrance—a secret door that seemed to lead into the mountain itself. Once Muhammad opened the door, there was light. Inside was a modern, well-lighted hallway to somewhere. Muhammad led them in and down a flight of stairs. He opened a door. Inside was a small control room of some kind—computers, radar screens, all kinds of high-tech equipment.

"What is this place, Muhammad?" asked Haddad.

"This is my laboratory," said Muhammad with a menacing smile. "This is the place that will allow us to bring the Zionists to their knees. This is the room that will change the course of history."

Muhammad began moving around the room, frenetically explaining what each piece of equipment did.

"You know, I designed all this myself," he said with a boastful look of self-assurance. "And, in a few hours, we're going to give this facility its biggest test. No one on earth will be expecting it. Everyone thinks the world is at peace. Even our friends in Damascus and Tehran will be surprised."

"Well," said Haddad, "could you fill us in on exactly what's going to happen?"

"At sun-up," said Muhammad, *"we nuke Tel Aviv!"*

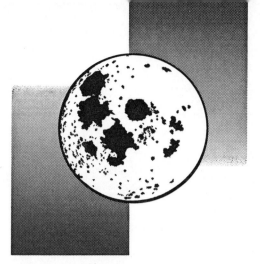

CHAPTER 5

Extra-Terrestrials and the Miracle

Ada was a beautiful young woman who helped her brothers tend their flocks in the days before the flood. She was so fair that many young men wanted her to be their wife. One day, a handsome and powerful prince came to meet with her father. His name was Belshar. He wore many jewels on his garments—rubies, topaz, diamonds, beryl, onyx, jasper, lapis lazuli, turquoise, emerald and gold. He was obviously a man of great means.

"I will pay more than a fair dowry for young Ada," said Belshar. "I want you to give her to me today."

"Well," said Ada's father, Jabal, "what's your rush? Can't we work this out? I'm very happy for you to take my daughter, but let's get to know one another."

"I'm here," said Belshar. "Ask me any question you like. I have nothing to hide from you."

"I'm sure you don't, sir," said Jabal. "But you can understand, Ada is my only daughter. I love her very much. Where will you live? Where will you take her?"

"I live nearby in the village of Enoch," said Belshar. "You will see your daughter again. Have no fear, old man. You are not losing a daughter, you will be gaining many grandchildren—strong and wise youngsters who will make you proud."

After a few hours of conversation, Jabal was persuaded. Belshar was a most impressive character—wealthy, accomplished, wise and exceedingly handsome. He was never at a loss for words. He was supremely confident. And his stature—tall, muscular and perfectly proportioned—assured Jabal that his daughter would never be threatened by strangers or bandits.

"So be it," said Jabal. "I will call in Ada now and tell her the good news."

Less than a year later, Jabal got word that he was a grandfather. He and his wife, Nama, decided to travel to Enoch, about 20 miles, to see their new grandson, Zelub. The daylong ride in the heat of the summer left Jabal and Nama thirsty and tired. But they couldn't wait to see their grandson when they arrived at Belshar's palace.

They were escorted in by servants and told to be seated in a large, well-appointed room. Gold urns and fine tapestries decorated the hall. Jabal and Nama had never seen such opulence before.

"To think," Jabal said with wonder, "that our daughter and our grandson should live like this!"

A moment later, Ada walked in to the room. She was not smiling. She was accompanied by two servant girls, one of whom was carrying the baby.

"Ada!" her mother cried, "it's so good to see you." She

ran up to her daughter and threw her arms around her. But Ada only returned a cold, lifeless embrace. There was little recognition and no happiness expressed in her face. It was Jabal who first noticed that something was wrong.

"What is it child?" he said. "What's wrong? Isn't Belshar making you happy? Are you ill?"

Ada gazed at her father and then shifted her glance to the baby.

"Is there something wrong with the child?" he asked.

"Oh, no, father," said Ada. "There's nothing wrong with the baby. The problem is everything is just a little too perfect."

She reached over to fold the blanket back to show her parents the child. Only a few weeks old, Zelub was already the size of a 1-year-old boy. He was fully alert, and, as the servants demonstrated to the amazement of the grandparents, already able to crawl and hold his head up—feats that would not be expected in normal children until they were many months older.

"What is the cause of this condition?" asked Jabal.

"Belshar is not a man," Ada said as she looked around fearfully. "He is not a human, and, therefore, neither is my son—your grandson."

"Whatever do you mean, child?" asked Jabal.

"I mean just what I said," replied Ada. "You gave me away not to a man—not to a prince of this world—but to a fallen angel, a dark spirit being who has merely assumed human form."

Just then Belshar walked into the room.

"Is this true?" asked Jabal.

Belshar shrugged, "Of course it's true."

"Then you deceived me," said Jabal.

"How did I deceive you, old man?" asked Belshar. "Did you ask me if I was human? Did I say I was? Did you ask me if I was an angel? I said nothing about what or who I am, did I? Anyway, you should be even more proud. Your grandson will grow up to be a great leader of men. His intellect and his strength will be superior to any mere earthling."

While Jabal was not aware of any situation like this before, this was not the only family plagued by such a development. In the times of Noah, as the population of the planet grew, some angels invaded the earth in the guise of men. Their supreme leader, named Lucifer, had devised an ingenious plan. He wanted to create a race of half angels, half men. In this way he thought that he could overthrow God's whole plan and make it impossible to carry out a pre-human judgment He had pronounced on all the angels who followed Lucifer, The Shining One, in his rebellion against God. So these rebellious angels assumed human form and beguiled women to marry them.

The children from these unions were incredible. God revealed to Moses the following account: "Giants [Hebrew *Nephilim*] were on the earth in those days, and also afterward, when the sons of God came in to the daughters of men, and they bore children to them. Those were the supermen who from ancient times were famous for their incredible exploits." (Genesis 6:4, Literal translation from Hebrew.) It is believed with good reason that Greek mythology came from the pre-flood legends that were passed down about these half angels, half men. They were indeed supermen—half extra-terrestrial. As this invasion spread, true humanity was almost wiped out. This is why it is emphasized about Noah that he was not only righteous, but that he was, "perfect in his geneology" (Genesis 6:9). In other words, he was not from a family who had intermingled with the fallen angels and caused him not to be truly human.

God was very angered by this development. If there were no true humans, there could not be a Savior sent to save them. One of God's great purposes in the plan of redemption was to teach the vastly superior angelic order that an inferior being like man, with only a fraction of the privilege and knowledge angels had, would accept His offer of salvation. This would prove that God was both loving and just in condemning the angels for their rebellion against Him.

God destroyed the world in the great flood, not only for the terrible wickedness that resulted, but also to preserve true humanity. All of the offspring from those "mixed marriages" died in the flood, and the angels who were responsible for those unions were bound in chains and cast into *Tartarus*, the great abyss—the darkest and most terrifying place imaginable. They are being held there while they await final judgment. It is written,

> *"And the angels who did not keep to their proper domain, but left their own habitation, He has reserved in everlasting chains under darkness for the judgment of the great day."* and *"For if God did*

not spare the angels who sinned, but cast them down to hell [tartarus] and delivered them into chains of darkness, to be reserved for judgment; and did not spare the ancient world, but saved Noah, one of eight people, a preacher of righteousness, bringing in the flood on the world of the ungodly…" (Jude 6 and 2 Peter 2:4, 5 NKJV).

"In the beginning, God created the heavens and the earth." The first verse of Genesis describes just how the heavens and the earth were originally created. The second verse describes the earth after a long interlude during which, apparently, some kind of catastrophic destruction took place. The rest of chapter one chronicles how God restored the chaotic earth to a habitable form that could sustain life.

It also says man was made in God's image. It says less about those others created in His image—the spiritual beings known as angels. These are true extra-terrestrials with unimaginable powers. Yet, it is impossible to understand man's predicament and fate without knowing something about the battles going on in the spiritual realm over man's soul.

Of course, God is eternal. He was. He is. And He will always be. His Son, too, has always been. He is the Alpha and the Omega. He was there when His father created heaven and earth. And He will be there always at His right hand.

Some time after God created the universe, He created the angels. They were as plentiful as the stars—in other words, too numerous to count. They were not like God's later creation, Adam and Eve, who had to rely on their two legs to transport their physical bodies around their beautiful garden. Humans were confined to planet Earth and the solar system. By contrast, angels could transport themselves anywhere in the galaxy at the speed of thought. They had great beauty in their own right. Their power was awesome. Their existence was sublime. They lived in the Garden of God in heaven, the prototype for the earthly Garden of Eden. Angels apparently had the run of the universe.

From the beginning, angels had the ability to rebel against God. The image of God in them consists of will, intellect, emotion, moral reason and everlasting existence. Though man has the same image of God, the angels' intelligence is vastly superior, and they knew God from first-hand daily experience.

In the angelic population, there is a hierarchy. Above all the rest was Lucifer, the "Star of the Morning." God momentarily pulled back the veil of mystery that shrouds eternity past when He revealed to the prophet Ezekiel that the real force behind the Prince of Tyre was one He calls the King of Tyre. The things attributed to this King go far beyond this earth and mere man. Ezekiel wrote,

> *"You were the seal of perfection, full of wisdom and beauty. You were in the Eden, the garden of God; every precious stone was your covering: the sardis, topaz, diamond, beryl, onyx, jasper, sapphire,*

turquoise, and emerald—all set in pure gold. Your voice had more range and beauty than a pipe organ from the day you were created.

"You were the Anointed One of the Cherubs, the highest order of angels, and the guardian of my throne; I Myself chose you; You were on the holy mountain of God; You freely walked on the fiery stones of holiness.

*"You were perfect in all your ways from the day you were created, **until** iniquity was found in you.*

"By the abundance of your pride you became filled with violence within, and you sinned; Therefore I cast you out as a profane thing out from the mountain of God; and I destroyed you, O Guardian Cherub, from the the midst of the fiery stones.

"Your heart was lifted up because of your beauty; you corrupted your wisdom for the sake of your splendor...."

When God created Adam and Eve, he announced to the whole angelic realm that he was going to prove through these inferior creatures that He was both just and loving in condemning the angels who rebelled. As far as humans go, there has not been another man or woman who could rival Adam and Eve for sheer beauty and human perfection.

This made mankind the specific target of Lucifer, who after God's judgment became known as the Devil and Satan.

Satan immediately set up residence on planet Earth. He

said to himself as he studied them, "The woman is the most vulnerable for two reasons; she is more emotional, and thus more easily confused; and she did not hear directly God's prohibition to not eat from the tree that gives the knowledge of good and evil."

As the evil genius carefully searched for the best strategy to approach the woman, he saw her weakness. "Aha! Now I've got you," he thought. "Your favorite pet is the serpent. It is so bright that the woman will not think it strange when it talks to her."

Eve had no idea of the lethal danger that lurked beside her. Satan is an invisible spirit being—however, he can invade and take over any physical creature except those who have been redeemed by God.

The next day, Adam left Eve alone and Satan instantly siezed the opportunity. Quick as a cobra, he moved in on Eve. With his awesome powers, he moved on Eve's mind to go play with her pet serpent by the forbidden tree.

"Now I've got you," Satan exulted to himself. He lunged into the serpent and took it over completely. The poor serpent didn't know what hit it. Eve did not notice the subtle change in the serpent's expression.

Speaking through the serpent, Satan said, "Did God really say that you couldn't eat from *every* tree of the Garden?" He said this to take her mind off the tremendous freedoms she had, and to focus on the one forbidden thing. Satan subtly injected the idea to make it look like God was holding out on them and wasn't so good after all.

"Oh, no," said Eve. "We may freely eat from all the trees

in the garden, but God warned not to eat of this one particular tree—not even to touch it—or we will die."

"Ahhh, now you've given me an opening" Satan thought. "I've trapped you now, Eve." She made the mistake of embellishing God's warning about the tree. God had been very explicit with Adam about the tree. Adam apparently added the idea of not touching it when he relayed the message, thinking it would keep Eve from even going near it.

"Oh, you won't die," said Lucifer as he touched the tree through the serpent. "See, there's no harm in touching it. I didn't die, did I? Here, you try it."

Eve summoned up her courage and cautiously touched it. Nothing happened.

"See what I mean?" asked Satan. "Now watch this." He picked a piece of fruit from the tree and ate it. "You see, I didn't die. God doesn't want you to eat from this tree because He knows you will have your eyes opened and you will be like Him, knowing good and evil. God just doesn't want you to become like Him.

"Come on Eve. Go ahead and eat the fruit—it's delicious. You are not going to die."

Eve thought, "Could God actually be holding out on us because He doesn't want us to become like Him?" She looked at the fruit. It did look delicious. "After all," she thought, "I didn't die when I touched it. The serpent didn't die when he ate from it. And I like the idea of being wiser—more knowledgeable. And the idea of being like God is strangely exciting."

So she grabbed the fruit and tasted it. It was good. She

did not die. She did not even get sick. So she brought some to her husband. He ate. As soon as he did, their eyes were indeed opened. For the first time, they became self-conscious and ashamed of their nakedness. They quickly sewed fig leaves together to make aprons for themselves.

It was God's custom to visit every evening with Adam and Eve in the garden. Shortly after Adam and Eve had eaten the fruit, they heard the sound of God's footsteps in the garden. They hid themselves from His presence behind some trees.

"Where are you, Adam?" God called out.

"I heard you in the garden and I was afraid," Adam said. "I am naked, so I hid myself."

"Who told you that you were naked?" God asked. "Have you eaten of the tree of which I commanded you not to eat?"

"The woman you gave me, she gave me the fruit and I ate it," Adam said defensively.

"What is this that you have done?" God asked, turning to Eve.

"The serpent beguiled me, and I ate the fruit," she said.

Turning to the serpent, God said, "Because you have done this, you will be cursed above all other animals. You will crawl on your belly and eat dust throughout your life. You will cause enmity between you and the woman and between her Seed and you. He will bruise your head and you will bruise his heel." In other words, you will wound Him, but He will strike you a mortal blow.

To Eve, God said, "Because of what you have done, I will greatly increase the pain of childbirth. Yet you will have intense desire for a husband and he shall rule over you."

To Adam, God said, "Because you listened to your wife and ate of the tree, the ground you walk upon shall be cursed. From now on, you will have to work hard for your food and your sustenance. The ground will not easily produce food—only thorns and thistles. You will have to eat the plants of the field."

God made Adam and Eve garments of skins for their clothing and drove them from the garden, assigning other angels the task of guarding the entrance to Eden. It's really a shame that a poor innocent animal had to die in order to provide a covering for man's guilt, but it was a specific type of what it took to bring forgiveness for sin.

God has allowed Satan and his legions a time of freedom before the final sentence is carried out. But they have used that freedom to try to prove God wrong in His "Operation Human Race."

There were many children like Zelub at the time. They were called Nephilim—meaning both "fallen ones" and "giants." Half-human and half-angelic, this new race produced such wickedness that it caused revulsion in God's heart, and the flood became an inevitability. The Nephilim helped create such horrible conditions on earth that God had the emotion of regret that he had created man.

"Semjaza, Azazel—I have a mission for you," Satan commanded two of his most trusted leaders.

"Yes, my lord," said Semjaza, "what can we do for you?"

"I want you to lead an army to earth and immediately cohabit with as many earthly women as possible," Satan said. "I want these unions to result in the birth of many healthy offspring."

"At once, lord," they replied. Azazel asked, "We will do this for you; can you tell us why? What is the purpose of these unions?"

"Let me explain," said Satan. "In future earth time—perhaps the next 100, 200 or 2,000 years, God has predicted He is somehow going to provide a way of forgiveness for all of mankind. This will undo my great victory in the garden and give man a chance to choose an eternal relationship with God. Anyone who accepts this Redeemer will, in turn, be forgiven and put out of our reach forever. And most important, this will demonstrate that God's sentence of eternal banishment for us is justified, because these inferior humans were willing to repent and accept His free provision of forgiveness.

"If I so mix our order of beings with the humans, God will not be able to condemn us without condemning His precious humans as well.

"My plan will accomplish one of two things. Because the human race will be too greatly mixed with us condemned angels to be saved, God will either have to forgive us all, or condemn us all. Thus He will have to admit His Operation Human project failed. He will have no other choice but to rescind our condemnation and forgive us, as I see it."

"You are absolutely brilliant, Lord Lucifer," said Azazel. "How can God ever defeat you?"

Of course, Satan miscalculated, as he often does. God first warned the world of the consequences of turning away from Him. Noah built an ocean-going barge over 200 miles from the nearest body of water and warned the world it was going to be destroyed by a great flood. He clearly warned that all who would not repent and believe in God's forgiveness would be swept away with the universal flood. After 120 years, only Noah and seven members of his family had accepted the gracious offer. Everyone else was destroyed.

It is important to see that one of the reasons Noah and his family were saved was the fact that his family geneology included no mix of angel and man in it. True, he was also a righteous man though faith in God's eyes, but had he or any members of his family been a product of such a mixed union, they could not have been saved. God literally said in the original Hebrew about Noah, "...Noah was a just man, perfect in his *geneology*" (Genesis 6:9).

Without a pure human race, there could not have been a savior, because the savior had to be a true man to qualify as a sacrifice for mankind's sin. The main reason for the flood was to decontaminate the human race—to purify it by eliminating the angel-men and the worst of them, the Nephilim. Many believe the factual basis for Greek mythology came from the accounts of the god-like beings known as the Nephilim.

Since mankind's creation, Satan's two principal roles have been to blind the unbeliever and to accuse, confuse and neutralize the believer. Satan still has access to God's presence.

An example of Satan's attack on believers is illustrated in the Book of Job. But no matter how much Satan hates God, he must still obey Him. When he is called, he wastes no time entering the presence of the Lord. Neither does he miss an opportunity to brag about the authority over the earth which Adam forfeited to him. In this role of accuser, Satan tries to convict believers before God day and night. This is the kind of access to heaven that God permits for His own reasons—even during the kind of all-out war that rages in the heavens and on earth.

The Bible warns about Satan's power over those who will not believe:

> *"And even if our gospel is veiled, it is veiled to those who are perishing. The god of this age has blinded the minds of unbelievers, so that they cannot see the light of the gospel of the glory of Christ, who is the image of God"* (2 Corinthians 4:3-4 NIV).

The invisible spiritual war raging all around us would make any military attack man can imagine seem like a popgun by comparison. Just as the archangel Michael wisely decided not to personally challenge Satan, human beings must understand their role in this struggle.

The Apostle Paul perhaps said it best:

> *"For though we live in the world we do not wage war with the weapons of this world, for the weapons of our warfare are not physical but have divine power to destroy strongholds of the mind. We destroy arguments and every obstacle raised by vain pride against the knowledge of God, and take every thought captive to obey Christ..."* (2 Cor. 10:3-6 HL).

🌓

Jeremy Armstrong wondered if he had made the right

decision as soon as he landed in Newark Airport, the closest to U.N. headquarters in New York City. While waiting
for his luggage in baggage claim, he got involved in a shov-
ing match between several local gang members. At six-
foot-two, Jeremy was about six inches taller than the
largest of the youths. But his fear was that they might be
armed. If they were, no weapons were ever drawn. He
kept thinking about Paul's letter to Timothy and how it
mimicked the times he was living through.

The cab ride to the U.N. took more than 40 minutes,
and Jeremy knew it was getting close to quitting time for
most of the staff. As he approached the building, he
noticed some words engraved in the cornerstone. He
stopped just for a moment to see what it said.

"...they shall beat their swords into plowshares, and
their spears into pruning hooks; nation shall not lift up
sword against nation, neither shall they learn war anymore..." it read. From his new Bible studies, Jeremy recognized the passage as from the book of Isaiah. He mused to
himself, "Gee, I thought that happens after the Messiah
comes to earth. I didn't realize the U.N. was the body that
was going to accomplish all this."

Though it was late, Jeremy had no doubts that he
would still catch his friend Zeke Charlton at work. After
hearing the news that Zeke's boss, Gianfranco Carlo, had
been assassinated in Israel by Muslim fanatics, he figured
Zeke would be on 24-hour-a-day duty for awhile. He was-
n't disappointed.

Just before 6 p.m., Jeremy was passed through an elaborate security system, including x-rays and metal detec-

tors, and was shown to Zeke's office. It was an impressive suite—something like what Jeremy would have imagined for the secretary-general himself—with a private library, kitchen, bedroom and multi-media conference room.

"Zeke," said Jeremy before even exchanging greetings with his good friend, "is this really your office? You must be as important as you think you are."

Charlton smiled and grabbed Jeremy, embracing him in a big bear hug. Zeke was not usually this friendly—not with anyone else. But his relationship with Jeremy was unique—built upon an unusual foundation. The two had served in combat together briefly during the Persian Gulf War. They were part of a special forces patrol that sneaked behind Iraqi lines to examine the strength of their fortifications just prior to the American land invasion. The small unit never actually tangled with enemy forces, but they did find themselves in an active minefield. And Zeke stepped on one.

He had the presence of mind to remain perfectly still—an achievement few can boast about no matter how much training they go through. Jeremy got the job of disabling the mine—thus saving not only Zeke's life, but his limbs as well. Charlton never forgot the personal risk Jeremy took for him. He vowed to repay him for it someday. He hoped this plum assignment might begin to even the scales.

"So how was your trip?" asked Zeke.

"Piece of cake," said Jeremy. "Anytime I get on an airplane and don't have to jump out of it in mid-flight, I consider that a good trip."

"I know what you mean," said Zeke. "Let's sit down for a little briefing and then I'll show you your office. It's not as nice as this, but I think you will be pleased. It beats the barracks you're used to."

"Hey, your bathroom beats what I'm used to," said Jeremy with a smile.

"OK, here's the deal, Jeremy," Zeke began. "You and I are going to be leading the greatest pacification program mission the world has ever seen. Carlo has laid the plans for the institution of the first real, true world government. We're on the fast track toward deployment now. There's no stopping it."

"Even Carlo's assassination isn't going to slow it down?" asked Jeremy quizzically. "I heard the news just as I was getting on the plane."

"Absolutely not," said Zeke with a great degree of self-assurance. "In fact, I can guarantee you it will only speed up the process."

"How, Zeke?" asked Jeremy. "Wasn't it principally the power of his personality that took us as far as we've come in the last few years?"

"Yes, that's true, Jeremy," said Zeke. "There are some things I can't tell you right now—some things you would-n't believe if I did. But just trust me, for the moment, and accept what I am telling you. We are moving fast and we are at the center of the universe here."

"So, what exactly do you want me to do?" asked Jeremy.

"Good question," said Zeke. "I couldn't really talk about it over the phone. I need you because, more than any-thing, I need someone I can trust absolutely and without any hesitation. I need you to be my right hand here. I need you to be my eyes and ears. I've got thousands of people reporting to me and sometimes all of the little details cause me to lose sight of the big picture. I want you to take on a lot of my administrative duties—to phase your-self into virtually everything I'm doing. Learn the players, learn the plan. Then we can begin to delegate to you as much of the work as you can handle."

"What exactly is the plan?" asked Jeremy.

"The plan is to facilitate world government—to root out the opposition and to clear every obstacle in our path," he said. "In a nutshell, that's what we're here for."

"I hate to ask such a stupid question, Zeke, but when did you become such a fan of global government?" asked Jeremy.

"Since I got to be such an instrumental part of making it happen," he said bluntly. "Jeremy, if things work out like I expect them to, we're going to be very important, very influential people in this new world we're creating."

Pope John Paul III and Elijah Ben David did not sleep that night. John Paul insisted to the medical team that had been treating Carlo that he needed to maintain a vigil by the body. The medical professionals were anxious to dis-connect the body from life-support and get it to the med-ical examiner where an autopsy could be performed.

"What's your rush?" asked the pope brusquely. "Aren't you certain the bullet to the head was the cause of death?"

No one in the hospital seriously questioned the pope. If he wanted to remain with the body for a few hours, so be it. The pope looked at Carlo. The top of his head was heavily bandaged. His face looked almost serene, except for the tube that was left sticking out of his mouth.

"Poor Gianfranco," he said to Elijah. "This time he calculated wrong. What was he thinking about? Did he really believe he would be resurrected? Had the power he was experiencing driven him to megalomania?"

"I don't know," replied Ben David. "I just know that Carlo told me not to lose faith, but to remain with his body after his official death." As the Pope stared out the window, he said, "Yes, I know. He told me the same thing."

Just then, a strange figure appeared in the room. It had the general form of a human, but they could see right through it. An awesome power emanated from his presence. It caused both the pope and Ben David to turn around. They couldn't believe their eyes. A glorious, multicolored aura radiated from the spirit being's form. The pope asked, "Who are you, Lord?" They looked in amazement as the figure smiled at both of them, then literally slowly merged with and disappeared into Carlo's body.

The pope moved quickly to Carlo's bedside. He got there just in time to see Carlo's eyes quiver and slowly open. Ben David's hair stood on end as he saw Gianfranco's mouth move. There was a look in Gianfranco's eyes that was totally different—other- worldly. It was an ecstatic look with overtones of something strange and almost sinister. Both the pope and Ben David shivered with a mixture of fear and excitement.

Then Carlo coughed—not loudly, mind you. Just the kind of noise one makes when trying to clear the throat. They were frozen with awe as Gianfranco reached up and pulled the tube slowly out of his mouth. It was true! Gianfranco Carlo was alive. They could see his chest beginning to rise and fall. He was breathing again. As he had predicted, a resurrection had occurred before their very eyes.

The pope jumped for the buzzer near Carlo's bed. He wanted to alert the staff, but most of all, he wanted to make certain he wasn't seeing things. Within seconds, a nurse was in the room, quickly followed by an orderly and, finally, a doctor. All of them did double-takes as they entered the room and saw Carlo breathing. They couldn't believe their eyes.

Now they hustled about re-connecting him to machines. His heartbeat was regular. His breathing was almost normal. When they first hooked up the brainwave monitor, nothing registered. It was simply a flat line. Then it suddenly it began to register extraordinary activity. In fact, there was far more brainwave activity than you would expect even in a fully conscious, uninjured and highly intelligent person.

The pope and Ben David watched as a smile formed on Carlo's face.

"How did you do it? Who was the mighty angel that took up residence in you?" they asked.

Carlo struggled to talk. He motioned for them to come closer. Speech was difficult because of damage to his throat by the tube.

Carlo whispered to the pope and Ben David, "Remember what I told you. The miracle has happened just as I predicted it would. This is why I specifically asked you both to be present after my official death. It takes two trusted witnesses to establish truth according to the Bible. You and Ben David must bear witness to the world about both my prophecy and what you saw and heard just now."

Zeke and Jeremy had basically pulled an all-nighter on their first evening together in New York. They caught about two hours of sleep in the office, then showered and shaved and got back to business. After all, there was a lot of work to do. Zeke's boss had been assassinated 24 hours earlier, and Jeremy needed to get acclimated to his new work environment, plus get caught up on the pressing developments of his assignment.

Zeke was introducing Jeremy to key staffers when he was paged on the intercom.

"Colonel Charlton, please dial one," the operator said in a serious monotone. "Colonel Charlton, please dial one."

"What is it now?" asked Zeke rhetorically before picking up the phone. "Yes," he said after dialing one, "this is Colonel Charlton. What! Are you serious? Stay on the line, I'm going into my office."

As Zeke hung up the receiver on the wall phone, he called to Jeremy to follow him, without even excusing himself from the other staffers.

"What's up, Zeke?" Jeremy said as he tried to catch up

to his fast-moving boss.

"You're not going to believe it," he said. "I don't even believe it."

"What won't I believe?" asked Jeremy as they entered Zeke's office and closed the door behind them.

As Zeke dashed for the phone, he smiled at Jeremy: "Carlo is alive!"

"You're right," Jeremy said, "I don't believe you."

Zeke picked up the receiver and pushed the blinking line that connected him with Jean-Claude DuMonde in Jerusalem.

"It's a miracle," DuMonde was saying, "even the Israeli Prime Minister/prophet Elijah Ben David and the pope agree. He was gone, Zeke, absolutely gone. He was several hours late for an autopsy. It's a miracle they didn't cut him up."

"Well, what's his condition?" Zeke wanted to know.

"Let's just say he's talking. He's in no real pain. He's alert," said DuMonde. "We thought he would be laid up and recuperating for some time, but he's recovering by leaps and bounds. There is just no explanation for all this! On the basis of the blood loss alone, he has no business being alive. He should be totally brain dead with the massive damage caused by the wound. And listen to this: He's arranging a bedside press conference with Ben David and the pope! One more thing, Zeke, and this is very important. The boss wanted me to pass along some instructions to you personally. I don't even know what they mean, but he said you would understand."

"Yes, J.C.," said Zeke, "what did he tell you?"

"He said, 'Tell Zeke to move ahead with Plan A—and quickly.' That's it, Zeke. That's all he said."

"I understand, J.C.," said Zeke. "That's all I need to know. Thanks for passing on the message. And, if you get a chance to pay my respects to the boss, give him my best. And tell him Jeremy Armstrong is on board."

"I will do that, Zeke," said DuMonde. "I better get going here and see what kind of hell is breaking loose. Looking forward to seeing you soon, Zeke."

"Bye, J.C.," said Zeke.

"Jeremy," said Zeke, "is this unbelievable or what? He's alive. He came back from the dead. If there's anyone left on this planet who still doesn't believe in this man, this should turn them around, don't you think?"

"Oh yeah," said Armstrong. "This will make him even more popular—even more powerful. It will make your plans move that much quicker and more smoothly."

"You figured that out pretty quickly," said Zeke.

"It's almost like a script," said Jeremy. "I remember back a decade ago when Yitzhak Rabin was assassinated by fanatics who wanted to stop the peace process. It had just the opposite effect. The opposition is always weakened by an event like that—they're placed on the defensive."

"Yes, and we need to figure out how to take advantage of the change in political climate this event creates," said Zeke. "Let's go over the plan, Jeremy, and see if you think we're missing anything."

Zeke dropped a voluminous report on Jeremy's lap. It was titled, "Consolidation of Power," and stamped "highly confidential."

"This is our blueprint for instituting all aspects of global government in the next 90 days," said Zeke. "This office, and your participation, Jeremy, are key to this timetable and to the success of this mission."

"Ninety days—are you kidding?" asked Armstrong.

"No, I'm not," said Zeke. "Anything is possible now. Carlo's resurrection has assured that."

"I will read your report tonight, Zeke, but tell me what you have in mind," said Armstrong. "What's the thrust of our work here?"

"Our job is troubleshooting, Jeremy," said Zeke. "We have to react fast and put out fires. We're also overseeing the area of opposition research."

"Opposition research?" asked Jeremy.

"Yeah, we need to find out who the troublemakers are going to be and then neutralize them," said Zeke.

"You mean neutralize them the way we used to neutralize the enemy in special forces?" asked Jeremy.

"Well, yes and no," said Zeke. "We don't always need to waste people in politics. Sometimes there are more effective means of neutralizing them. The point is, we want to minimize the obstacles to our goal."

"So, who would you say represents the biggest threat to your goal?" asked Jeremy.

"Without a doubt, I would say it's the religious fanatics," said Zeke. "It's not even so much the Muslims. They actually play right into our hands with a lot of what they do. But the real obstacles are those little pockets of evangelicals and fundamentalist Christians you find every once in a while. There aren't too many left, but the ones we encounter are the most determined to stop our plan."

"Why do you suppose they are so against world government?" asked Jeremy.

"They're just superstitious," said Zeke. "They keep clinging to certain Bible prophecies which they say predict that Satan will control a world government—that he will literally indwell and take over the body of a man who will rule the world. That gives them the creeps, so they're opposed to any kind of world government—even the most benevolent. Some of them have gotten hold of some books left behind by those Christian fanatics who disappeared. It has caused no end of trouble in some areas."

"Well, Zeke," said Jeremy, "given the latest developments in Jerusalem, with our world ruler waking up from the dead, these concerns are only going to intensify, don't you think?"

"Gee, I never thought about that, Jeremy," he said. "That's a good point. We'll have to keep an eye on those groups. Maybe you should take personal charge of that mission. I'll get you a briefing paper that will provide you with background material on all of the key suspects."

Three days later, the world prepared to tune in to the most highly publicized press conference in history. Gianfranco Carlo would be sitting up in his hospital bed in Jerusalem to make a special address to the people of the world. With him also would be the Israeli Prime Minister Elijah Ben David and Pope John Paul III, who were with the secretary-general throughout his ordeal. Questions from the world press would be entertained by satellite.

In New York, Jeremy watched at home in his new apartment.

"Good evening ladies and gentlemen, people of the world," began the pope, who was standing next to Gianfranco Carlo's hospital bed. "I speak to you tonight from Jerusalem, the center of the world, the city of peace, the city of the prophets, the jewel of the Holy Land. Three days ago, an assassin's bullet struck down my brother and friend, Gianfranco Carlo, the leader of the European Union and the secretary-general of the United Nations. I was there. I saw it. Many of you saw it on television. From the moment I saw the head wound and the blood, I was certain my friend was dead. But, as you know, Gianfranco Carlo is very much alive today.

"My friends," the pontiff continued, "I am here tonight to tell you that I believe Gianfranco Carlo is alive tonight because of a miracle. Make no mistake about this. He did not survive that gunshot wound. He truly died. He was pronounced dead. He was dead for several hours. I sat next to him in the hospital after he was disconnected from the monitors and the oxygen. He was gone. And he came back—just like Jesus did 2,000 years ago.

"That's right, my dear brothers and sisters, I am here tonight to tell you that Gianfranco Carlo was resurrected—raised from the dead for a great purpose. This is what Jews and Christians and Muslims and others have been waiting for so long—our Messiah, our Christ, our Mahdi, our Krishna, our Buddha. He is finally here. His name is Gianfranco Carlo. I suggest we listen to him tonight—hear what he has to say."

Then Ben David took the microphone, "Sons of Abraham, Isaac and Jacob. I am here tonight in the name of the God of our Fathers to bear witness to several miracles I personally witnessed. Gianfranco predicted to me long before it happened that he would be assassinated. He predicted he would die and then be miraculously raised from the dead. Tonight I bear witness, according to the test of Moses in the Torah, these prophecies have been fulfilled exactly. Gianfranco's resurrection is a true miracle. He himself asked me to stay with his body and witness these things before his assassination. I now bear witness that he is a Prophet, he is alive by a miracle and that he is the 'Anointed One of God' for the Gentile world. He saw to it that there would be two reliable witnesses to these facts in accordance with the Torah. I therefore submit to him as his Prophet."

"Thank you, Holy Father, and thank you my Prophet Ben David. I called on you both to be my witnesses because your honesty and religious authority are unimpeachable.

"Thank you all over the world for your heartfelt prayers over the past few days," began Carlo. "They have meant so much to me—as have your cards and flowers, enough to fill several hospitals, I would imagine.

"Yes, my friends, it is a miracle that I am alive tonight. Let me tell you what death is like. I have been there. I remember very vividly passing through a tunnel. There was light at the end—very bright light. When I reached the light, I heard the voice of God tell me: 'You must go back, my son. Your work is not yet finished. You will be fully healed—fully resurrected. And when you are whole again, you will have extraordinary powers. You will be able to see the future. You will be able to detect a lie from the truth. You will be able call fire down from the sky to devour your enemies.'

"Well, my dear friends, it is my sincere hope that I no longer have enemies on the earth. I believe we can all work together in this global village of ours. Aren't we all better off cooperating with one another—sharing our resources, ideas and technology for the overall good of mankind? What's the point of war, violence and hatred? What is to be gained from those horrible conditions?

"That's why I believe it is so urgent that we speak together tonight. While recovering in my hospital bed these last three days, I have been hard at work. I have been talking with world leaders in America, Great Britain, France, Germany, Japan, Russia, China, Africa and the Middle East. There is a growing consensus among all of our important regional leaders that it is time for a better way. Nationalism served its purpose in its time. But the day of the nation-state is over. The day of world government is here. The promised day of beating swords into plowshares and spears into pruning hooks has finally arrived.

"Over the next few days I will be announcing a series of electrifying plans designed to make you—each and every one of you—freer, safer and more prosperous than you ever imagined you could be. That is the goal of our New World Order, our new global ethic. We are here to serve you, to improve your lives, to ensure peace.

"And last but not least, I promise to lead you into an era of greatly enhanced consciousness. A quantum leap in spiritual awareness is about to happen—and I have been appointed by the almighty Lord of this world to make it happen.

"That is all I have to say tonight, my friends, except to add: It's good to be alive again. We have so much to look forward to here on this planet. Now, I understand we can take a few questions from the international press."

Press secretary Ron Piereson stepped forward to explain that the questions would be transmitted to the secretary-general and holy father in Jerusalem by satellite from studios in Washington, Rome and Beijing.

"The first question is from Sam Crawford with CNN," said Piereson. "Go ahead Sam. Can you hear me?"

"Yes, this is Sam Crawford in Washington. Secretary-general Carlo, to what do you attribute your miraculous recovery?"

"Good question, Sam," said Carlo. "First of all, let's not forget that I did not 'recover' from the gunshot wound. I died. This is an important distinction. I am here tonight—alive and getting well—because my father in heaven wants me here, directing human affairs, providing leadership, making the tough decisions in this age of uncertainty. My Lord assured me that we have a chance—perhaps our first, perhaps our last—a chance to achieve lasting peace in the world. My role is to foster that peace and to enforce it, harshly if necessary. But we can create a new world for our children and our children's children. I believe God has given me the authority and the power. All I need now is your cooperation and your belief."

"Followup, if I may, sir," said Crawford. "Are you telling us that you represent the Second Coming? Are you the Christ, the so-called Messiah—God incarnate?"

"Simply put, Sam, I am. Though I am still Gianfranco Carlo, I have been indwelt by God's spirit. I know there will be many skeptics out there. But I look forward to demonstrating my new power and authority in the very near future. But just to give you a foretaste, so you understand how serious I am about what I say, I would like you all to look out your windows now, go outside and look at the southern sky..."

Jeremy had been sitting in a near trance listening to Carlo's words. He was stunned—and scared by them.

"What have I gotten myself into now?" he wondered to himself. "And what is this business about the southern sky?" Jeremy didn't know if he could even see the southern sky from his apartment balcony. He wasn't even certain which way was south in his state of New York disorientation. But he went outside on the patio anyway. There were people all over the street staring up at the image. It was Carlo, all right. How did he do it? An image of his face, as clear as a television image, appeared as he said in the southern sky. He appeared to be talking, though he could only be heard on the televisions that were on in every building and every living room in the city. It was possible, then, to sit outside, watch Carlo give his speech from the sky and actually hear every word from the battery of TV sets on in the area—all tuned to the only program on anywhere in the world at that moment, "The Gianfranco Carlo Show."

Jeremy sat in a chair on his deck and listened to the image in the sky: "Yes, my friends, this is just a sample of what I will be showing you in the days ahead. It is not meant to scare you or frighten you, I only want you to understand how serious I am and who I truly am."

Jeremy studied the image, trying to figure out how he did it. Was it a projected image? He didn't think so. Was there a huge flat-screen monitor suspended in the atmosphere? He didn't think so. This was curious indeed.

"Maybe," thought Jeremy, "this is a miracle. But, if it is, somehow I don't think it's a miracle of God."

For the first time in a long time, Jeremy allowed himself to remember what his mother and dad had taught him as he grew up. They were among the Christian fanatics from all over the world who had disappeared unexplainably. He became strangely disturbed and uneasy.

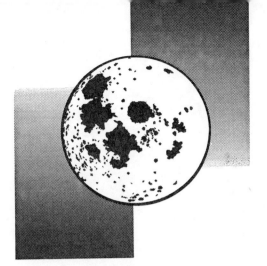

CHAPTER 6

Ezekiel's Hook

C aptain Isaac Barak was in the bunker at Palmahim when he heard it—the sound he had hoped he would never hear. It was a high-pitched and bone-chilling buzzer, a pulsating variation of the kind used to signify the end of a period in an American basketball game. This one, however, indicated the ultimate horror. It was the signal that a ballistic missile was streaking toward Israel.

Barak instantly took command, "Bearings?" he said in a cool confident voice.

"From Lebanon toward Tel Aviv—low trajectory and coming fast!" shouted Sgt. Joshua Schwartz, trying to conceal his terrible anxiety. His whole family was in Tel Aviv.

It was as easy as that to identify the projectile. Back in 1996 Israel had launched the Amos-1 communications satellite aboard a French Ariane rocket from the European Space Agency's French Guiana complex. The 961-kilogram,

$350 million satellite was one of the best investments the Jewish state ever made, because, along with the Arrow program and the 335-kilogram Ofek-3 satellite boosted into orbit by an Israeli rocket, it represented a primitive first step toward the creation of a genuine anti-missile shield. It was Amos-1, however, in geosynchronous orbit above Zaire and providing round-the-clock surveillance of the Arab world, that spotted this missile.

Faced with critical decisions that involved hundreds of thousands of lives—all of which had to be made in seconds—Barak could only wish General Oved were here in the bunker. There was no time to call him before impact, only time to notify Jerusalem.

"Put the Arrow in the bow," said Barak. "Mobilize MIRA-CL as backup. Men, I don't need to tell you, we have no margin for error."

Barak picked up the hotline to Prime Minister Elijah Ben David. In seconds he had him on the line.

"Mr. Prime Minister, this is Captain Isaac Barak at Palmahim. A missile is headed from the Bekaa Valley toward Tel Aviv. We are prepared to attempt intercept. Do we have your permission to launch?"

"Dear God," he whispered. "Do your best, Captain," said Ben David. "Millions of lives may hang in the balance."

As soon as Ben David disconnected with Barak, he picked up his own hotline to Secretary-General Gianfranco Carlo's hospital room in Jerusalem. He got right through.

"My Lord," said Ben David, "I've just received word that at least one missile is headed from Syrian territory in the

Bekaa Valley toward Tel Aviv. We aren't certain, but it probably has a nuclear warhead."

"Listen carefully, Ben David," said Carlo. "Don't waste a moment. Launch a retaliatory nuclear strike at Damascus immediately!"

"At once, my Lord," said Ben David as he hung up the phone.

It was impossible to overstate Carlo's new authority in the Middle East—and especially in Israel. Nothing major happened in foreign policy or security issues that Carlo didn't know about. Indeed, Elijah Ben David had helped Carlo to acquire that authority, especially in Israel. Usually he made the call on anything controversial. It was not surprising that even Prophet-Prime Minister Ben David should call him on such an urgent matter—especially one that would be so important to the entire world. It would have been unthinkable for him not to have made the call, and even worse not to have listened and obeyed.

The prime minister didn't like making the next call, but orders were orders. Since Carlo had guaranteed Israel's security with U.N. forces, he had become the de facto head of government. He was also, of course, the most important political leader in the world. Ben David wasn't about to second-guess him. He picked up the phone—another hotline—to Dimona, Israel's not-so-secret nuclear missile base.

"This is Prime Minister Ben David," he said. "Launch the Doomsday Missile (code word for a five megaton thermonuclear missile) on Damascus. This is not a drill. I repeat this is not a drill. Launch 'Doomsday' on Damascus.

Here are the authorization launch codes…27, 64, 66, 8, 31."

Back at Palmahim, sweat was running off Barak's brow. It was not that warm. It was the stress of knowing how many lives were in his hands.

"Schwartz," he said, "you will be responsible for the coordinates on the Arrow. I will take control of MIRACL. As soon as you think you are locked on, go for it. You won't get a second chance, so make it your best shot."

Barak sat next to Schwartz so he could monitor his progress and set up a shot for MIRACL in the event it was necessary. Barak truly hoped it didn't come to a test for MIRACL, hardly a proven anti-missile weapon. Though it had been successfully tested in computer simulations, it had never actually been fired at a live missile.

"Fifteen seconds," said Schwartz as he lined up his coordinates. "I have missile lock. Ten, nine, eight, seven, six, five, four, three, two, one…missile fired!"

Schwartz held his breath. It would take only seconds to determine if it was hit. The radar screen showed nothing.

"Come on!" said Schwartz.

"Please, God!" said Barak.

"It's a miss!" sobbed Schwartz.

Captain Barak knew the chances of saving Tel Aviv now were slim to none. But he had one shot left and he was going to take it. He carefully worked out his coordinates for the MIRACL. He found the missile on the screen. "I have missile lock," he said. But before he fired he said aloud: "O God of Abraham, Isaac and Jacob, though I walk through the valley of the shadow of death, I shall fear no evil. Use Your angels to guide this laser beam to its target. Save Your people, Israel, as You promised You would through our holy Prophets. Amen...*FIRE !*" Barak shouted.

There was silence in the room. It seemed like there was silence all over the world for the next two seconds. Then he saw an image of the incoming warhead disintegrate on his screen.

"Bull's-eye," shouted Schwartz. "It's a miracle!"

How does one feel when he has just saved the lives of more than a million men, women and children? Barak knew in that moment what few would ever experience. He fell to his knees before everyone and loudly praised and thanked the God of his fathers. Everyone was startled because Isaac Barak had never been a religious man. (He had always been openly contemptuous of the constantly meddling orthodox rabbis. He was turned off of religion by their arrogant, holier-than-thou attitude.)

Even the usually cold United Nations observers in the bunker were dancing for joy. And tough Sgt. Schwartz was crying. His whole family had been saved.

Then Barak remembered. "O my God! I must call Jerusalem immediately. They could be seconds away from launching a retaliatory strike on Damascus. I've got to make sure they understand we knocked the incoming warhead down."

"Mr. Prime Minister, this is Barak," he said. "The missile is destroyed. We got it with our experimental MIRACL system. Repeat, *the missile has been destroyed!*"

"What?!" asked Prime Minister Ben David. "I can't believe it!"

"Mr. Prime Minister," said Barak. "What's the matter? If I

didn't know better, I would say you sound, well, distressed. Don't you understand? I'm telling you the missile headed for Tel Aviv has been knocked down. Our city is saved!"

"I understand, Captain," said Ben David. "I'm happy you have spared the lives of hundreds of thousands of our countrymen. You shall get our top medal for valour and a promotion. Bless you for...er...ah...what you have done. But I am just aghast at what *we* have done. I have already fired the Doomsday missile at Damascus by direct order of Secretary-General Carlo himself. Damascus no longer exists."

"Lord help us," said Barak. "The whole Muslim world will declare a jihad against us."

"Yes, Captain," said Ben David, "we will need His help more than ever now. The rage of the Muslim world will now burst into flames of war. God bless you, my brave son, and may He protect Israel."

Barak retreated to a private room, and there, of all things, he found a Bible. He randomly opened to the Prophet Isaiah, looking for some comfort. He was utterly shocked when his eyes fell upon these verses:

"An oracle concerning Damascus: 'See, Damascus will no longer be a city but will become a heap of ruins. . . The fortified city will disappear from Ephraim [an Israeli tribe whose land extended from the Golan Heights to Damascus], *and royal power from Damascus; the remnant of the Syrians will be like the glory of the Israelites,' declares the Lord Almighty...In that day men will look to their*

Maker and turn their eyes to the Holy One of Israel" (Isaiah 17:1, 3, 7 NIV).

Jeremy Armstrong and Zeke Charlton called a special meeting of their top intelligence analysts to evaluate the international ramifications of the Damascus attack.

"Damascus is gone," began Harif Harrare, a U.N. Arabist. "Hundreds of thousands are dead or dying. The entire city is incinerated. Refugees who lived nearby are streaming away from the city in all directions. Tens of thousands will die later from radiation exposure. President Hassan is dead. So are his sons and most of his ministers. They had no warning, no time to prepare or retreat into shelters."

"What about the rest of the world?" asked Charlton. "Are any of the other Arab countries, or Iran, likely to make a move? Is anyone trigger-happy out there?"

"Iran is loading chemical and nuclear warheads on their missiles as we speak," said Colonel Simon Lefebvre, a British expert on Islam. "They are in a fury right now, but I don't think they will want to get nuked. So they are not likely to act alone. None of the other Arab countries—not even Iraq—are likely to make a move by themselves. Of course, Syria has been decapitated. Israel's biggest immediate threat is from within its own borders—the millions of Palestinians and other Arabs living with the Palestinian Authority. They pose a serious security threat of a different kind. The riots have already begun—Molotov cocktails, even random shootings."

"How about outside the Middle East?" asked Armstrong. "China, Russia...what are they thinking about this? What are they likely to do?"

"That's a good question," said Dr. Peter Demetrio, a Sino-Russo expert. "Russia sees this as a cold blooded, unwarranted nuclear strike on one of its closest strategic allies in the Middle East. You know, Russia has defense pacts with Syria that require it to respond to 'aggression' of this kind. I only hope Carlo can continue to charm the Russians the way he has in the past. Boris Gudonov has always had his eye on the Middle East. He wrote a book several years ago called *Russia's Destiny in the Persian Gulf.* What does that tell you about his long-term ambitions? He has never completely trusted Carlo. He may perceive this attack as Carlo's way of further dominating a sphere of influence that rightfully should be Russia's."

"OK," said Charlton, "I thank you all for your input. Unless there's something else someone wants to add, I will prepare my report for the boss."

Zeke had less than 30 minutes to prepare a fax for Carlo. He could almost envision his boss checking his watch about now. Yet, he wasn't at all sure about what he had to report in concrete terms. Everything was fluid. No one could predict what would happen next. This was the gravest challenge to the New World Order that Carlo had yet faced.

As Charlton retired to his office to work on his report, Armstrong decided to dive into some of the background material that had been piling up in his own office—specifically reports on the terrorist groups that may have had a hand in firing the original missile at Tel Aviv. He had asked Zeke to requisition a competent assistant to help him get organized—sorting files, setting up his computer programs, etc. He had plenty of clerical help, but what he needed was a trusted and gifted aide—someone with some foreign linguistic abilities and a head on his shoulders.

Armstrong got more than he bargained for in the form of Erin O'Hara. She had all the ingredients, all right, and then some. She also just happened to have gorgeous long red hair that framed a exquisitely beautiful face, sparkling green eyes and a figure that could win the Miss Universe contest. So it was small wonder that Jeremy had trouble keeping his eyes off her and his mind on his work. But there was no denying she knew what she was doing. She was very intelligent, resourceful, thoroughly knew the entire section operations and was serenely self-confident.

Jeremy couldn't remember ever being so attracted to anyone before. Was it the stress he was under? Was it because he had not had time for romance in several years? Was it the fact that the world was coming apart and he needed a diversion? Or had he finally found the woman of his dreams? He wasn't sure. He had been attracted to other women before, but never as strongly as this. Usually women were quickly attracted to him. But there was no clue as to whether this lady was attracted to him at all. She was professional and respectful, but cooly aloof.

"So what do you make of the day's developments?" he asked her.

"Well, Colonel, I'm beginning to wonder if there is anything we can do to prevent the world from destroying itself. To the Muslims, Israel's nuking of a major historic Islamic capital was the final blasphemy."

"You hit that one right on the button, Ms. O'Hara," he said. "And please, knock off the 'Colonel' business. 'Jeremy' will do just fine."

That brought a slight smile to her face—not an easy achievement in times like this. She seemed to be a very serious young lady. "Please call me Erin, Colonel...I mean Jeremy," she said, looking up at him with those dancing green eyes.

"I don't know," she said. "This may sound like heresy around here, but I'm beginning to question this whole idea of 'world government.' I don't see it working. And I just don't buy into this deification of Gianfranco Carlo. His restoration to life seems to have caused the whole world to follow him blindly. There's something about all this that just strikes me as...well, wrong."

That brought a large grin to Armstrong's face. This was the first person he had met at the U.N. who shared his feelings of silent skepticism toward Carlo and the new world government.

"You know," said Armstrong, "I couldn't agree with you more. But those kinds of thoughts are very dangerous to express these days—at least outside of these four secured walls."

"Oh, I know," she said. "I don't know why...but I just sensed I could trust you. I hope I'm not out of line."

"Not at all," he said. "I was beginning to feel like maybe

I was crazy. If I am, it's great to have such beautiful company," He said with a wink.

Erin laughed. She was surprised at how quickly she was being drawn to this man. He was very straightforward, honest, kind, intelligent and had an almost boyish charm. His manner showed he was used to taking command and leading, yet he wasn't cocky—in fact, he had a humility about him that was disarming. She had looked up his service record before coming to work with him, so she would understand his exact needs and objectives. She was amazed that he had extensive combat experience and had received almost every medal for bravery in battle the U.S. and other countries awarded. He was also one of the few living recipients of the Congressional Medal of Honor. "Of course, the fact that he is ruggedly handsome doesn't hurt," she mused to herself.

"This certainly does seem like a madhouse, doesn't it?" she said. "I don't just mean the U.N., but this whole new world order. It's like one big insane asylum where everyone spies on the other."

"Erin," Armstrong said, "I know we have just met, and we have a lot of work to do. But would you consider taking a break and having dinner with me? I'm starved."

"Why Colonel...I mean Jeremy, I'd just love to," she said in her most charming southern drawl.

That was it—Jeremy was smitten. When Erin turned on her charm, he was so captivated he could hardly find the door. But he did manage to hide his flood of emotions, open the door and gallantly bow in his most charming impersonation of a Kentucky Colonel.

In Jerusalem, Carlo had left his bedside office and was back in his U.N. headquarters—a suite of offices inside the new Jewish Temple complex. There had been lots of objection to offices of any kind inside the rebuilt Temple. But the complaints all but subsided when they were leased out to the U.N. After all, the worldly Jewish leaders reasoned, the Temple is a place of peace and the U.N. is the most aggressive agent for peace on earth.

"It's a match made in heaven," declared Prime Minister Ben David at the ribbon-cutting ceremony during the opening of the posh new U.N. Jerusalem headquarters.

This morning, though, Gianfranco Carlo's demeanor was anything but peaceful. He had just received a call from President Gudonov in Russia.

He rehearsed the entire conversation in his mind, "You have left me in a very uncomfortable position," thundered Gudonov in his thick Russian accent.

"Control yourself, Boris," said Carlo in his most friendly manner. "Remember your blood pressure problem."

These two had never truly liked each other. They barely got along. Gudonov had reluctantly accepted Carlo's authority when he took the ten most powerful nations out of the EU and made them his base of power. Those ten nations now were the center of the New World Federation.

Gudonov had recently said on CNN, "The Almighty Ten is acting like the 'new Imperial Roman Empire.'" Then

Gudonov thundered, "Russia never got a fair deal from the EU and the rest of the world, and now much less from this almighty United States of Ten. Moscow has been treated like a second-class citizen in your new world order." His face took on an ominous expression as he continued, "Don't push the Russian Bear too far. You might just see him go into action with a terrible rage. I warn you before the world audience tonight, we Russians will not tolerate this treatment any longer. And don't forget, Comrades, we still have the largest arsenal in the world."

Carlo had been informed of that chilling message, so he listened very carefully to Gudonov as he vented his anger about the Damascus holocaust. "President Hassan was not only our close ally," Gudonov exclaimed, "He was my personal friend. You and your bastard daughter, Israel, murdered him in cold blood!"

"Now, Boris, let me remind you that we acted in self-defense," said Carlo. "We acted within the confines of international law. Syria had fired first. Our analysis of the wreckage of that missile indicates that it carried a multiple megaton thermonuclear warhead that would have obliterated Tel Aviv as completely as Israel's missile devastated Damascus. I am as saddened as you are about the consequences of those actions, but...."

Gudonov broke in: "Enough! You know as well as I do that Hassan didn't fire that weapon. It wasn't launched from Syria. It came from Lebanon."

"And you know very well," retorted Carlo, "that Hassan has maintained complete authority over Lebanon—especially the Bekaa Valley—for the last two decades...."

"I'm not going to debate this with you Carlo," Gudonov broke in. "But your so-called New World Order is rapidly deteriorating into a New World Disorder. You are presiding over nothing but chaos. I'm not going to stand by and let you dictate terms to us Russians."

"Oh no?" said Carlo. "And just what do you plan to do?"

"You'll see," said Gudonov ominously. "You'll see soon enough."

"Don't threaten me, Gudonov—it might prove to be a great folly", warned Carlo. "And don't threaten me and the Russian people" thundered Gudonov. "Don't forget for a moment, Gianfranco Carlo, Russia is still a great power with the largest arsenal on this planet. So I'm not threatening, I'm promising." Gudonov then angrily hung up. Carlo stared out the window for a long time as he realized he was about to be plunged into the greatest test of his career.

At the bunker in Palmahim, General Oved entered, walked straight over to Captain Barak and gave him a long, sincere hug.

"Son," he said, "you did it. I'm proud of you. This was the moment we had prepared for, and you came through with flying colors. Don't blame yourself for the foolishness of others. Those innocent people in Damascus would be just as dead if you had failed. Remember, there would be hundreds of thousands in Tel Aviv who would be dead as well. You bear no responsibility for the death and destruction in Damascus."

"Thank you, General," said Barak. "I can reason this out in my head, but in my emotions I still feel somehow responsible."

"That's crazy, Isaac," Oved replied. "The only thing you are responsible for is saving the lives of over a million innocent civilians. If there were any justice in this crazy world, Israel would be erecting monuments to you today."

Then Barak looked around to see if anyone could hear him. He said to the general, "I had the strangest experience right after hearing about Damascus being nuked. I went aside and looked for comfort in the Prophet Isaiah. My eyes fell on the page to which I had randomly opened—it declared that Damascus would be totally destroyed and never built again. Now here is the real punch line—the context indicates this event would shortly precede the coming of the Messiah to save Israel from a holocaust. General, that could only have been fulfilled at this moment in history. Damascus has never been destroyed before. Even if it had been, the prophecy says it will never be rebuilt again. With the radioactivity permeating what was Damascus, there is no possibility of it being rebuilt. General, I am beginning to believe that there really is a true personal Messiah and that He is about to come to earth. Furthermore, I believe Prime Minister Elijah Ben David is a false prophet."

The general was so startled that his mouth fell open. Then he said, "Isaac, that is truly amazing, but for heaven's sake be careful. You could be summarily executed for what you just said. We must find some time to secretly study this and determine what we should do."

Barak hated to change the subject because the general

was visibly moved. "Sir, I believe it's important to report a very strange meeting I had with DuMonde today."

"Yes," said the general with an anxious tone, "what did he say?"

"It appears Carlo and company want to take over the bunker here," he said.

"Did he say that?" asked the general.

"Not in so many words," explained Barak. "He said it would be necessary to station more 'observers' here and that a full investigation would begin tomorrow. I got the distinct impression that they have already concluded their investigation and have decided that Israelis can't be trusted to defend themselves anymore. I also think he is trying to pass the blame for the Damascus debacle entirely upon us."

"Let's go into your office," the general said, looking over his shoulder in fear their conversation was being overheard. Once inside, the general closed the door.

"Captain," he began, "I think it's necessary for us to appear to cooperate with the U.N. Go along with whatever they suggest. Do not question their judgment. Do not offer any protest."

"Yes, general," said Barak, "but what will this accomplish? Are we to write off our plan to defend Israel? Israel is in more danger today than ever before. You know very well that these U.N. 'observers' will not even attempt to intercept another incoming missile unless it's headed straight for Carlo's head."

"Yes, my son, I know this," the general said. "You are exactly right. But I think we must feign cooperation so that we can still retain access to this facility. Do you understand what I mean?"

Barak thought for a moment. He smiled.

"Yes, General, I think I know exactly what you mean."

"By the way," the general said nonchalantly, "You are now Major Isaac Barak, and I've recommended you for Israel's highest medal for valour."

Back in New York, Charlton got off the phone with DuMonde in Jerusalem. He had his marching orders.

"What's the matter, Zeke?" asked Armstrong. "You look like you just saw a ghost."

"I'm afraid I'm seeing lots of them," said Charlton. "Look, Jeremy, we've got a new priority from the boss. It seems there's some new dissent breaking out—here in the States, in Europe, even in Israel. He's worried about these fanatical Christians running around saying that he, the pope and Elijah Ben David are nothing but false prophets and ravenous wolves in sheep's clothing. He wants us to crack down on them—big time."

"Well, what do you mean by 'crack down,' exactly?" asked Armstrong. "What can we do here in New York?"

"He's giving us carte blanche to use the military—anything we need," said Charlton. "Resources are not a problem. He just wants us to start rounding them up—wherever they are—and to 'terminate them with extreme prejudice,' as he put it."

"You can't be serious!" said Armstrong.

"Yes, I'm very serious," said Charlton. "I hope you don't have a problem with that."

"Well, yes, Zeke, as a matter of fact, I do have a problem with that," Jeremy said. "Do you know why? Because I think I'm near becoming a Christian myself! I 'm beginning to agree with them."

"Jeremy," said Charlton, "you don't know what you are saying. Quiet down. I don't want to see you executed. Think about this carefully, and for God's sake don't say anything about it to anyone. I need your help. We have orders. We're soldiers, remember?"

"We're soldiers?" asked Armstrong incredulously. "Is that what soldiers do, Zeke? Do soldiers round up innocent men, women and children and 'eliminate them'? I suppose the Nazi SS who presided over the concentration camps in Germany were soldiers just following orders too, huh?"

"Now look, Jeremy, you're really out of line," said Charlton "When did you get all fired up about religion, anyway? When did you become some kind of a Christian freak?"

"I'm not the religious nut, Zeke," said Armstrong. "Your boss, who thinks he's God—he's the religious nut."

"OK, that's enough," said Charlton, "You're temporarily relieved of your duties here. I want you to go home, calm down and think this over. Decide if you want to be on the winning side or the losing side, Jeremy."

Jeremy went home, but not before telling Erin what had happened. They had a very special evening the night before. The one thing Jeremy would miss about his short-lived term at the U.N. was Erin.

"I'll call you later," she said. She couldn't hide her sense of extreme sadness over the news that Jeremy would be leaving the U.N. She was most of all surprised at how rapidly Jeremy had become so dear to her. She felt like she had loved him for years.

"Please do call," Jeremy said, "but be very careful. Watch your back and trust no one."

Boris Gudonov didn't waste any time getting his ducks in order after his conversation with Carlo. He feared Carlo's long reach in international affairs. He feared his awesome military machine, which included the combined nuclear arsenals of Europe, the United States, Israel—and perhaps China. And he especially feared what everyone in their right mind feared about Carlo—his amazing supernatural powers. After all, this was a man who, on all appearances, actually came back from the dead. Some suspected it was a fraud—a staged publicity stunt designed to increase his power. But Gudonov was not among them. He knew there was something special about Carlo—something fearful, even hideous.

So Gudonov got right to it. He knew if he was to act against Carlo, he would have to do it quickly. He would have a limited amount of time to coordinate his efforts with a few key allies. His best shot, he believed, was striking quickly at the Middle East, taking control of the oil fields and the indispensable land bridge (on which Israel sat squarely in the middle) that connected Europe, Asia and Africa. This would paralyze Carlo and the western world, which was still so dependent on petroleum. It would also block any surprise offensive against them, because their southern flank would be not only protected, but in position to make a devastating counter-attack in the event of an attack through Europe. His first call was to Ayatollah Makhubar in Iran.

"My friend," Gudonov said through a translator, "I am deeply grieved by Carlo's actions in striking at your close ally Syria. I do not believe he can be trusted. He has chosen sides with the Zionists. He flaunts this decision by living in their Temple. Tehran could be next. Do you want to wait? Or do you want to act with me?"

"Mr. President," the ayatollah said through his Russian translator, "Carlo is a blasphemer of the highest order. He calls himself the savior of the Muslim people—our redeemer. There is no convincing evidence to me that he is the Mahdi the Muslims have waited for. To me, he is an infidel, a false prophet and a murderer of the Islamic people. Tell me what your plan is. I am eager to join any attack against the Zionist Entity and Carlo...."

Later, Gudonov made several more calls—to the leader of Turkey, also disenchanted with the way his nation was treated as a third-rate member of the European alliance. Ankara was on board. All of the former Soviet republics in central Asia were with Moscow—especially with the blessing of the ayatollah, who declared the mission a "Jihad" or "Holy War." Egypt was an easy sell. The United

Arab Republic had a historically close relationship with Syria—having even considered mergers on more than one occasion. Its peace treaty with Israel was rejected by the devout Muslim masses long ago.

Gudonov persuaded, Iran, Egypt, Kazakhstan, Turkey, Libya, Algeria, Tunisia, Morocco, Mauritania, Sudan, Iraq, Saudi Arabia. Now Gudonov was certain he had a formidable force with which to stand up to Carlo. He knew he needed to mobilize fast. It would not take Carlo long to hear the rumors. He had ears everywhere. Gudonov needed the element of surprise to win. It would have to be a lightning-like strike. If he could defeat Carlo in the Mideast and control the oil fields, he would have the bargaining power to reassert Russia's authority.

Gudonov's logistical problem was troop movements. He needed to begin moving masses of troops into position for a quick dash to the south, but he knew full well that anything of this scale would immediately be detected by Carlo's elaborate satellite surveillance system.

"The only way to go," his top general said, "is to soften up the target with a barrage of strategic nuclear missiles. After that attack, we'll move in."

It made sense to Gudonov. He told his allies to mobilize for a sudden coordinated strike. Each would have its own separate initial target. All would eventually converge on Jerusalem, which, the Islamic coalition insisted, would not be targeted by nukes. The holy sites must be preserved, they said. Moscow agreed, though if it had been up to Gudonov, he would have blown the entire city away—holy sites or not.

Armstrong was home in his New York apartment of only a few weeks. He looked around. It barely even looked familiar. Jeremy had not spent much time at home during his stay at the U.N. Almost all of his waking hours—and many of his sleeping hours as well—were spent at the office, addressing one crisis after another.

Armstrong began packing his bags. There was no going back, he thought. He would not be a party to some international witchhunt against Christians. He simply would not do it. In fact, the way he was feeling right now, Jeremy was going to do everything in his power to thwart Carlo's plans against Christians.

Just then the phone rang. Jeremy hoped it would be Erin. There were only two things warming his heart these days—one was his deepening faith in God and his personal Bible study, and the second was the way he felt about Erin and the way she seemed to feel about him.

"Hello," said Jeremy hopefully.

"Hi," said the familiar female voice that gave Jeremy heart palpitations every time he heard it, "it's me," said Erin.

"Where are you?" Jeremy asked.

"I'm home," she said.

"Erin, I need to see you right away," he said. "Can you meet me?"

"Of course," she said. "Where?"

"I don't think it's safe for you to come over here," he

said. "I'm probably being watched. Meet me at Mikuni—
it's a sushi bar at the corner of 33rd and Third. Can you be
there in 20 minutes?"

"I'll be there in 15," she said.

In the short time Jeremy had been in New York,
Mikuni had become his favorite hangout. Not only did
they make a dynamite spicy tuna hand roll, but he had
befriended the owner, a young Japanese-American restaurateur who, like Jeremy, had been discovering the Bible.
Even the name of Tony Suzuki's restaurant meant "kingdom of God." Armstrong felt like he was part of that kingdom when he ate there and chatted with Tony and his
family members. Jeremy imagined there were angels surrounding this place. It was his refuge in this turbulent and
dark time and place.

By the time Jeremy got there, Erin was already seated
at the sushi bar.

"I told you I'd be here in 15 minutes," she said with a
smile.

With all the stress Jeremy was under—all the things on
his mind—he couldn't hold back a smile when he saw
Erin.

"Let's go sit at the corner table," he said. "I have some
serious things I need to talk to you about privately."

"OK," she said, warmly taking him by the arm as they
walked across the dining room.

"Erin," he said as he clutched her hand, "I realize we
haven't known each other very long. This may sound
ridiculous to you. As beautiful, bright and charming as you
are, you've probably had many men throw themselves at

you. But...I don't know how to say this exactly ..."

"Just tell me, Jeremy," she said smiling.

"I'm in love with you," he said while looking down at the floor.

"Now that didn't hurt too much, did it?" she asked, as she put her arms around him. "Surely you know I feel the same way about you. So why was this so difficult, my brave soldier?"

"The problem is...our world is falling apart," he said. "Not just the big world out there with Carlo and the nuclear weapons going off, but our little world, too. I've got to leave here, Erin. I'm through at the U.N. And I feel like I've got to do something to stop Carlo and Zeke and their evil plans to eliminate Christians. Of course, that's a very dangerous business. So it's a crazy time to fall in love."

"Jeremy," she said, "imagine how much harder it would be to take on the whole world all alone."

"No," he said, "I'm not dragging you into this. This is my fight. It's a no-win situation."

"Do I sound like I'm being dragged into something?" she said. "I was the one who took a chance and first talked openly about my doubts concerning Carlo and company. Do you think I'm doing this to please you?"

"No," he said, "I know you are as sincere in your convictions about this as I am. But I don't think you realize just how dangerous these people are and how evil are their intentions. I also think there's something about this struggle that goes far beyond this physical world. There are supernatural elements to it. In a way it's a spiritual struggle, too. I'm convinced from my reading of the Bible that the only way to protect ourselves is by putting on a kind of spiritual armor. We need to call on help from God and His angels. Fighting alone as humans we're helpless. Carlo with his supernatural powers knows this. He's not alone."

"I want to learn all about that," Erin said. "Jeremy, there's one thing I have learned in the last few years of observing this crazy planet we live on: I know there's got to be more than this life. I know it's not Carlo. I know he's a phony. I know the hatred he has in his heart—the ruthlessness. He talks persuasively of peace, but he's a warrior at heart. I know your heart, Jeremy. I know it's different. If there's a God who can show me how to be more like you, then I want Him in my life."

"Sweetheart, you know there isn't anything you could say to me that would be more meaningful than what you just said. That is just the nicest, kindest and most loving thing I have ever heard. But I still feel strongly that you should not get involved in my fight against Carlo. First of all, I don't even have a strategy yet. Second, I know it's dangerous just talking about resistance and rebellion in this present environment, much less to actually become an agent against them. I have seen their plans. Within days, Carlo will be instituting a new system of buying and selling that will enable him to have almost total control of people's lives. Already they have begun implanting computer chips in people's hands after they swear allegiance to Carlo. They numbers all begin with his special computer code—666. I mean, what's next? He's a complete totalitarian."

"OK, Jeremy, you tell me what to do," said Erin. "Should

I continue working at the U.N.? Should I collaborate with these draconian plans? Should I be a part of the problem?"

"Well, do you think anyone—Zeke or anyone else—suspects we're as close as we are?" asked Jeremy.

"No," she said, "I really don't. We've been quite reserved, and, of course, there hasn't been much time for anyone to notice anything."

"That's good," he said. "I think you could be most valuable right where you are—feeding me information and keeping me apprised of what they're up to. It's dangerous, but just living in this world right now is dangerous, too. Our only hope is changing it and making sure we're right with God. Erin, I need to go back to Southern California and report back to my unit so I'm not considered AWOL. I don't know what they'll have me do or where they will assign me. But I want you to know I love you and it's for keeps. No matter what happens, please remember that. I will call you whenever I can. I will write you, too, but not at the office. I have some books I want to leave with you—some things that I think will fascinate you and give you a little deeper understanding of God. I can't tell you how important it is to read your Bible—read it every day. Pray for God's intervention in your life and mine. Pray hard. Pray as if your life depended on it—because it does."

Jeremy was right about Carlo's new economic plan. He was ahead of schedule. While Gudonov in Russia placed his faith in arms and military alliances, Carlo believed the real strength was in economic control. So he was tightening his grip on power. He understood the old saying about the power of the purse strings. Within a few days of the nuclear attack, he instituted a new system of buying and selling in Israel, the U.S. and throughout most of western Europe. He used as his excuse the "war on terrorism"—the kind of international terrorism that had resulted in the attack on Israel and its retaliation on Syria. There would be no more incidents of this kind, he promised.

Eventually—within weeks, not months—it would be a worldwide system. No one could buy or sell merchandise or services or hold employment without receiving a computer chip implant in the hand or forehead. And to receive that implant, you had to swear allegiance to Carlo and his one-world system and reject all other loyalties, including faith in other gods. All of this, supposedly, to ensure that terrorists could no longer buy the material necessary to build the kind of weapon that was fired at Tel Aviv.

The U.S. armed forces had not yet instituted the implant program, so Jeremy was exempt—for now. Erin, as a U.N. employee, had not yet been asked to get the implant. She was able to buy most of what she wanted at the U.N. by simply having her paycheck debited. But she did notice that Tony Suzuki and Mikuni was out of business the next time she went by the restaurant. She was sure it was because he refused to get the implant. That would be Tony, she thought.

Erin was hearing rumors of an underground economy already forming. Some people were refusing to participate in Carlo's new system. But the vast majority did. There was no question in her mind that she would not participate if and when she was faced with that choice. Something Jeremy had told her stuck in her mind: "My reading of the Bible," he had said, "suggests that if we take that step and even symbolically accept Carlo as God, we give up any chance of knowing the true God." She didn't know exactly what she would do, but Erin was certain she would take her chances at survival.

When Jeremy reported back to his unit in Southern California, he was told he could be shipped off at a moment's notice for a special assignment in the Middle East. Jeremy was not happy about that. For one thing, the Middle East seemed to be going to hell in a handbasket. For another, it sounded far from Erin O'Hara. She was on his mind—day and night. He wondered if he would ever seen her again in this lifetime.

He didn't have to wait long for the suspense to end. His orders came through within a few days. He would be taking his elite unit of 26 men to Palmahim, Israel. There they would be principally responsible for security at an anti-missile bunker. It didn't sound like very exciting duty to Jeremy, but then again, there was enough excitement in the world right now. Jeremy's main goals were to subvert Carlo in any way he could and to reunite as quickly as he could with Erin. Neither goal had great potential for success.

When Jeremy disembarked from his C-17, he was struck with how similar the climate in Israel was to Southern California's. He felt right at home. He had a briefing scheduled with Jean-Claude DuMonde, a name that had been familiar to him back in New York. This was someone Zeke had regular contact with. He wondered if he was, perhaps, being "set up" in some way with this assignment. Somehow, though, as misguided as Zeke was right now, he still couldn't believe he would wish Jeremy harm.

"Lieutenant Colonel Armstrong," said DuMonde, "your assignment is to ensure that no one but trained, select and trusted U.N. personnel are permitted to operate the anti-missile facilities at Palmahim. Is that clear?"

"Well, not exactly, sir," he said. "Where is the threat coming from? Who will be attempting to use that facility?"

"As you know, the nuclear strike at Syria was prompted by a first strike at Israel," he said. "That missile was destroyed in mid-flight by those at Palmahim. To ensure the proper balance of power, it is necessary that only our personnel—not nationalists of any stripe—have access to that facility."

"It sounds to me like the Israeli team who knocked down that incoming missile that was on a low trajectory are the only competent people to man it," Jeremy replied. "After all, no one else has ever intercepted and destroyed a missile, especially under those circumstances. Who is in charge now?"

"It is under our control, but there is still limited access by that Israeli Defense Forces team," said DuMonde. "That must be terminated immediately. That will be your first assignment. Then your job will be to secure against any intruders finding their way into the bunker."

"Am I likely to encounter armed resistance?" asked Armstrong.

"I don't believe so, but it is a possibility," said DuMonde. "It's a possibility for which you should be prepared. You know these Israelis, they can be real cowboys sometimes."

"How would you suggest we handle this?" asked Armstrong. "Should we begin with the diplomatic approach and simply meet with the Israelis and tell them how it's going to be? Or should we just shut down access immediately?"

"I believe the diplomatic approach should be attempted," said DuMonde. "But you should be ready to act at the slightest sign of opposition. Now let's head over to Palmahim. Are you ready?"

"There's no time like the present—let's get on it." said Armstrong.

Jeremy's American troops, wearing U.N. insignia, and DuMonde's small entourage of U.N. officials traveled in a small car and truck convoy for the 30-minute ride to Palmahim. DuMonde's group was in a Mercedes limo leading the way. Armstrong's men were loaded into two troop trucks that followed, with Jeremy in the first truck. They would have to pass through Palestinian Authority territory. There had been trouble here recently—riots, random shootings, firebombings—mostly a response to the Israeli nuking of Damascus.

Jeremy, sitting in the front passenger seat of the truck, noticed some suspicious activity ahead. There appeared to be some people in civilian clothes darting about perhaps

100 yards in front of the vehicle and on his right-hand side. He instinctively prepared for action. As his truck pulled closer he heard the familiar pop and hissing of a rocket propelled grenade (RPG). A split second later, the back of his truck exploded in flames. He could hear his men screaming in agony. As the truck rolled to a stop, Armstrong jumped out to assess the damage and the casualties, but was greeted with small arms fire. He ran for cover on the other side of the truck. His driver had already been hit.

He feared another RPG could hit the second truck at any second. He could see his men running for cover as they exchanged fire with their unseen assailants hiding behind rocks and trees 25 to 30 yards off the road and up a small incline. It was a perfect spot for an ambush. He checked to see where DuMonde and the Mercedes were. He could see them speeding off, apparently unhit.

The only weapon Jeremy had with him was his trusty Browning automatic pistol and some grenades. Only four men made it out of his truck, and they too were ducking for cover behind the burning remnants of the truck. He did a quick head count and figured he had 17 men still standing. It appeared, based on the number of rounds being fired, that his unit outnumbered the attackers. But Jeremy's men had lousy position. So far, there had been no more RPG attacks, so his second truck was still operable. But he didn't dare load his men into it because they'd be sitting ducks for another RPG round if the ambushers had one.

Jeremy led his four survivors from the first truck back

to the larger group behind the second truck.

"Get away from the truck," he told his men. "Get cover below the embankment on the road. I'm going to try to call in an airstrike on these guys."

Jeremy wasn't even sure who to call, having just landed in Israel two hours earlier. But he decided the best bet was U.N. headquarters in Jerusalem. After a considerable amount of wasted time, he got through to a French military commander. He described the situation and their coordinates to the best of his ability. Within ten minutes, three attack helicopters swooped in, fired some missiles in the vicinity of the attackers, and the firefight was over.

Armstrong had some badly wounded men who were quickly loaded back into the remaining truck. Before they drove off, though, he and a small group of troops checked out the area that had been held by their attackers. They found five bodies, all Muslims dressed in civilian clothes. They had only one rocket launcher, and had apparently fired their only round.

"You were brave but foolish," Jeremy said as if he expected the dead Palestinians to hear him.

Five minutes later, Jeremy and his troops had found their way to Palmahim, only five minutes down the road. He located medical facilities for his wounded and took the rest of his men to the bunker.

"Colonel," said DuMonde when he saw Jeremy approaching, "I hope you're OK. How are your men?"

"Well," Jeremy said, "Six are dead, three are badly burned and may not make it. This is not my favorite way to start an assignment."

"I'm so sorry," DuMonde said. "Things are hotter than I imagined here. Your work is going to be cut out for you. I hadn't even considered the possibility of a terrorist attack on the bunker here, but with this kind of activity so close, I suppose it would be wise to plan for that too."

"Yes," said Jeremy, "I'll tell you one thing for sure, I'm going to need some armor here, and I need to know how I can call for backup and support more quickly. The red tape I had to cut to call in that airstrike was totally unsatisfactory."

"I understand, Colonel," DuMonde said. "I will make the necessary arrangements for you. Whenever you're ready, we should go meet General Oved."

"I'm ready," said Jeremy.

"Let's go, then."

It was a short walk, and on the way DuMonde filled Jeremy in on the personality he was about to encounter.

"General Oved is, well, a little old-fashioned, Colonel," said DuMonde. "He still believes in the nation-state. His first loyalty is to Israel rather than the greater world community. You'll find him to be a charming man. But don't underestimate him—he is as clever and courageous as he is charming."

Jeremy decided that he had already liked General Oved for years. He was just the sort of commander he loved.

"General," said DuMonde attracting his attention away from Major Barak.

"Yes, J.C., how are you? I understand you ran into some opposition a few minutes ago down the road."

"Yes—some friends of yours, General?" J.C. joked.

"No," laughed the general, "not friends of mine."

"General, I would like you to meet Lieutenant Col. Jeremy Armstrong of the Tenth Detachment of the U.S. Special Forces. He's been assigned to the U.N.'s new security detail here at Palmahim."

"Nice to meet you, Colonel," said the general. "Always a pleasure to be around American special forces troops. It makes me feel more secure," he said with a wink at Barak. When the U.N. sends someone of your caliber to guard us, it's kind of a backhanded compliment. Oh yes, I am familiar with your brilliant record."

"Thank you, General," Jeremy said. "It's a pleasure to meet you. I've also heard some nice things about you from Mr. DuMonde."

"Yes, I'll bet you have," the general laughed. "He probably told you how 'old-fashioned' I am because I see my job as defending my own country." Then the three men all laughed.

"General," said DuMonde, "the reason we're here is a matter of some seriousness. The colonel's assignment is to take over control of the bunker from the IDF. We feel the U.N. technicians now have a handle on the operations aspects of Palmahim and are well-qualified to protect your country. Carlo is directing us to ensure that only U.N. personnel are in a position to intercept from now on."

"Isn't this amazing," said General Oved grimly. "I guess my men just did their job a little too well for Carlo—is that it? Maybe we should have let that missile strike Tel Aviv. Then Carlo would have had more of a moral justification for nuking the Syrians. Is that it?"

"You know me, General," said DuMonde. "I'm just here to follow orders. I trust you will order your men to cooperate with us fully."

"Of course, J.C.," said Oved feigning complete submission. "Consider this my unconditional surrender."

"Well, that's hardly the proper terminology, General," DuMonde said. "After all, we're all on the same side here. We all want the same thing."

"Oh, yes, of course," said Oved jovially. "I keep forgetting. Major Barak, please write down a memo that the U.N. is on our side. I must post it in my office."

"Then I will leave you and the colonel alone to work out all the details," said DuMonde. "Colonel, I will see you tomorrow morning, when I hope our transition here will be complete."

"See you, J.C.," said Oved. "Colonel, why don't you come with me, have some lunch and we'll figure all this out. There's someone in particular I want you to to become acquainted with. Major," he called to Barak. "Come have lunch with Lt. Col. Jack Armstrong."

"How do you do?" said Barak as he shook Jeremy's hand.

"I'm great," said Armstrong, "but, for the record, it's not Jack, it's Jeremy."

"Oh, sorry about that," said the general. "You just remind me so much of that mythical all-American hero."

"Thanks, then—I'll take that as a compliment, I think," laughed Jeremy.

"Captain," said the general, "let's have some food

brought into the conference room for the three of us. We have some important issues to discuss with the colonel."

Jeremy Armstrong sensed he was in for the greatest dilemma of his life. And he already loved the general—he just couldn't help it. Warriors always seem to admire other true warriors.

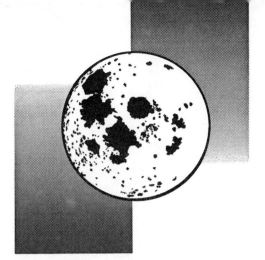

CHAPTER 7

Magog's March

As a U.N. employee, and a high-ranking one at that, Erin O'Hara lived in a different world than most Americans in the early part of the 21st century. For one thing, most of her basic needs were met. The U.N. building was like a self-contained island—its own police, grocery stores, department stores, etc. Ironically, U.N. employees still did not have to subject themselves to the indignities that the agency required of the rest of the world—most notably the hand implants that authorized buying, selling and employment.

That was reason enough for Erin to remain at the U.N. She also stayed so that Jeremy would know where to call her when he got the chance. She got her first call from him several days after he arrived in Israel. He briefly recapped his adventures, including the firefight right after he landed. She was worried about him—very worried. There was little he could say to calm her fears. For that matter, he was just as concerned for her safety. With Carlo in charge of the world, New York could be as dangerous as the Middle East.

"There's a lot I have to tell you," she said. "Is it safe to talk now?"

"I don't know," said Jeremy. "Let me try to find a more secure line later. Also, make sure you watch what you say in your office. The walls have ears at the U.N."

"Yes, I understand," she said. "Oh, my darling, call me soon. I'm so worried about you. It's hard for me to sleep or function during the day just thinking about all the dangers you're facing. And I know you—you have such a warrior's heart that you get angry if there's a battle and you're not invited."

"I'm worried about you, too, darling," said Jeremy.

"I miss you so much," said Erin. "I wake up and dream you're holding me."

"I miss you, too," said Jeremy. "I adore you."

"I love you, too," she said.

It was not easy for Erin. Like Jeremy, she was alone in the world. Her family members, including her mom, older sister and younger brother, all disappeared in the same great mysterious event in which Jeremy's mother and sister vanished. They both believed their families had been swept up to heaven to avoid the ugliness the world was now facing. Jeremy and Erin both wished they had listened a little more attentively when their families tried to tell them about Jesus and how He voluntarily died in their place to purchase a pardon for them.

Now it was not even safe to admit to anyone that you thought about Jesus, much less believed in Him. Erin was walking in lower Manhattan one day when she heard a woman screaming. She looked over to see what the commotion was all about. There were police officers nearby. The screaming woman was telling the police to arrest her companion because she was a Christian. The accusation alone was enough to have the woman taken away in handcuffs. Erin wondered what the penalty was for conviction on such an offense.

To preserve her sanity—and her life—she spent most of her time inside the U.N. It also gave her more of an opportunity to keep tabs on Zeke and Carlo. It was clear that the persecution of believers on the streets of New York was a direct result of the orders given by Carlo in Jerusalem. It was also clear that this was a worldwide phenomenon. Carlo saw his biggest threat not from the Muslim fanatics who had shot him and fired a nuclear missile at Tel Aviv, not from the Russians who were threatening him, but from the sincere Christian believers simply trying to live their lives and be left alone. That told Erin a lot about the man's character.

Erin had been transferred to another department after Jeremy left. That suited her, because she did not have to play a direct role in the persecution of believers in her new job. She found out, however, that the man replacing Jeremy was a ruthless confidante of Carlo's—Shimon Isikoff, a former Mossad officer. The son of Holocaust survivors, ironically he relished his role as persecutor of Christians.

Through her eavesdropping and intercepted memos, Erin learned that concentration camps had been set up around the world to handle the new Christian converts so demonized by Carlo. She suspected some were death camps, but she did not yet have confirmation. There were even rumors that Christians were being beheaded without mercy. Clearly, it was very dangerous to share one's faith in Jesus Christ anywhere in the world.

But the most interesting fact she discovered was that Carlo was indeed expecting an imminent all-out Russo-Muslim attack on the Middle East. The thought of it made her heart sink. Jeremy was at ground zero of a certain holocaust. And to make matters even more unbearable, she couldn't get a warning to him. For days she waited for him to call. She could not sleep or eat fearing for his safety. Finally, one night about midnight, she got the call she had been so anxious for.

"Hi sweetie," Jeremy said.

"Oh my darling, thank God it's you," she said. "I must to tell you what's about to happen. Please tell me you're on a secure line."

"Yeah," he said, "I think it's pretty safe to talk for a few minutes. What's up?"

"Jeremy, you've got to get out of there right now," she said. "The Russians have gotten together the most radical Muslim nations and are planning an all-out invasion of the Middle East at any moment. Carlo fears it will be the first unrestricted use of neutron and thermonuclear warheads. It could literally be the beginning of that horror our parents called *the war of Armageddon*."

"Wow," he said, "that's pretty bad. But, you know, honey, I can't just leave. I'm a soldier. That's why I'm here."

"Please don't tell me this," she said. "It's going to be a bloodbath, Jeremy. How are you going to protect yourself?"

"Well, honey, the good news is I'm stationed in one of the most heavily fortified bunkers in Israel. It's the principal anti-missile site. It may indeed be targeted by the Russians—if they know anything about Israel's defenses. But it would literally take a direct hit to get us. It's as safe a place to be as there is in this little country."

"It's reassuring to hear that, but I am still so fearful for you," Erin said. "I wish we could just run away together—maybe to another planet or something."

"Yeah, I know, but isn't that about what our parents said Jesus was going to do in that thing they called the Rapture?" he said. "Anyway, if it's any consolation, you're all I think about—night and day. You're my reason for wanting to stay alive—you and God, that is."

"I feel the same way," said Erin. "I've been reading all the material you left me and constantly studying the Bible. Our families must have been right, Jeremy. Why didn't we listen to them?"

"I really have a feeling we were left behind for a special reason, honey," he said. "And just remember, no matter what happens, we'll see each other again. We'll be together."

"Are you sure, Jeremy?" she asked.

"I'm certain," he said.

Armstrong hit it off well with General Oved and Major Barak. (General Oved had promoted Barak to Major after his incredible intercept of the nuclear missile.) They understood each other. After hearing the way the general spoke to DuMonde, Jeremy had enough confidence to let Oved know that he shared his cynicism about the U.N. He told him about his experience in New York. It was risky, of course, to share information like that with anyone, but Jeremy knew he needed to begin finding some alliances if he was to be a force for good in this world.

Oved and Barak openly shared their fears with Armstrong. They told him there were two problems with the U.N. taking over the bunker. First, their technicians were incompetent and would be unable to intercept a missile no matter where it was headed. And second, the U.N. would sacrifice certain Israeli cities and probably attempt to protect only Jerusalem—where Carlo himself was stationed.

The three of them hatched a plan. Jeremy told Barak to stay close by the facility so that he could be summoned quickly if and when an attack was signaled. Jeremy's men would then simply summon him and, by sheer force, place him in control of the bunker. After the attack was over, of course, they would all have to flee. Oved and Barak knew the countryside well and had plenty of friends who would shelter the fugitives, including Armstrong's 17-man Special Forces unit. At least the plan would give Barak one more chance to save the nation. After that, they figured, it would all be in God's hands.

"I think it's already in God's hands," said Oved.

They all shook their heads. They also shared their experiences with angelic visitations and messages. And they all agreed that they felt a strong angelic presence continuously with them now. Armstrong also let his friends know that he had reason to believe that the Russians were at that moment massing for an attack on the Mideast.

"The next time that buzzer goes off, Isaac, I think it's going to be a whole volley of incoming Russian missiles," he said.

"We've been preparing for them," Barak said, winking at the general.

"Jeremy," the general said, "you are a true blessing from God. I wonder sometimes if you, too, might be an angel."

"Well, General," he said, "my mother never had any trouble distinguishing me from an angel. I can assure you of that. But I'll tell you what, guys. I sure would appreciate it if you would pray with me some time. There are so few people I can trust in this world right now. I trust you fellows. I know we pray to the same God."

"There's no time like the present, Jeremy," said the general.

"Heavenly Father," began Jeremy, "You know how my heart is burdened for the safety of the one I love. Please send Your angels to protect Erin. It's so hard being apart in times like this, Lord. But having the assurance that You love her even more than I do gives my heart some peace. And bless, guide and protect my new brothers here in Israel—Isaac and Oved. Thank You, Lord. Amen."

"Amen," said the general. "Thank you for our unexpected American ally."

"Amen," said the major.

Jeremy broke up his 24-hour watch at the bunker into three shifts. He commanded one—from 8 a.m. until 4 p.m. Lieutenant Rafer Landry took the next shift, from 4 p.m. to 12 midnight. And Sergeant Ralph Freeman took the overnight shift. Each of them understood what to do in the event that buzzer went off. Major Barak and his most trusted assistant made sure at least one of them was always within 100 meters of the bunker. They didn't have to wait long to test their battle plan.

Within weeks, the buzzer went off in the middle of the night on the Sabbath. Freeman first summoned Barak, then Armstrong and Landry. Rafer Landry had his men lock up the surprised U.N. techies in a secure room in the bunker. He ripped out the phones so they couldn't call anyone. Barak came in and sized up the situation. It was a coordinated salvo of three ICBMs headed from the Ural Mountains of Russia toward Dimona, the Israeli nuclear missile silo base.

"Arm three Arrows," Barak barked.

Then another buzzer went off…and another.

"I need more help," Barak said as he concentrated on his aim.

Just then, Armstrong came in. He had been observing the U.N. techies' exercises on the Arrow and had practiced long hours with Barak in its operation. He hoped it would be enough to intercept the incoming missiles. It would have to be enough.

Barak determined that at least two more ICBMs were headed toward Israel. The coordinates indicated Haifa and Tel Aviv were the targets.

"These guys know where to shoot," Armstrong said.

Barak did the sighting and the lock-ons. He would then turn over his seat to Armstrong for the final countdown and firing. This would allow Barak to target several missiles at a time—an absolute necessity under these extraordinary conditions.

"I hope we don't run out of missiles before they do," he said. It was no joke. Two more missiles were sighted. "At least we have a little more time with these then we did with the flat trajectory of the Syrian missile. And I'm not going to bother calling anyone this time."

The hotline phone was ringing off the hook. Barak knew it was either the president or Carlo's office. Under the circumstances, he wasn't about to answer it. "Cut that damn thing off," Barak ordered.

Armstrong was in the final countdown process on the first missiles. Before he pulled the trigger, he said a little prayer, just as Barak had done with the terrorist missile. It worked. "Bullseye! You got all three of them," exclaimed Sgt. Schwartz. "Yes!" both he and Barak cried at the same time. "Praise the Lord," added Jeremy.

"Yes, praise Him indeed," added Barak. "But keep your concentration—more are on the way."

Just then, four U.N. soldiers, summoned by Carlo from a nearby facility, walked into the bunker demanding to know what was going on.

"We're trying to save the world," retorted Armstrong. "In fact, we're saving your lives. Right now you have a choice—help or die."

"My orders are to seize control of this facility," said the

leader, raising his sidearm toward Armstrong.

Sgt. Freeman didn't wait another second. He fired four shots which instantly took out all of the U.N. intruders before they could fire a single round.

"I guess they answered that question," said Freeman.

"Thank you, Sergeant," said Jeremy very calmly, without even taking his eyes off the radar screen. "I knew that Texas quick draw would come in handy some day."

Armstrong's men removed the bodies of the U.N. troops, placing them in the secure room with the techies and their comrades.

"They weren't as cooperative as you fellas," said Sgt. Freeman, as he locked the door behind him.

Armstrong knocked down another incoming missile. But the next one was even more critical, seeing as how it was headed directly for their bunker. Everyone held their breath.

"Isaac," said Armstrong, "maybe you should handle this one."

"No," he said, "you're doing just fine, Colonel."

"Got it!" Jeremy cried. "Six for six. Isaac, are we a team or what?"

Arrow was proving its mettle. Barak had not yet needed his MIRACL backup system. But the trouble was, missiles just kept coming toward Israel. Barak and Armstrong were successful at knocking down the first six, but the seventh eluded the Arrow. It was headed for the Galilee region of northern Israel. Barak zeroed in on it with the MIRACL system.

"3, 2, 1—it missed!" he shouted. There wasn't time for

another attempt by either the Arrow or MIRACL systems.

"I think it's the Tiberias area," said Barak near tears.

"Pull yourself together men," said Armstrong. "You did the best you could. There's still many more missiles headed our way. Don't lose your discipline now."

The team knocked down three more in a row, then couldn't keep up with what was incoming. Another missile hit the West Bank area near Ramallah.

"The Russians are killing a lot of Arabs tonight," said Barak. "I thought they were friends."

Another missile hit Jordan. It seemed like a relatively unpopulated area. But they just kept on coming.

"Do you notice they're not firing at Jerusalem?" asked Barak. "The Russians' Muslim friends want to walk in there and take over. They don't want it radioactive."

By the time the missiles stopped coming—about 45 minutes later—Isaac and Jeremy had shot down 17 out of 20. Of the three that sneaked through their defenses, one hit Galilee, one hit the West Bank and another hit inside Jordan close to the border. It was a pretty good job, but a lot of people were still dead as a result of the attack. There was no time and no room for celebrating, no matter how brilliant their performance had been or how miraculous was the damage control.

General Oved knocked on the door as things were winding down.

"We've got to get out of here—now!" he said. "More U.N. troops are on their way. We'll all face the firing squad for what we've done. Clear out with what you've got and bring all the weapons and ammo you can carry."

The general had located six civilian cars to accommodate himself, Isaac, Jeremy and 17 of Armstrong's troops. Each driver was given different directions with some rendezvous points. Fifteen minutes after they had all cleared out, U.N. armored personnel carriers and troop transports with a full platoon arrived. When they found the dead U.N. troops and debriefed the survivors, Carlo was informed.

He was fit to be tied. He demanded that the renegades be found at all costs. He even diverted troops away from preparing fortifications for the coming Russian invasion to search for them.

In Moscow, President Boris Gudonov was perplexed by the reports he was getting from the Middle East.

"Only three of 20 missiles reached targets?" he asked. "And not one hit the Dimona facility, which means that Israel still has all of its strategic missiles intact. There must be something wrong with our information. Carlo doesn't have a defense shield that effective. Is he using his supernatural powers again?" he scoffed.

This was worrisome. The nuclear attack Gudonov unleashed on Israel had been thought by some of his advisers to be too big—in that it would render the area unsafe for his own invading troops. Now, however, it appeared the attack was far too small. It would not have softened up the area enough for the conventional attack. But that did not deter Gudonov. He would use theater nuclear weapons when he got to the area. The invasion must begin—now!

Russia led the way, with coordinated movements by all of its allies. Gudonov and his allies hoped that if they limited their nuclear attack to the Middle East Carlo would not want to escalate it by striking back at Russia Otherwise, France, Italy, Spain the U.K. and the U.S. would be targets and a full-scale global nuclear war would be under way.

Carlo was smart. Instead of launching a nuclear attack on Russia, with its massive arsenal of warheads and missiles, he chose to strike back at Iran, Egypt and Libya, thus crippling these nations' ability to sustain a massive long-term invasion and taking out their limited nuclear arsenal. Now Russia had a choice: Would it invite a nuclear strike on its own cities and silos by responding to the attack? Or would it concentrate on its primary objective, winning the war for the Middle East?

Gudonov chose the latter, a fact that did not endear him to his Muslim allies, who sought revenge for the utter destruction of their major cities. But nothing would deter Russia from its historic goal of dominating the Middle East. This was the moment Gudonov had been waiting for—and dreaming of—for a long time.

His battle plan included the following:

Iraq would fire its awesome arsenal of chemical weapons at Israel. In addition, Baghdad would unleash its secret biological weapons designed to spread cholera, tuberculosis and the plague. Iran would shut down the Persian Gulf by closing it at the Straits of Hormuz using its Russian-built Kilo submarines and Hawk anti-aircraft missiles, Silkworm missiles and anti-ship cruise missiles.

Though Syria was devastated—in essence decapitated—by the nuking of Damascus, the nation still had hundreds of Soviet-made Scud, SS-21 and shorter-range Frog 7 missiles stockpiled. Now was the time to use them, Gudonov told the new Syrian leadership, which was itching for revenge. Syria had been involved in every Arab war against Israel. Even after the nuclear attack, its army was among the largest in the region. It had 808,000 troops available for the invasion, along with 4,500 main battle tanks and 591 combat aircraft.

And then there was Egypt. For so many years, Cairo was perceived to be in the pocket of the West. For one thing, there was the cash. The Camp David Accords seemed to make Egypt reliant on billions of dollars of western subsidies. But in the late 1990s, Egypt's moderate leadership was overthrown by radical Islamists, making it, overnight, the most dangerous nation in the Middle East.

Why? Egypt maintained a tremendous arsenal supplied by the United States. Egypt's stock of main battle tanks increased in the 1990s to more than 4,000. The quality of its air force increased dramatically. It also stockpiled more than 2,500 anti-tank guided weapons. How did Egypt so quietly become a military power while it was talking peace?

From 1980 through 1998, American taxpayers transferred about $40 billion to Egypt. About $25 billion of that aid was in direct military assistance.

Gudonov was also counting heavily on support from

the Saudis—and not just cash and oil. After the Persian Gulf War of 1991, Riyadh went on an arms shopping spree of unprecedented proportions. The desert kingdom purchased $30 billion of arms in the following year. But that was simply an acceleration of a trend that had been ongoing for a quarter of a century. During that time, the Saudis transformed their army, air force and navy, spending $250 billion in the last 10 years alone. The quality of the purchases had been notable, with Riyadh trying to make up for its lack of manpower with high-tech weaponry, particularly for its air force.

Iran, meanwhile, had armed forces numbering 863,000, with more than a half-million on active duty. The country had 1,245 main battle tanks and 295 combat aircraft. A real coup for Gudonov was teaming Iran with Turkey—traditional rivals on the international stage. With Turkey joining Syria, Lebanon, Egypt, Saudi Arabia. Jordan, Yemen, Libya, Iraq and Iran, Russia's Middle East allies could mobilize an army of more than 6 million men.

These armies could field 25,000 main battle tanks, including T-72s, M1A1 Abrams and Britain's Chieftains. That was more than the United States could have mustered back in the 1980s through 1997. They could scramble 4,000 first-rate combat aircraft, including F-16s, MIG 29s, MIG 31s and Mirage F-1s. Iran had some Backfire bombers that could reach Mach 2 and attack targets are far as 3,000 miles away.

That was the force the Russian, German and central Asian armies joined to attack Israel. No wonder Gudonov had confidence. Including the Russian forces, Gudonov was mobilizing a coalition of more than 10 million troops to march on Jerusalem.

But Carlo had a few surprises of his own.

Isaac, General Oved, Jeremy and his men all found each other at the first rendezvous point. They had traveled north, directly toward Galilee, and could already begin to see the destruction caused by the nuclear blast. With everyone else in the vicinity fleeing in the opposite direction, travel toward the disaster area was fast and easy. But it was clear they could go no further in that direction. They holed up for a few days on the lake with some of Gen. Oved's trusted friends.

"The Russians will be coming in a few days," said Oved. "There will undoubtedly be more missile attacks, some theater nuclear weapons and lots of conventional fighting all through this valley. We've got to find some real shelter for that firestorm."

"Do you have any ideas, General?" asked Barak.

"Yes I do," he said. "You know, for years during the 1980s and even into the '90s, the northern-most communities in Israel—just south of the Lebanese border—were constantly under attack from Katyusha rockets launched by terrorists. For the people who lived in those communities it became such a way of life that many of them built bomb shelters. There were even some larger community shelters that were built under schools and civic centers. A long time ago, I toured those facilities. I don't know what ever became of them, but I think it's worth a look to see what kind of condition they're in."

"Sounds like our next move," said Jeremy.

"I think I should take two or three of your men, Jeremy, and check it out first thing tomorrow," the general said. "We'll stop first at a place called Metulla."

"Good idea," said Armstrong.

Jeremy's mind, though, was really far away—in New York, as a matter of fact. He was wishing he could figure out a way to get word to Erin that he was all right. It was nearly impossible to make an international call out of Israel tonight. The nuclear blasts had disrupted normal communications. In addition, every survivor in the Jewish state was trying to use the phone at the same time. And everyone in the rest of the world who knew someone in Israel was trying to call in. The circuits were jammed.

Armstrong decided the best idea was to write a letter to Erin. While it could take a long time getting to her, he could at least pour out his heart and tell her how he felt about her. When she found out he survived the first volley of nuclear weapons, it would give her confidence that he would really make it through whatever was coming.

"What a heck of a time to fall in love," Armstrong thought. "The world we know is coming to an end, and Erin and I are desperately trying to just let each other know that we are alive."

"What are you writing?" asked Barak.

"I'm writing to my girlfriend, Isaac," he said. "We never really got a chance to get together with all this stuff going on in the world. But something tells me we are going to have a life some day. If we ever get married, Isaac, I'd like you to be there."

"There's nothing I would rather do," Isaac said. "Except perhaps have you there for my wedding."

"Do you have someone special?" Armstrong asked.

"No, I have not had time to find someone," he said. "Now maybe there won't be anyone left for me," he said only half-joking. "Tell me about your woman."

"Well, she's a woman all right," said Jeremy. "She's beautiful—the most beautiful female my eyes have ever seen. I would trade every other joy in my life just to be with her for a month. Do you know what I mean?"

Isaac just smiled. He was getting the picture.

"Listen, I have a better idea than trying to get that letter through to her," Isaac said. "I saw a computer in the other room. Why don't you try to e-mail her?"

"I'm glad your computer wizardry has made love a little easier," said Jeremy smiling broadly.

Jeremy typed the following letter on the e-mail screen:

Dear Erin:

You must be worried sick by the news you're hearing. I just wanted to let you know I made it through the nuke attack. It's a long story and I won't bother you with it now, but I am safe. My men and I have gone AWOL and are looking for a safe place to ride out this storm. I've got a couple of Israeli friends—good friends—helping us.

I know the next wave of missiles will be even worse, but I have confidence God is watching out for us. I'm praying for you every day. Let's live through this ordeal just so we can be together, if only for a little while. What do you think?

I will try to reach you again as soon as communications normalize.

All my love,
Jeremy

Erin read the e-mail note and cried with joy. She read it again and again. She wished there was some way she could just respond. She also wanted to tell him what she was hearing at the U.N.—that the worst was yet to come. The satellites had picked up major troop movements. Not only were the Russians launching a full-scale invasion of the Middle East, but the satellites also revealed that the Chinese—fearing they would be cut out of world power—were mobilizing to do the same. This war could destroy planet Earth.

Erin had made some decisions about her life, too. She wished she could tell Jeremy about them. Perhaps she should just take a chance and e-mail him enough information so that he wouldn't worry too much about her.

Dear Jeremy:

I don't know if you're going to get a chance to see this. But I have no other way of reaching you.

You need to know that the Russian invasion may not be the end. The Chinese are mobilizing, too. Depending on how the Russians fare, Beijing may send its entire army after the oil fields. Our spy satellites have seen millions of Chinese troops mobilizing.

Second, you need to know that I am leaving New York. I don't think it's safe anymore—especially not for me. I have made some contacts in the Christian underground and will be leaving for a secret rural camp with plenty of provisions and shelter. I need to ride out this storm, too.

All my love,
Erin

"O Lord Jesus," Erin prayed, "I never knew it was possible to love a man the way I love Jeremy. I know the world is about to come apart, but please bring my darling and me together again, even if only for a short time. And above all, keep our faith strong for the trials that are coming."

Gen. Oved returned from Metulla with good news. He had found an old, abandoned shelter large enough for all of them and then some. All they would need was enough bottled water and other provisions to last indefinitely. It wasn't the kind of shelter that would survive a direct or near-direct nuclear hit, but it would make it through anything short of that.

"I think we should get moving immediately," he said. "We have a lot of work to do before the Russians get here." Everyone agreed. Gen. Oved knew of several old IDF supply depots where weapons, ammunition and survival rations were stored. They would check them out on the way to Metulla.

●

When the Russians arrived, they came with a scorched-earth policy. The orders from Gudonov were clear: "You may destroy anything except Jerusalem. Save that for our Muslim friends."

Before the troops and the armor moved in, they blazed their trail with tactical battlefield nuclear weapons. They indiscriminately killed anything and everything in their path—Israeli citizens, Arabs, farm animals, wildlife, crops and trees. They were not interested in occupying this territory. They only wanted to destroy it. The Russians' interest was in the oil fields beyond Israel. They would win favor with the Arabs and Iranians—the entire Muslim world—by destroying the Jewish state, this constant source of irritation for them.

The Russian-led Muslim confederacy swept through northern Israel first. They burned and they killed and they destroyed. But they did not stay. They moved through quickly—on to the next target. Thus, they missed the two dozen people in the big shelter under Metulla. They probably missed many others in smaller home-based shelters as well. It did not matter to the Russians. They had bigger objectives on their mind as they cut a swath of destruction through the center of Israel's Jordan River Valley and neared Jerusalem.

Then, just as it began to appear that the Russians had

done it, all hell broke loose. The Israeli nuclear arsenal took out Tehran and other Iranian cities. Under the command now of Carlo and the U.N., they took out Tripoli. Baghdad was reduced to smoldering embers. Mecca and Medina and Riyadh went up in smoke. Cairo was history.

The Israelis used their fourth generation neutron warheads to destroy the elite Russian forces sweeping down the Jordan Valley toward Jerusalem. the warheads had a limited, predictable radius of intense radiation, so they were ideal for use against the massed hordes of Russian and Islamic troops. They destroyed only protein-bearing living flesh, not the rest of the environment.

Carlo had bought some time. In addition, he unveiled some other secret weapons in his arsenal—unmanned bombers that disintegrated enemy positions with laser beams, hypersonic Aurora fighters that soared into the skies at 12 times the speed of sound, and info-bombs that sought out and confused Russian military computers.

And worst of all was the HAARP weapons that could be focused on specific regions where troops were assembled and literally drive them so crazy that they attacked each other.

"Who dares to make war with me," thundered Carlo. The "peacemaker" had become a warmaker and seemed to be even better at the new role.

But just to make sure his point was not missed, Carlo ordered a massive nuclear strike, using U.S. and European weapons, at the land of the ancient tribe of Magog— Russia. The idea was to destroy Gudonov's ability to strike back in anger at Carlo for his convincing defeat. This caused something that had never been seen before. So many thermonuclear warheads exploded in near proximity of time and locale that a self-generating chain reaction enveloped the entire European part of Russia and turned everything up to the Urals into a lake of fire.

Carlo used the sophisticated HAARP weapon system based in Alaska to jam and cripple Russia's computerized command and control centers. They had no more ability to detect the incoming missiles. They were literally "blind." By the time Gudonov in his super-hardened shelter realized what was happening, it was too late to respond in any meaningful way.

Oh, he did manage to get off a few nuclear missiles and hit New York, London, Paris, Los Angeles and Chicago. But materially, no real damage was done to Carlo's war machine.

After it was over, Carlo asked Pope John Paul III to make a televised speech to the world calling for "restraint" and "forgiveness." The pope declared Carlo to be the savior of the world. He promised help would be coming to the millions of victims of burns, disease, radiation sickness and other maladies associated with the man-made global disaster. Then Israel's Prophet Elijah Ben David said that it was Carlo's divine powers that had saved the world.

A few days after the Russians had swept over them on their one-way journey, Gen. Oved, Barak and Armstrong ventured out of their dark shelter to see the sunlight. But it wasn't nearly as bright as they expected. Dark clouds hung low around the earth, reducing the sunlight by more the 50 percent. The oft predicted nuclear winter was now becoming a reality.

"I feel like I'm still underground," remarked Armstrong.

"It's as if the earth has already been entombed," said Barak.

Nevertheless, even the putrid air of nuclear holocaust was an improvement over the recycled air they had been breathing in the shelter. But the group wasn't going anywhere. The cars that brought them to this site were now reduced to cinders. It was clear that the shelter was still going to be home for awhile. Armstrong took all of his men foraging for useful supplies. They came back hours later with nothing—nothing! That's what was left—no crops, no fruit, no vegetation of any kind, no fresh water, no animals.

When they returned, Jeremy saw Gen. Oved and Barak sitting on the ground weeping—sobbing uncontrollably—and throwing dust on their heads. He ran up to them as fast as he could.

"What's the matter my friends?" he asked. "What has happened?"

Barak still could not contain his sobbing long enough to get a word out, but Oved managed to fight back the tears.

"Jeremy," he began, "remember the angel I told you about—the encounter I had at my home?"

"Yes, of course," said Jeremy. "How could I forget?"

"He was here," Oved said, still choking back his emotions. "He was here—he appeared to both Isaac and me at the same time."

"He did? What did he say to make you weep like this?" asked Jeremy.

"He told us that *Jesus of Nazareth, the Lord Messiah*, had intervened on our behalf and on behalf of the Jewish people to save Israel. Jesus Christ, Jeremy, do you hear me? Not that false prophet, Ben David, nor the self-appointed god, Carlo, but the Lord Jesus, the Messiah of Israel and God's almighty Son."

"Yes, of course I hear you," Jeremy said. "This is truly amazing. Did the angel quote any prophecy from the Bible about this?"

"Yes," exclaimed Oved and Barak in unison. "He quoted this from Zechariah:

> *"And I will pour on the house of David and on the inhabitants of Jerusalem the Spirit of grace and fervent prayer; they will look upon me whom they have pierced; they will mourn for Him as one mourns for his only son, and grieve for Him as one grieves for his firstborn"* (Zechariah 12:10).

Choking back tears again, Oved said, "Then we were shown a vision of the Lord Jesus with gaping wounds in his side and his hands and feet. We couldn't control our grief as we realized that we had rejected Him and forced His crucifixion."

"The angel told us not to be sad, because Jesus was still the king of Israel and the Jews were still His chosen people. The covenant made between God and the descendants of Abraham, Isaac and Jacob were irrevocable. Israel will last forever, just as God promised Abraham."

"This is quite a revelation to us, as you can imagine," said Barak, finally able to speak. "Jeremy, you must have known this all along. But we have been living in denial of who our true Messiah is."

"What else did the angel say?" asked Jeremy.

"He said that the Messiah, Jesus, is coming very soon to deliver those who have believed in Him and received the pardon for sin he gave His life to provide for us," Oved said. "He is going to clean up this mess of a world and restore it all. But—He also told us there is greater trouble still to come."

"The Chinese?" Jeremy asked.

"Yes," Oved said. "And terrible plagues and earthquakes and storms. We have not lived through the worst of it by a long stretch. Thank God we still have plenty of water and dry rations," said Oved. "We may be here for a very long time."

"Yes," said Barak, "thank God—thank the Lord Messiah...Jeshua. By the way, how did you know about the Chinese?"

Jeremy chuckled as he answered. "My mother made me read a frayed old book from the 1970s called *The Late Great Planet Earth*. I thought the author, named Lindsey, was a total nut case at the time. But most of what he interpreted from the Hebrew prophets is now coming true."

Erin had found her way to her new Montana survivalist shelter—in the nick of time. New York had been devastated by the nuclear attack. Carlo's U.N. braintrust had been destroyed. Erin wondered about Zeke and others she knew there. The U.N. had an underground shelter. But the attack was so sudden, who knows if they had any warning?

Meanwhile, she was around lots of believers for the first time in her life. They spent most of their time in the candle-lit underground bunkers reading scripture, studying the Bible and praying and fasting. The fasting made the dry rations last longer and taste better.

But Erin just wished she could hear from Jeremy. It was terrible not knowing what was going on. He was a world away, but he may as well have been a universe away now that communications had broken down. The only news Erin's group got from the outside world was via a short-wave radio.

They knew all about the Russian invasion, the way it was turned back and the way the Russians then unleashed their nuclear fury on the West.

It's all laid out in Ezekiel," said Matthew, a young lawyer in another lifetime. "Look here…it says,"

> *"Son of man, set your face toward Gog, of the land of Magog, the prince of Rosh, Meshech and Tubal, and prophesy against him and say, This is what the Lord God says: Behold I am against you, O Gog, the prince of Rosh, Meshech and Tubal; and I will turn you about, and put hooks into your jaws, and I will bring you forth, and all your army, horses and horsemen, all of them clothed in full armor, a great company, all of them with buckler and shield, wielding swords; Persia, Cush* [black Africans]*, and*

Put [Muslim north African nations of Libya, Tunisia, Algeria, Morocco and Mauritania] *are with them, all of them with shield and helmet; Gomer and all his hordes; Beth-togarmah from the uttermost parts of the north with all his hordes—many peoples are with you"* (Ezekiel 38:2-6).

"This is the very alliance that attacked Israel—Russia, Iran, Libya, Algeria, Tunisia, Morocco, Turkey, and so on," said Matthew. "And here it is predicted in the Bible hundreds of years before the birth of Christ! Just listen to how clear this is:

"Be prepared and prepare all those with you, you and all your hosts that are assembled about you, and be a commander for them. After many days you will be mustered; in the latter years you will go against the land that is restored from war, the land where people were gathered from many nations upon the mountains of Israel, which had been a continual waste land; its people were brought out from the nations and now dwell in false security, all of them. You will advance, coming on like a storm, you will be like a cloud covering the land, you and all your hordes—many people with you.

"Thus says the Lord God: On that day thoughts will come into your mind, and you will devise an evil scheme and say, I will go up against the land of unwalled villages; I will fall upon the quiet people who dwell securely, all of them dwelling without walls, and having no bars or gates; to seize, spoil and carry off plunder; to attack the waste places which are now inhabited, and the people who were

*gathered from the nations, who have gotten cattle
and goods, who dwell at the center of the earth,
Sheba and Dedan and the merchants of Tarshish
and all its villages will say to you, Have you come
to seize spoil? Have you assembled your hosts to
carry off plunder, to carry away silver and gold, to
take away cattle and goods, to seize great spoil?*

*"Therefore, son of man, prophesy, and say to Gog,
This is what the Lord God says: On that day when
my people Israel are dwelling in false security, you
will bestir yourself and come from your place out
of the uttermost parts of the north, you and many
peoples with you, all of them riding on horses, a
great host, a mighty army; you will come against
my people Israel, like a cloud covering the land. In
the latter days I will bring you against my land,
that the nations may know me, when through you,
O Gog, I vindicate my holiness before your eyes.*

*"This is what the Lord God says: Are you he of
whom I spoke in former days by my servants the
prophets of Israel, who in those days prophesied for
years that I would bring you against them? But on
that day, when Gog shall come against the land of
Israel, says the Lord God, my wrath will be roused.
For in my jealousy and in my blazing wrath I
declare, On that day there shall be a great shaking
in the land of Israel; the fish of the sea, and the
birds of the air, and the beasts of the field, and all
creeping things that creep on the ground, and all
the men that are on the face of the earth, shall
quake at my presence, and the mountains shall be
thrown down, and the cliffs shall fall, and every*

wall shall tumble to the ground. I will summon every kind of terror against Gog says the Lord God; every man's sword will be against his brother. With pestilence and bloodshed I will enter into judgment with him; and I will rain upon him and his hordes and the many peoples that are with him, torrential rains and hailstones, fire and brimstone. So I will show my greatness and my holiness and make myself known in the eyes of many nations. Then they will know that I am the Lord" (Ezekiel 38:7-23).

"Do you see what God is saying?" asked Matthew.

Erin had never understood that passage before. She never guessed it would have such relevance to her life. The man she loved was under those torrential rains of hailstones, fire and brimstone. This was very real. This was not some story in an old dusty book.

"Yes," she said, "I see it."

"There's much more," said Matthew. "The next chapter in Ezekiel explains that the Lord would strike down Russia's weapons—just as many of its missiles were shot down. It also predicts that Russia and other lands will be scorched with fire as a result of this attack. It has all happened already! And listen to this: It says Israel will be burning the weapons from this war for the next seven years. It will take the Israelis seven months to bury the nuked dead soldiers."

"Can we pray together, Matthew," said Erin. "This is all very real to me because the man I love is over there, under these clouds, under this firestorm. Will you pray for me that he is somehow miraculously sheltered?"

"Sure, Erin," Matthew said, "Let's pray: Heavenly Father, we ask a special protection and guidance for Jeremy Armstrong. We ask You to send Your elect angels to protect him and guide him through the devastation and destruction You are allowing in that land—the land of Your special chosen people. Let Jeremy be a light in the darkness, Lord. Let him figure in Your grand plans to save mankind—to redeem us all for Your glory. In Jesus' name, Amen."

"Amen," said Erin. "Thank you so much."

They were having a revival meeting in the shelter at Metulla. All of Jeremy's elite corps had become believers. Those who were skeptics before, changed their mind when they heard the testimony of Major Barak and General Oved.

They were reading the Bible and singing songs—traditional Jewish songs as well as Christian hymns.

"I need some prayer," said Jeremy to Isaac, General Oved and Freeman.

"Yes, Jeremy, what for?" asked Oved.

"For Erin," he said. "The worst part of all this for me is not knowing what she is going through. Here we are in the 21st century and we're living like cavemen—with no way of communicating or traveling. I just want to hop on a 747 and fly to New York to see her. But that's impossible. There are no flights except bombing missions. There are no communications except those directing the warriors toward their next target. Help me find some peace in this experience. Pray with me that God will watch over Erin and that His angels will protect her the way they have protected us."

"Heavenly Father," began General Oved, "In the name of Your Son, Jeshua, we pray that You will hear the troubled heart of our brother Jeremy. Give him peace, my Lord. Assure him that You love Erin even more than he does. Let him know that they will be together again— soon. No harm will come to her because we believe You and Your angels are more powerful than our adversaries. We thank You in Messiah Jeshua's name. Amen."

"May I?" asked Freeman, who had hidden the fact that he was a pastor's son.

"Please do," said Jeremy.

"O Lord, I bless thee that the issue of the battle between thyself and Satan has never been uncertain, and will end in victory. The Savior-Messiah broke the dragon's head, and we contend with a vanquished foe, who with all his subtlety and strength has already been overcome. When I feel the serpent at my heel may I remember Him whose heel was bruised, but who, when bruised, broke the devil's head.

"Heal us, Lord, of any wounds received in the great conflict; if we have gathered defilement, if our faith has suffered damage, if our hope is less than bright, if our love is not fervent, if our souls sink under the pressure of the fight. O thou whose every promise is balm, every touch life, draw near to thy weary warriors, refresh us, that we may rise again to wage the strife, and never tire until our enemy is trodden down.

"Give us such fellowship and faith with thee that we may stand against Satan, our lower natures and the world system, with delight that comes not from a creature, and which a creature cannot mar.

"Then shall my hand never weaken, my feet never stumble, my sword never rest, my shield never rust, my helmet never shatter, my breastplate never fall, because my strength comes only from the Holy Spirit."

Jeremy couldn't understand some of Ralph Freeman's church language, but he was thankful that the Lord did. He sat there amazed that he was comforted and at peace in the gathering gloom of a nuclear holocaust.

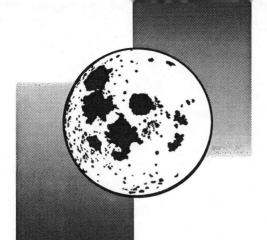

CHAPTER 8

Asia's March

And the sixth angel sounded, and I heard a voice
from the four horns of the golden altar
which is before God, one saying to the
sixth angel who had the trumpet,
'Release the four angels who are bound
at the great river Euphrates.'
And the four angels, who had been prepared
for the hour and day and month and year,
were released, so that they might kill
a third of mankind. And the number of
the armies and of the horsemen was
two hundred million; I heard the number of them.

REVELATION 9:13-16

ehind the scenes in this world, there's an enormous spiritual battle taking place. Angels are the foot soldiers in that war. Not only do they have a life of their own and assignments in a war for control of heaven, but they also play a vital role in the history of men. Armstrong learned that. Oved discovered it, and so did Barak.

What they didn't realize, however, is that fallen angels in particular have a special interest in and assigned authority over certain places in this world, as well as in men's hearts. These are what the apostle Paul called, *"the princes of powers and principalities."* Some of them, for instance, may play upon people's emotions—jealousy, fear, anger. Others actually preside invisibly over countries and large geographical areas of the earth.

Once the prophet Daniel sought answers from God about why the Jewish people had not returned to Israel. He prayed and fasted for what seemed like an inter-

minable period before a holy angel appeared to him. The
angel explained:

> *"God was not indifferent to your prayers. He had*
> *heard you on the first day you prayed, but my*
> *appearance here to deliver the answer was delayed*
> *for twenty-one days because I was detained by the*
> *prince of the kingdom of Persia."*

Of course, no mere mortal could detain an angel. The
prince this spiritual being was referring to was a demon
who had special influence in Persia. The direct intervention of the Archangel Michael was necessary to free the
angel involved in this conflict with this powerful demon
in Persia. When he had delivered his message to Daniel,
the angel said his next assignment was to fight the prince
of Greece.

In this kind of spiritual warfare, good and bad angels
fight in hand-to-hand combat. Winners move on to other
battles. Losers are sometimes cast into a pit or bound and
shackled, limiting their influence to a certain part of the
world.

One of those intense spiritual battles took place thousands of years ago east of the Euphrates River. Four
demons had gone too far, God decided. For the most part,
Satan's minions were permitted to tempt and torment on
earth. But sometimes they exceeded their authority.
Sometimes they made God so angry, like those who min-
gled with earthly women before the flood, that He
ordered His elect angels to do battle—to bind those rebellious spirits. And that's what happened east of the
Euphrates River one day, a long time ago. Angelic swords

clashed, chains clanged and locks clinched.

When the battle was over, the four powerful fallen angels were bound and their authority limited to the eastern side of the river. For centuries after, they were restricted from exercising their influence on the western side. God just didn't permit it—holding them in check with His superior numbers of angels and His own will.

The effect of this bondage—and the presence of those demons at the river throughout much of human history—has been significant. The Euphrates has always been the dividing line between Asia Minor—what we call today the Middle East—and Asia, or the Far East. To the people of the Middle East in biblical times, Asia was a vast, unknown world. Though China represented one of the first great civilizations, Asia has always been something of a mystery to the Western mind. In part, this mystery has been due to this unseen barrier between East and West—not just a great river, but a divinely enforced spiritual gulf.

Asia has erupted from time to time, enlarging its sphere of influence and threatening to spill over its power and might into the outside world. But something unexplained always hindered its progress—some unseen force. Likewise, the western world always found it troublesome and difficult to spread its way of life, particularly its faith, in Asia, where paganism and pantheism found their deepest roots.

So, even though the Chinese invented gunpowder, rocketry and other great human breakthroughs, they were never able to become the kind of world power one might expect through such achievements. They still only went so far. The Japanese, too, remained a separate society right up until the time Admiral Perry sailed in and persuaded them to open up for trade. Historically, too, India, the world's largest democracy, was held back by a religiously imposed caste system and the worship of many gods and idols.

In the Book of Acts, the apostle Paul wrote about how he relentlessly tried to take the message of Jesus Christ into Asia, but the Holy Spirit wouldn't let him. The apostles Thomas and Matthew were sent there and both died as martyrs. There were reasons for all that. And one of the principal reasons was the presence of those powerful demons perched on the eastern side of the Euphrates, frustrated by their imprisonment yet determined to make the most of it by frustrating Godly men.

Shortly after the crushing defeat of the Russians and their allies in the Middle East, God chose to unshackle those four demons and permit them to fulfill their destiny of unparalleled destruction beyond the Euphrates—just as He had predicted He would. These were fierce beasts. They roared and growled like a mighty herd of lions. They cursed and blasphemed. They swore vengeance for their long imprisonment. And they went off to carry out their historic mission—to kill one-third of mankind.

It was a dark day around the entire planet. Clouds of debris kicked up from the limited nuclear exchanges of the past months still hung low over the earth, obscuring nearly a third of the sunlight and casting a deathly pall over humanity. Yet, no one in the world knew just what was happening. No one—not even Armstrong, Oved or Barak—had any idea of the magnitude of the development that had occurred that day. No one, that is, except Carlo, who, ironically, would have to face the consequences for what was being unleashed.

When the evil angels left the riverside, they took off with fury and determination. If this was to be their final stand, they thought, they would make the most of it. They would take as many people with them as they could.

The damage to the planet's environment from the first nuclear exchange was already incalculable. Famines were breaking out on every continent. Weather patterns were severely disrupted by the constant cloud cover. Radioactivity was causing sickness in regions downwind from the blasts. Disease was rampant. Drought was killing as many people as any other cause. And now the four powerful demons of the Euphrates would wreak even more havoc on humanity.

One of those demons immediately began whispering in the ears of leaders in Ankara. Turkey had controlled the flow of water into the Euphrates River through a series of huge dams and reservoirs. Now it decided it was time to preserve its most important natural resource. It stopped the water at its source, reducing one of the world's greatest rivers to a trickle. Thus, one of the great physical obstacles to invasion of the Middle East by an unbelievably huge Asian army was removed.

Already an Asian alliance had been emerging. Carlo himself had precipitated this with his plan to carve up the earth into ten geographic spheres of influence. Asia quickly became the fastest growing economic entity on the planet. With such potential, the people of Asia and their leaders deeply resented the idea of being controlled by a dictator from Europe, even though it proved to be very profitable for them. Carlo's plans were now holding them back from their destiny, they believed. Despite his power, or perhaps because of it, they cursed him.

Spearheaded by the technologically advanced Japanese and the sheer numbers and awesome military might of China, India and North Korea, this new force—practically unscathed by the nuclear exchange between Russia and the Western nations—recognized that an historic opportunity had come. Japan's rise as an economic superstar and China's emergence as an even more formidable military and political power contrasted sharply with the growing image of the United States as a has-been power, destroyed by the collapse of its economy due to an obscene national debt. To Asians, the U.S. was little more than a den of criminals, drug addicts, broken families and rebellious youths.

One of Japan's time-honored proverbs is: "Move with the powerful." That meant only one thing in the late 1990s and the early part of the 21st century. It spelled China. The mutually destructive battle between Russia and the West had left this new Asian alliance the most powerful force on Earth. Without a presence in the Middle East, the Asian leaders understood they ran the risk of losing their access to the lifeline of industrialized life—oil.

A tactical decision was made in Tokyo, Beijing, New Delhi and Pyongyang to swoop in and invade the Middle East. It began, like the last battle, with a nuclear attack.

This time, however, there were no sacred cities. There was no effort to preserve landmarks and places of worship. This was all-out, unrestricted, no-holds-barred war.

"This place is beginning to feel like home," joked Barak, referring to their bunker.

They had spent the better part of a year now in this shelter. They no longer worried about U.N. troops coming to search for them as deserters. That time was long past. Their only earthly concern—like that of everyone on the planet these days—was survival.

They were far better off than most. They had stored tons of dry provisions and IDF survival rations. It didn't taste good, but it kept them alive. They also had enough water to drink, though almost none to wash. That made living together in confined quarters for weeks or even months at a time a little unbearable. But no one would have preferred to be on the outside looking in. It was hell out there. They could hear and feel the bombs exploding on almost a daily basis. Occasionally they could even hear armored columns passing overhead—always in one direction, east to west. How much more could there be to this Asian army, they wondered.

When they would hear nothing for a few days, someone would take a peek outside to see if it was safe to venture out. But there was little to see and nothing to salvage from the outside. It was dark constantly these days. Candles and gaslight kept it nearly as light in the underground shelter as the cloud-shrouded sun kept it up above.

One thing they could get outside occasionally was a shower from Mother Nature. But most often, the heavy rains were accompanied by ungodly hailstorms. It was unlike any hail the Israelis and Americans had ever seen. It could kill. Better to stay underground at times like that.

Armstrong recalled from his training in theater nuclear warfare survival tactics that open-air hydrogen explosions were not only accompanied by intense fireballs and destructive radiation, but also by freakish rain and hailstorms. He remembered stories about ships at sea reporting large dents in armor plating as a result of such storms. The hailstones are apparently caused by the great atmospheric turbulence the blasts create. A thermonuclear explosion is like a big compression hammer that pushes the atmosphere's humidity, compresses it and shoots it into the upper stratosphere. When you compress air with humidity, then throw it into the stratosphere at 60 or 70 degrees below zero, what happens? All of that compressed moisture freezes, then returns to earth in chunks of ice that weigh between 75 to 125 pounds.

"In Revelation, the Bible talks about hailstones weighing as much as a hundred pounds falling down on men," Armstrong told his companions. "That's undoubtedly what people up there are experiencing. God help them. This bunker looks better and better when you consider the alternative."

The most unnerving part of life in the shelter was the rocking and creaking. Sometimes it sounded like the earth above them was going to come crashing down. Often they couldn't even tell whether it was a bomb landing, armor crossing over them or an earthquake. There seemed to be lots of earthquakes. And the idea of being buried alive did not help anyone sleep better.

"Here's what the prophet Ezekiel had to say about these times," said Barak:

> *"And the fish of the sea, the birds of the heavens, the beasts of the field, all the creeping things that creep on the Earth, and all the men who are on the face of the Earth will shake at My presence; the mountains also will be thrown down, the steep pathways will collapse and every wall will fall to the ground.... And with pestilence and with blood I shall enter into judgment with Gog; and I shall rain on him and on his troops, and on the many peoples who are with him, a torrential rain, with hailstones, fire and brimstone."*

"Wow, does that sound familiar," said Jeremy.

"Yes it does," said Ariel Oved.

The group spent lots of time poring over scripture and praying. They had all shared an intimate experience with the living God, and no one had any doubts any more about what they were living through or any inhibitions about expressing their faith. For one thing, there was little else to do—nothing else to distract them from learning about their Maker.

Every day, though, Jeremy would write in his journal. He kept notes as if he were writing letters to Erin. He was beyond worrying about her now. He had placed his paralyzing concerns for her in God's hands. He simply couldn't handle thinking about it anymore. It was too overwhelming. It would make him so nervous, he was impossible to be around.

"My watch says it is 8 p.m.," Jeremy wrote. "The calendar says it is August 19, 2011. But times and dates don't seem to have much relevance down here in the dungeon. Our sleep patterns are shot. The darkness and our physical inactivity encourages sleep. But extended periods of explosions and shaking can deprive us of real sleep for days at a time.

"I wonder what's going on up there? Sometimes I wish we had a periscope. The ancient prophets—Ezekiel, John, Daniel—seem to have had a better look at this time we are living in than we have.

"I also wonder what it's like for you. Are you as safe as I am? Do you have food and water? Do you have adequate shelter? One thing gives me comfort: I'm sure there is not as much fighting going on in the States. I'm sure conditions are bad. But I hope you have days when you can take a walk in the sunlight."

Erin and her group lived an existence which, in many ways, paralleled Jeremy's. Much of their time was spent underground. They were very fortunate to have shelter so sturdy. There were still trees and foliage surrounding them in the Montana mountains. But the severe climatological changes were a worldwide phenomenon. They almost never saw direct sunlight anymore. There were torrential rainstorms and hailstorms, and they even had a little snow that August. But it was followed the next day by 90 degree heat.

Extremes like that made it next to impossible to enjoy any fresh food. The lived on grains that they could keep dry in large, airtight storage containers in their old bomb shelter.

"How much longer can we go on like this?" Erin asked Matthew one day.

"As long as the Lord allows us," he said. "You know," he said, "we're not just passive players in this war up there. We have a real part to play in this struggle. This is not just a battle between men, it's between the princes of powers and principalities. We can be of tremendous moral support to the angels of light. Nothing gives them more power than our prayers."

"You're right, Matthew," said Erin. "You're always right. It would be so much easier for me to keep my priorities straight, I think, if I just had some information about Jeremy—if I knew where he is and how he's doing. It preoccupies my mind and makes me anxious to think about all the time that has gone by."

"I know what you mean, Erin," Matthew said. "I'm so grateful Denise is here with me. I don't know what I would do if we were separated through this ordeal."

Denise walked over just as Matthew was finishing his sentence.

"Are you talking about me?" she said with a smile.

"Yes, of course," he said. "Erin is feeling blue again,

honey. I think we should pray with her."

"Oh that would be so nice," said Erin. "I really need it today."

"We all need it, every day," said Denise.

"Heavenly Father," began Matthew, "we know so little about what is going on up above us. But we do know this: Your will is being done on this planet. You will bring Your kingdom to earth in your own timing. We pray that the torment and agony of our loved ones will be minimized during these days. We pray that Jeremy Armstrong will be surrounded by Your guardian angels day and night until he is reunited with Erin. We pray that Your son, Jesus, will return soon, Lord, and that He will bind Satan and redeem this earth for all time for Your glory. Amen."

"Amen," said Erin.

"Amen," said Denise.

Just then, a disturbance occurred at the other end of the shelter—near the entrance.

"Someone's upstairs, someone's trying to get in!" exclaimed the watchman on duty.

"Who is it?" asked Matthew.

"We don't recognize him. It's just one man," said the guard.

The survivalists had rigged a periscope of sorts that allowed them to peer at anyone who approached the entrance to the shelter. Each person underground took a turn looking into the viewfinder to see if the stranger was someone they knew. Erin, Matthew and Denise walked over for their turns. Matthew didn't know the man, nor did Denise. Finally, it was Erin's turn.

"Oh my!" she said the instant she looked. "That's Zeke Charlton, my old boss from the U.N.!"

Carlo sat in his Temple, an evil smile on his face. He was beating back this offensive by the Chinese. His stockpiles of nuclear weapons were far from depleted, but the Chinese seemed to be relying more on manpower in the last few weeks. His calculations showed they had exhausted their arsenal.

Ben David and Pope John Paul III were seated across from Carlo, as was Juan Montez, Carlo's secretary for international security.

"I've done it," Carlo told them with glee. "They are finished. There's no one left to challenge my authority on this planet. Their blood is running deep. Our reports tell us the entire Jordan River Valley is red with the blood of my enemies."

"I don't understand something," interjected Montez. "Before the Chinese exhausted their nuclear stockpile, why didn't any of their missiles strike Jerusalem? My intelligence reports tell me that several missiles were headed here, that they could not be stopped by our anti-missile battalions, yet they never reached their target."

"I stopped them," insisted Carlo, who knew better, but was becoming increasingly megalomaniacal. "I stopped them with my sheer willpower."

"I see," said Montez, hiding his skepticism.

Ben David looked askance at Carlo. He, too, knew better. He knew where the real power came from. They had both known for a long time that Jerusalem would not be destroyed by man. And they knew why.

"What's next?" asked the pope.

"It's time for the fifth seal to be opened," explained Carlo. "It's time for us to go after all those who have been disloyal subjects. Anyone who has not sworn allegiance to us must be rounded up and eliminated at once. We will never have another chance like this."

Carlo was referring to the Book of Revelation, chapter 9, verses 1-4:

> *"And the fifth angel sounded, and I saw a star fall from heaven unto the earth; and to him was given the key to the bottomless pit. And he opened the bottomless pit, and there arose a smoke out of the pit, like the smoke of a great furnace; and the sun and the air were darkened by reason of the smoke of the pit. And there came out of the smoke locusts upon the earth and unto them was given power, as the scorpions of the earth have power. And it was commanded them that they should not hurt the grass of the earth, neither any green thing, neither any tree, but only those men who have not the seal of God in their foreheads."*

Since Carlo saw himself as "God," what he meant to happen was the wholesale persecution of all those who refused to accept him as such.

"How high should this priority be?" asked a surprised Montez, who understood exactly what he meant. "Drought, nuclear dust, starvation and disease are killing hundreds of thousands a day."

"I'm quite aware of that," shot back Carlo. "It's all going just as planned. Now I want it clear that under no circumstances should our resources be squandered on trying to save people. Our No. 1 objective now becomes the elimination of all opposition. Is that clear?"

"Yes, of course," said Montez, a once willing and able assistant who now obeyed Carlo out of sheer fear.

"He'll be coming for us soon," Carlo said, looking at the pope, "and I don't want Him to have any friends here when He arrives."

Ben David nodded in tacit agreement. The pope looked at both of them, wondering just what was going to happen next.

General Oved, Armstrong and Barak agreed that, since it was quiet upstairs, now might be a good time to send a scouting party out. But since previous missions of this kind had turned up little in the way of useful information or salvageable goods, they agreed this one should explore further from the shelter.

"The team should leave at the crack of dawn and plan to be back an hour before sundown," said Armstrong.

"The problem is, Jeremy, we don't really know when either of those things occurs for sure," said Barak. "We can make some guesses based on the time of year, but it's been awhile since any of us were even conscious of the sun coming up or going down."

"You're right," Isaac. "We'll figure out a specific time for sunup and then have someone outside actually monitoring it. We'll just have to hope we're not too far off on the sundown estimate."

"I would suggest the team travel south-southeast," said Oved. "With the amount of time they have on foot, they should be able to get to the lake and see what that part of the country looks like."

By "the lake," Oved was referring to the Sea of Galilee. It was the closest heavily populated region—or at least it had been. They had no idea what they would find outside the immediate area in northern Israel and southern Lebanon. The next morning, the team left. It included Major Barak, who knew the countryside well, Jeremy and five of his men.

For the first few hours, the unit found almost nothing alive. Northern Israel, once a relatively lush and verdant area, had been reduced to desert. It wasn't just nuclear weapons that had punished and transformed the land. Everywhere they looked they saw evidence of large-scale conventional warfare and troop movements. Only rusting hulks remained of entire Russian armored columns. Weapons were everywhere—artillery pieces, small arms, unexploded shells, even a few helicopters.

It reminded Jeremy of a verse he had read in Ezekiel, chapter 39, verse 9: *"And they that dwell in the cities of Israel shall go forth, and shall set on fire and burn the weapons, both the shields and the bucklers, the bows and the arrows, and the handspikes, and the spears, and they shall burn them with fire seven years."*

"Seven years," he said to Isaac. "That ought to be about

right, judging from what I'm seeing here."

"Well," said Isaac, "what do you expect? Ezekiel was a good prophet."

The squad stayed close to main roads so Barak could keep his bearings. It was eerie when they would come to a residential area that was completely deserted—or where everyone had been killed.

They found lots of human remains. There were dead Israeli civilians killed by Russian troops, bombs, artillery and tactical nuclear blasts. There were plenty of dead Russian soldiers, all apparently killed by Carlo's neutron nukes. And where there were bodies, there was stench— and flies. The men placed bandannas over their noses when they marched through such areas.

But the most noticeable thing about their walk was the sound. Total silence. There were no birds singing. No traffic noise. No voices other than their own. No hum of engines or industry. Just absolute quiet. That, too, was eerie.

As they got closer to the lake, the troops met their first survivors. They were kids living a kind of "Lord of the Flies" existence. Barak talked to them in Hebrew and learned that they had survived the holocaust by hiding in caves. They lived off the food they found on the bodies of dead soldiers.

A few miles further, they found the remnants of civilization. While sitting on a hill looking down through the binoculars, they could see a community rebuilding near the edge of the lake. But they dared not get closer because of the presence of U.N. troops in and around the area.

"Well," said Jeremy, "We've been gone almost four hours, maybe we should start back."

"Yes, you're right," said Isaac.

And just as he did, they heard the sound of vehicles driving quickly up the road toward their position.

"Take cover," yelled Jeremy.

They were U.N. troops—two truckloads of them—and they appeared to be looking for something. Jeremy guessed that the kids might have tipped them off about the presence of other soldiers in the area. Fortunately, they drove right past them. But this was going to make getting back before dark trickier than they had expected—especially if this patrol continued to search for them.

Worse yet, Isaac, Jeremy and the troops were tired. Having been confined to their shelter for so many months on a survival-oriented diet, they didn't realize how out of shape they were. Their endurance for such treks had been severely reduced. Jeremy began to doubt they could get back before sundown, which, under the circumstances, was a scary thought. Could Barak even find the shelter in the dark? Would they find a suitable place to camp for the night? And what if the bombs started flying again?

They began the long walk back. About 30 minutes later, they heard the unmistakable sound of a chopper approaching from the south. Jeremy waved his men toward cover. The chopper flew over low and deliberately. It was definitely on a search mission for them, thought Jeremy. He wasn't sure they could obscure themselves with the chopper at such a low altitude. The terrain did not lend itself to hiding places. There were no standing structures and no trees—only some small rock formations and some disabled Russian armor.

After buzzing around for what seemed like an interminable period—probably only about 15 minutes—the helicopter took off southward again at high speed.

"Not a good sign,"Armstrong told Barak."He must have spotted us."

"Well, I guess we better get moving again."

"Yes," said Jeremy, "and keep looking for places to make a stand if they come back for us."

Thirty minutes later, they heard the sound of chopper blades echoing in the stillness again. This time, though, when they looked behind them there were three Comanche attack helicopters headed straight for them. They scrambled quickly for cover.

Jeremy had been thinking about what they could do if faced with this prospect. The only weapons he had in his arsenal that might be effective were RPGs. He had never hit a moving helicopter with one and figured it would be a challenge. But it was worth a try.

"Rafer" he yelled to Landry, "use your RPG." He got the high sign as Rafer got set up, while Armstrong armed his. At least he had plenty of grenades if he missed.

As the choppers flew into attack formation, they began spraying the area with machine gun fire. Then the rockets started flying toward them. Their cover was absolutely inadequate defense against an airborne attack. They wouldn't have much time.

Jeremy fired the first shot—a miss. Rafer quickly fired a second and hit the lead chopper, which burst into flames and crashed to the ground. That was enough to make the other two helicopters back off a little and regroup out of range. They continued circling the area about a half-mile away.

"They want to keep us pinned down here until the cavalry can arrive," said Jeremy. "We can't just sit here and wait to be outgunned and outnumbered."

"What do you suggest?" asked Barak.

"Landry and I are going to have to attack them," he said. "I'm going to take one extra man. You take the rest of them back to the shelter. We'll try to catch up with you later."

"I don't like it, Jeremy," said Barak.

"You got a better idea?" Armstrong asked.

After thinking for a minute, Barak gave Jeremy a hug and said, "Go get 'em tiger, Jesus will give you the fighting skill of David." He rounded up the four other men and began moving quickly north.

The choppers spotted the men on the move and began to fly slowly toward them, still keeping enough distance to remain out of range of RPG fire. So Armstrong, Landry and Jason Black crept closer and closer to their attackers. When they were close enough, but apparently undetected, they opened fire.

Once again, Rafer knocked out chopper number one. Jeremy stood in the open, waiting courageously for the third chopper to get closer. Bullets were hitting all around him. The gunship's infrared beam was locked squarely on Jeremy's chest, but he held his concentration. At the last second, he took careful aim and fired. The chopper disappeared in a fireball.

"Wow, Jeremy," Landry said, "would you mind telling me how you kept those bullets from hitting you? That was a 30 millimeter Vulcan six barrel machine gun. Hundreds of bullets guided by an infra-red beam locked on your chest were coming straight at you. Yet they divided and went down both sides of you—as if an invisible hand shielded you. No wonder you got the Medal of Honor. That was the bravest thing I ever saw. It must have been something like David running at Goliath with a sling shot."

"I just knew that I had to hit that chopper or we were all dead," Jeremy replied. Then I heard the angel's voice again saying, "Fear not! Stand still and wait until they're in range, for not a bullet will hit you. Behold, I have already delivered your enemies into your hands." Rafer and Jason stood there amazed and speechless at what they had just heard.

The threesome was about 20 minutes behind the rest of the squad and began trotting to catch up. Barak saw the two choppers explode, so he kept his unit moving slowly to give Jeremy's team a chance to make up time. They regrouped shortly afterward and continued to make their way north. They were now well behind schedule with little chance of making it back before dark. But they would get as close as they could.

"Maybe we can just feel our way home," Jeremy suggested.

An hour later, with many miles still to go and the dim

light rapidly fading, they heard the sound they hoped not to hear—the rumble of troop trucks off in the distance. Jeremy pulled out his binoculars and looked in the direction of a dust cloud to the southwest.

"Yep," he said, "there they are."

"How many?" asked Rafer.

"Hard to say," Jeremy replied. "It looks like at least two truckloads—probably a full platoon's worth."

"What's your plan, Colonel?" asked Barak.

"Well, I would say we only have one option—ambush them before they see us. Here's the plan: Rafer, you set up over there behind those rocks. They will have to come up this road. Now, be sure you hit only the first truck with your RPG when it reaches this point. Isaac, you stay with Rafer and use your Uzi to pick off any survivors from that first truck. The rest of us will be over there—behind them. When they start jumping out of the second truck, we'll get the rest of them."

"Why not just knock them both out with RPG's?" asked Barak.

"Because, Major, the second truck is our ride home."

Sure enough, Rafer's deadly accuracy came through again. One RPG shot at about 300 meters and the truck burst into flames. Barak didn't have that many survivors to finish off. And, just as planned, the men in the second truck began jumping out right after the explosion. But some of them ran for cover before Armstrong and company could hit them. So, a one-hour firefight ensued before the remnant of the attackers was driven off or killed.

It was almost totally dark now. As tired as the men

were, they were glad they had some transportation.

"I'm not sure I remember how to drive," said Jeremy. "Rafer, why don't you do the honors. Isaac, you better sit in the front seat with him and be his navigator. But remember, don't get too close to the shelter. We need to ditch the truck at least four clicks away so these buzzards don't find us."

"OK, Colonel," said Isaac, "but just one question: I have heard this term before in American war movies, but just how far is a 'click'?"

"Sorry about that, Isaac," he said. "It's about half a kilometer."

Isaac found a good spot to dump the truck about two miles from the shelter—a place from which he was confident he could find his way in the dark. They made it without further incident.

All was quiet above the shelter for the next several weeks. Armstrong and company went outside often now. They got so comfortable with the idea of being above ground that they nearly became overconfident that things were normalizing in the world. Though things were far from pleasant up there, being above ground gave the men a chance to exercise and breathe air that hadn't been breathed before—even if it was a little high in radioactivity.

One day, while everyone was above ground talking, laughing and breathing what passed for fresh air in those days, they almost failed to notice the rumbling sound in the distance. It was not an earthquake, but later, when everybody scrambled back down into the shelter, it would feel like one. It was the largest armored column anyone had ever seen, and it was passing right by them—a parade that lasted not for days but for weeks. Day and night, night and day, Chinese tanks and armored personnel carriers streamed over the Lebanese border and into northern Israel. It interfered with their sleep and it prohibited any visits above ground.

"How could anything on earth stop that force?" asked Barak.

"We're not talking about something earthly when we're talking about Carlo," said Armstrong.

"That's true," said Oved, "but I don't think Carlo has enough nukes to stop that kind of conventional force. And how is he going to defend Jerusalem from the Chinese tactical nukes?"

"The Bible tells us to pray for the peace of Jerusalem," reminded Barak. "I think that would be a good idea, right now."

"Do you mean that we should pray for Carlo?" asked Armstrong.

"No, of course not," said Barak. "But Carlo is an aberration. The city must not be destroyed because of him."

"You're right," said Jeremy, "God will have to intervene in this battle or everyone will perish."

Back in Montana, after getting over their initial apprehension, Matthew and Erin decided to see what Zeke Charlton wanted. He was clearly all alone. He did not appear to be armed. And, even if he was, he would have been outgunned by those in the shelter. They opened the hatch and put a gun to Charlton's head.

"What do you want here?" demanded Matthew.

"I…I…my name is Zeke Charlton," he began. "I had one of my employees followed here a while ago—Erin O'Hara. I mean you no harm. I want to join you."

"OK, come down here and let's talk," said Matthew, still keeping the gun on Zeke. Once they had relocked the hatch and seated themselves down in the shelter again, Matthew said: "Now…explain yourself."

"Well, as I said, I had Erin followed when she left the U.N.," Zeke said. "It was my job to persecute all those who refused to accept Carlo. We had intercepted some of Erin's calls and suspected she might be leaving. Originally my intention was to follow her and destroy all those hiding out here. But, as I studied more and more about what Christians believed, I think God began to work on my heart. I had seen Carlo at his worst. His inhumanity and ruthlessness always bothered me. When my best friend left and told me he was a Christian, it really got me thinking—and, I guess, praying. Anyway, once we had located this spot, I told my men to forget they ever found it. And I knew that some day I would try to come here myself. So here I am."

"Erin, what do you think?" Matthew asked.

"I think he's sincere," she said. "I know this man loved

Jeremy—almost as much as I do. He could have had him killed, but he didn't."

"Are you a believer now?" demanded Matthew.

"Yes, I am," said Zeke. "I'm not sure I know fully what that means. But there is no question in my mind—after having looked evil in the face—that I choose God, not this phony messiah Carlo."

"Zeke," Erin interjected, "What do you know about Jeremy?"

"I think he's very much alive," Zeke said. "I know he was attached to an antimissile bunker in Palmahim, Israel. There was something of a coup there. Apparently Jeremy and his men helped some Israeli military people take over the bunker. They shot down a bunch of Russian missiles, and then they all took off, leaving behind them a trail of dead U.N. soldiers. Carlo searched the ends of the earth for them but, as far as I know, he never found them. Of course, that area has been hit harder than any other area on the face of the earth. But if I know Special Forces Lt. Col. Jeremy Armstrong—and his survival ability—I wouldn't bet against him finding some place to ride out this storm.

"I heard about an incident up in Galilee just before leaving my post that could only be Jeremy's kind of operation," Zeke said with obvious admiration. "The communique reported that a small group of renegade soldiers had shot down three of our most advanced helicopters from a range of 300 meters with only RPGs. They then destroyed a whole platoon of crack U.N. soldiers, stole a truck and got away without a trace."

"Now I would bet a month's pay that was Jeremy and some of his hand-picked men," Zeke said cheerfully.

"Oh Zeke," said Erin. "Jeremy's going to be so happy to see you again. "Do you really think we'll get that chance to be reunited?"

"If anyone can live through all this, it's Jeremy. He is a natural born warrior—did you know he's part Apache?" said Zeke. "Anyway, I have to see him again—if only to punch him on the arm and apologize."

Life only got worse for those who managed to live above ground. Virtually all the drinking water in the Middle East was poisoned by several years of chemical and biological warfare. Even the seas were devoid of life in the area. The desolation witnessed by Armstrong and company was nothing compared to what was wrought upon the land after the Asian invasion. No one bothered killing civilians anymore. Both sides knew they would just die anyway—of starvation, disease, thirst and neglect, or as a result of crime.

The Chinese army hurtling toward Jerusalem was slowed by tactical nuclear weapons. The Chinese, in turn, fired their own nukes at Carlo's forces—even at Jerusalem. But it was obvious to everyone that something totally supernatural was protecting Jerusalem. Carlo knew it was not his anti-missile weapons. He had no defenses against the long-range nuclear artillery shells the Asian coalition fired at the capital. Yet they seemed useless against God's holy city. The Chinese were baffled.

Carlo's nuclear attacks on the Chinese, however, were devastating. The only factor that sustained the war was the sheer size of the Asian force—an army 200 million strong. If any troops survived the firestorm Carlo created for them, he made certain they would have no homeland to return to. Beijing and every major Chinese city—as well as most of the rural countryside—were ionized.

The prophet Isaiah saw it as clearly as anyone alive in the 21st century when he wrote:

"Behold, the Lord lays the Earth waste, devastates it, distorts its surface, and scatters its inhabitants. And the people will be like the priest, the servant like his master, the maid like her mistress, the buyer like the seller, the lender like the borrower, the creditor like the debtor. The Earth will be completely laid waste and completely despoiled, for the Lord has spoken this word. The Earth mourns and withers, the world fades and withers, the exalted people of the Earth fade away. The Earth is also polluted by its inhabitants, for they transgressed laws, violated statutes, broke the everlasting covenant. Therefore, a curse devours the Earth, and those who live in it are held guilty. Therefore, the inhabitants of the Earth are burned, and few men are left."

The devastation was hardly isolated to the Middle East and Asia. The Chinese fired every ICBM they had at the western cities in America and Europe. Nuclear winter turned out to be more than a theory. The result was a complete breakdown of the Earth's environment. In the storms that followed, hailstones of a hundred pounds or more rained down on men. A large part of the polar ice caps melted, inundating most of the world's islands. Even the topography of the continents was rearranged as mountains were leveled, volcanos erupted, and giant craters dotted the landscape.

But, miraculously in some cases, people did survive. Erin's group in Montana weathered this man-made disaster that lasted some three and a half years. A surprising number of Jews in Israel survived—given that this was ground zero in the worst holocaust the world would ever know. And others, like Armstrong and company, found their little sanctuaries and made it through. Was it human resourcefulness or God's will? No one was quite sure—until, that is, the Day of the Lord.

Carlo and Elijah Ben David knew it was coming. The pope knew it, too. They had known it all along. The script had been written centuries earlier. And they knew that script as well as anyone—including the authors. But they were so deceived by Satan's deceptive powers they actually thought they could win against the Lord of Lords, Jesus the Messiah. This holocaust was Satan's final opportunity to vent his fury toward the human race which God had used as the final case to prove Satan's guilt. So, as he had done all through history with other tyrants, he used Carlo's, Ben David's and the pope's lust for power and desire to be like gods to capture their wills. Then he used them for his destructive purposes—keeping them deceived until their final, inevitable moment of ruin.

"It is finished," Carlo cried on the Lord's day. He was mimicking what the Lord had said on the cross. He was still mocking, still defiant. Ben David used his Satanic powers to call fire down from the sky. He then declared Carlo to be God Almighty.

This was the final blasphemy for the Lord. After seven years of torture and death, God had seen enough. He sent back His Son, accompanied by mighty angels declaring Him Lord of Lords and King of Kings. But even the sight of Jesus Christ descending from the clouds in dazzling glory before all the world and Jerusalem wasn't enough to cause the Evil Trinity of Carlo, Ben David and the pope to repent. Even the sight of the Mount of Olives splitting in two when Jesus' foot first touched down where He ascended to Heaven some 2000 years before—with all its deafening sound, including the greatest earthquake in the history of the planet—was not enough to bring Carlo, the Evil One incarnate, to his knees. In fact, Carlo, the Beast, was driven to greater insanity. He decided he might as well try to turn all the remaining weapons and armaments against the Lord Himself. He also called upon his fallen angels for one last stand—a violent clash of swords and wills over Jerusalem.

As Jesus stood on the Mount of Olives and strode toward the Temple, Carlo ordered his remaining tactical nukes to be fired directly at Him. Of course, it was futile. The Lord deflected the missiles out into space with his raised hand. Carlo ordered his troops to fire their artillery shells, encased with biological and chemical weapons. The Lord disintegrated them harmlessly with a wave of His hand. Carlo ordered his troops to fire everything they had at the Lord and His heavenly host. The bullets and shells fell harmlessly to the ground.

Those humans who continued to follow Carlo's orders to attack God Himself died horrible deaths. With as little as a glance upon the Son of God coming to earth in all His glory, their flesh was stripped from their bones, their eyes from their sockets, and their tongues from their mouths. But the final battle still came down to spiritual hand-to-hand combat. Carlo and his demons had to be physically and spiritually restrained—shackled and cast into God's horrible bottomless pit. Meanwhile, no human who accepted the false messiah survived.

Above Jerusalem in the clouds, the angels fought a fierce battle. But the demons were badly underpowered. And God's will was strong. The elite angels were emboldened by the continual prayer of those human spirits who returned to earth with Jesus—those who never tasted death. Among them were Jeremy's mother and sister, and Erin's family.

Miraculously, all over the world, people could see this spiritual war taking place in and over Jerusalem by simply looking into the sky wherever they were. Jeremy, Gen. Oved, Major Barak and the rest came out of their dank dungeon and into the dim sunlight to witness this event. In Montana, Erin and Matthew and the rest came out of their cramped and depressing shelter into a gray and hazy new day. They, too, could see the most important event in history taking place in the Big Sky—like some giant Cinerama movie screen.

As they recalled the unprecedented events that had happened in the last several weeks, it fit exactly into what the Apostle John wrote in the Apocalypse. They read from parts of chapters 16 and 19 aloud:

"Then the seventh angel poured out his bowl into the air, and a loud voice came out of the temple of heaven, from the throne, saying, "It is done [finished]*!" And there were noises and thunderings and lightnings; and there was a great earthquake, such as had not occurred since men were on the earth. Now the great city* [Jerusalem] *was divided into three parts, and the cities of the nations fell* [i.e., all the cities of the world were destroyed]. *And great Babylon* [the Vatican along with Rome] *was remembered before God, to give her the cup of wine of the fierceness of His wrath. Then every island fled away, and the mountains were not found. And great hail from heaven fell upon men, every hailstone about the weight of a talent. And men blasphemed God because of the plague of the hail, since the plague was exceedingly great.*

"Then I saw heaven opened, and behold, a white horse. And He who sat on him was called Faithful and True, and in righteousness He judges and makes war. His eyes were like a flame of fire, and on His head were many crowns. He had a name written that no one knew except Himself. He was clothed with a robe dipped in blood, and His name is called The Word of God. And the armies in heav-

en, clothed in fine linen, white and clean, followed Him on white horses. Now out of His mouth goes a sharp sword, that with it He should strike the gentiles. And He Himself will rule them with a rod of iron. He Himself treads the wine press of the fierceness and wrath of Almighty God.

And He has on His robe and on His thigh a name written:

KING OF KINGS

AND LORD OF LORDS.

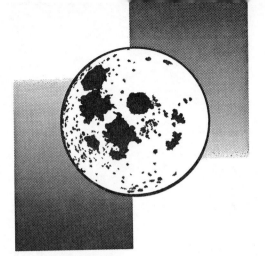

CHAPTER 9

The Conquering King

Good was as close to Abraham as He ever has been to any man—before or since. He trusted him, shared information, even accepted counsel from him.

But so serious were the troubles in Sodom and Gomorrah, and so grave were His plans for dealing with them, that the Lord wasn't certain he should confide in Abraham. He even had a little debate with Himself about it: "Shall I hide from Abraham what I am about to do, seeing that Abraham shall become a great and mighty nation, and all the nations of the earth shall bless themselves by him? No, for I have chosen him, that he may charge his children and his household after him to keep the way of the Lord by doing righteousness and justice; so that the Lord may bring to Abraham what he has promised him."

So God spoke to Abraham: "Because the outcry against Sodom and Gomorrah is great and their sin is very grave, I will go down to see whether they have done altogether according to the outcry which has come to me; and if not, I will know."

Abraham petitioned the Lord: "Would you destroy the

righteous of Sodom and Gomorrah along with the wicked? Suppose there are fifty righteous people within the city. Would you still destroy it and not spare the fifty? I can't imagine that you would do that—treat the righteous in the same way you treat the wicked. Far be it from you to do that! After all, you are the judge of all the earth. Surely you will do what is right in Sodom and Gomorrah!"

"If I find at Sodom fifty righteous in the city, I will spare the whole place for their sake," said God.

"Forgive me for my impertinence, Lord," said Abraham. "After all, I know that I am nothing but dust and ashes and have no place to speak to you in this way. But, suppose five of the fifty are lacking. Would you destroy the whole city for the shortcomings of five?"

"I will not destroy it if I find forty-five righteous ones there," said the Lord.

"Well, suppose only forty righteous are found there," said Abraham. "Would you destroy the city?"

"For the sake of forty I will not," said the Lord.

"Please don't get angry with me, Lord, but what if only thirty righteous are found?" Abraham asked.

"I will not destroy the city if I find thirty righteous there," God said.

"Again, pardon me for asking, but suppose only twenty are found?"

"For the sake of twenty I will not destroy the city," God responded.

"Please don't get angry with me Lord if I ask you just one more question: Suppose only ten righteous are found?"

"For the sake of ten I will not destroy it," God said.

God then sent two angels to visit Sodom that night. When they got to the city's gate, they met Lot, who was sitting there. Lot bowed humbly before these messengers of the Lord and begged them to spend the night at his home.

"No," they said, "we will spend the night in the streets."

"Please, my lords," Lot begged, "I pray you to come to your servant's house where you may wash your feet, spend the night and rise up early to continue your business."

"Very well," they said.

Lot prepared a magnificent meal for the angels. After they had eaten but before they lay down for the night, a commotion developed out in the street. It seemed every man in the city had surrounded the house. They began calling to Lot.

"Where are those men who came to you tonight?" they shouted. "Bring them out here so that we can get to know them better."

Lot understood what these men wanted. They were planning to rape the angels. He went out to plead with them to leave the angels alone. But the mob became angry and began threatening Lot himself. One of the angels reached outside the door with one hand and plucked Lot up, brought him inside and bolted the door. They also struck the mob blind.

"Do you have anyone else here in this city?" the angels demanded of Lot. "Are there any sons-in-law, daughters or anyone else? If so, bring them out of the city immediately, for we are about to destroy this place."

Lot ran out to find the men who were planning to marry his daughters: "Hurry up," he told them. "Get out of this city with me now. The Lord is about to destroy this place."

But his would-be sons-in-law only laughed, thinking that Lot was joking with them. They wouldn't be coming. At dawn, the angels awoke Lot and told him to take his wife and two daughters out immediately so they would not be destroyed along with the city. They even took them by the hand and led them safely out of town.

"Flee for your life," they told Lot. "Do not look back or stop anywhere in the valley. Flee to the hills or else you will be consumed."

"Would it be all right if I go to that little city over there?" Lot asked. "I can't make it to the hills."

"I will grant you this favor, also," said one of the angels. "I will not destroy that little city. But hurry up, for *I can do nothing until you arrive there.*"

Then, when Lot was safely distant, without warning, fire and sulfur rained down on Sodom and Gomorrah from heaven. Everything in the cities and in the valley was destroyed—men, women, children, plants and animals.

Lot's wife did not listen to the angels' warning and turned to look at the firestorm. Just the sight of it caused her to die on the spot where she stood, her skin and living tissue consumed instantly. Abraham, meanwhile, up in the hills, looked down toward Sodom and Gomorrah and saw only a mushroom cloud.

When Jesus descended from heaven to Jerusalem, it appeared to the remainder of humanity that he was encircled in white cumulus clouds. But they were not clouds as we usually think of them. They were not clouds of water vapor. Instead, they were clouds of believers dressed in white linen returning to earth like some invincible army of witnesses. They would not need to draw a sword or carry a gun. They just needed to be there to see the greatest event in the history of the world.

There was nothing slow or deliberate about His coming. It was as sudden as lightning strikes, but much brighter and more spectacular. Everywhere, all over the world, people cried and mourned when they saw Him. Why? Because they saw that He was indeed the One. It was unmistakable now. Carlo was an impostor. This was the man who had been crucified nearly 2,000 years earlier for their sins. He still bore the wounds! You could see the holes in His hands and feet, the scars where the lashes fell, the wound in His side where the lance entered, the gashes on His head where the crown of thorns had been thrust.

But Jesus did not come back to be pitied. He came back to judge those who had rejected Him. So the crying and mourning was not just for Jesus. They cried, too, for themselves. All those who had believed in Carlo and accepted his implant were doomed. They had committed the unpardonable sin. There was no hope for them.

When Jeremy and company witnessed this event, they recalled the words of Zechariah 12:

"Then the clans of Judah shall say to themselves, 'The inhabitants of Jerusalem have strength through the Lord of hosts, their God.' On that day I will make the clans of Judah like a blazing pot in the midst of wood, like a flaming torch among sheaves; and they shall devour to the right and to the left all the peoples round about, while Jerusalem shall still be inhabited in its place, in Jerusalem. And the Lord will give victory to the tents of Judah first, that the glory of the house of David and the glory of the inhabitants of Jerusalem may not be exalted over that of Judah. On that day the Lord will put a shield about the inhabitants of Jerusalem so that the feeblest among them on that day shall be like David, and the house of David shall be like God, like the angel of the Lord, at their head. And on that day I will seek to destroy all the nations that come against Jerusalem. And I will pour out on the house of David and the inhabitants of Jerusalem a spirit of compassion and supplication.... On that day there shall be a fountain opened for the house of David and the inhabitants of Jerusalem to cleanse them from sin and uncleanness."

"We've got to go to Jerusalem, right now," Jeremy said.

When Jesus' feet touched down on the Mount of Olives, splitting the hill in two, it created a giant crevice running east and west. While one would expect people to run from such a natural disaster, oddly, this phenomenon had the effect of attracting many of the survivors in Jerusalem. The believing Jewish remnant, already protected miraculously and supernaturally by the Lord and empowered with new spirit by His return, understood this giant crack in the earth created by the quake to be a place of refuge. So they ran to it by the thousands.

They, like Armstrong and company, recalled the prophecy in Zechariah and believed the great cavern was opened up for their protection from the terrible devastation that the Lord was about to pour out on the godless armies of the world. In other words, this new faultline was to be used as a kind of natural bomb shelter.

It didn't take long for Barak, Oved, Armstrong and his men to reach Jerusalem. Their first instinct, upon clearing out of their shelter for the last time, was to run for that old truck, hoping against hope that it would still be operable after the Asian invasion. When they got there, it was gone. But, there were some other abandoned vehicles nearby. They loaded themselves in and headed south for Jerusalem. They had no idea what might lie between them and their destination, but they were certain, given the promises of God, that on this day they would be empowered to deal with any adversity. And they were.

They couldn't believe the extent of the destruction they witnessed on their trip through Israel. It was much worse than what they had seen on their previous excursion to the lake. Israel was practically lifeless for dozens of miles at a stretch—no men, no animals, not even vegetation had survived the fallout of two massive nuclear and conventional invasions.

About five miles outside Jerusalem, though, they began seeing some people. There was panic everywhere— refugees fleeing to and fro in utter confusion. They knew they had to go, but where? Then Armstrong's two-vehicle convoy, a smaller transport truck and a Jeep armed with a machine gun, nearly ran smack into a heavily fortified U.N. highway blockade. They stopped about half a mile away to regroup and strategize how to bypass it.

"We could go back and try to find another route into Jerusalem," said Barak, "but my guess is they will have those roads blocked as well."

"What if we went off-road for a few miles and hiked into the city?" asked Armstrong.

"That would be fine," said Gen. Oved, "except we still don't know what kind of opposition we will see. If we have to make a run for it or fight, I'd rather have the vehicles with us than to be on foot."

"Well, then, suppose we just break through the barricade?" asked Armstrong.

"Are you crazy?" Oved asked. "They've got APCs blocking the road, machine-gun emplacements, they may even have the road mined up there."

"Look, I know it's crazy in the conventional sense," said Armstrong. "But this is a new world we're in now. Remember what Zechariah wrote? He said the house of David and the inhabitants of Jerusalem would be given supernatural strength at this hour. Now, Gen. Oved and Isaac, I know you are part of the house of David, and I believe the rest of us are, too, through our faith in Jesus. If we call upon the Lord for the power, I believe we can drive right through that barricade and go all the way to Jerusalem. No one can harm us if we believe and claim that protection as our own."

Isaac and Gen. Oved looked at each other.

"Let's pray," they said.

Erin, Zeke, Matthew and Denise also began making their plans for a pilgrimage to Jerusalem. Even though it was still a war zone, they believed in the promise of God in Zechariah. They believed they would be safe there—that there would be special protections for believers. And they wanted to see Jesus. Erin also hoped to see Jeremy.

It was not the easy trip it would have been under normal circumstances. There were no commercial international airline flights—only military and a few private ones—from anywhere in the United States. So, the big question was: How do we get there?

Zeke still had lots of military connections. Now that Carlo had his hands full contending with Jesus, he figured it might be safe to poke his head up from underground and make some inquiries with friends at some air bases. He was certain he could hitchhike on a flight to Israel. The hard part would be arranging transportation for three civilians.

So he decided to invoke his old title and position, even though he had left it many months before. After all, was a soldier at a U.S. Air Force base likely to know about staff shakeups months ago at the U.N.? It was certainly unlikely, given all the turmoil in the world during that time period.

Zeke got lucky on his first try. He arranged for the four of them to fly to Israel on a military transport plane leaving Aberdeen Air Force Base in South Dakota a week later. Zeke had come to Montana in a U.N. car, which he had stashed about two miles from the shelter in a dilapidated old barn he found on his way. Fortunately, it was still there…and it still ran. The four of them piled in with some food and supplies and took off for South Dakota the next day.

All Erin had in mind was just to see Jesus face to face —and the possibility that she was would see Jeremy, too.

⬤

"OK, let's go for it!" said Jeremy.

The truck would take the lead position as they approached the barricade. The Jeep would follow close behind and be prepared to spray cover fire at those at the barricade if they pursued the fleeing vehicles.

"Buckle your seat belts," Jeremy joked as the truck began to pick up speed. Freeman was driving, Jeremy was bracing himself for the impact in the front passenger seat. Most of the other men, including Gen. Oved, were holding on to something in the back of the truck. Some were reciting the Lord's Prayer. Barak and two Americans were riding in the Jeep.

The truck was hurtling toward the barricade at 95 kilometers an hour when the first warning shots rang out in front of them. Freeman pointed the truck at the weakest spot he could identify in the barricade, at least at the speed he was traveling. There seemed to a narrow opening between two armored personnel carriers straight ahead of them. It wasn't wide enough for the truck to make it through, he realized, but if his velocity was high enough and his truck strong enough, he might be able to push them out of the way and make it through without too much structural damage to the truck.

The U.N. soldiers scurried out of the way when they saw the truck was not stopping. They stopped firing and ran to protect themselves. The impact of the truck on the APCs nearly lifted Jeremy right out of the cabin. The men in the back were piled up on the floor. But the truck made it through and was still running. The Jeep passed through the same opening with no trouble.

Barak, manning the machine-gun, turned around to cover them. No one was in pursuit. They were too stunned by the brazenness of the attack. Zechariah was right. Outnumbered and outgunned, the house of David had triumphed. Now it was on to Jerusalem.

At what had been the Mount of Olives, believers continued to flock to the cavern, all under the watchful eyes of Jesus. He signaled to them to come—to hurry to safety.

"Come!" he said, standing over the scene on the mountain. "Hurry, my children."

Armstrong's caravan pulled up at just that moment. Everyone disembarked from the truck and Jeep and just stared up at Jesus. They were close enough to see his wounds. Then they quietly knelt down before Him in prayer. But there was much commotion all about them. Hundreds of people were making their way, as fast as they could, to the cavern the quake had created. It didn't seem like a natural thing to do, but Jesus was telling them it was all right.

Jeremy and the rest began making their way toward the shelter, too. When they got there, they saw that this was no natural "accident." Perfect stairs were carved into the hard granite leading down a deep crevice. There was light down there, but no fixtures—just natural light that seemed to have no source.

Barak also wondered why it was still perfectly light outside, given the hour—9 p.m. The sun was not in evidence, but, somehow, there was still daylight, at least over Jerusalem.

"This place is fantastic," said Jeremy, looking around and admiring how clean everything was and how perfect was this underground shelter. "The last few years would have been a lot more pleasant if we had a place like this to stay, huh?" he said.

"Let's be grateful for what we had," said Gen. Oved, as they continued walking down the stairs that seemed never-ending.

"Oh, believe me, I am," said Jeremy. "Not only to you, General, for finding that site, but to God for making it available and safe for us. We were very, very fortunate—

very blessed. If we ever had any doubts about that, they should have been dismissed on our trip here."

"You guys are making me miss our dungeon already," joked Barak.

Finally, after about five or ten minutes of descent and hundreds of steps, they reached a wide-open area with a perfectly flat, smooth floor surrounded by several rooms. Again, there was what appeared to be natural light everywhere with no visible source. There were fountains in the center of the room that people were drinking from—even wading in.

"Well, this is certainly an improvement over our humble shelter in Metulla," said Oved.

Oved and Barak were meeting many people they knew—old friends, men they had served with, even some relatives. There were warm hugs and lasting embraces. They introduced people to Jeremy and his troops, but there were so many new faces that no one remembered names.

About an hour after they had arrived in this fantastic God-made shelter, an ear-splitting noise that sounded like another earthquake halted everyone in their tracks. The ground was rumbling, but not shaking violently. From their vantage point, those in the shelter could not see what was happening above them. Jesus descended the steps and looked over the crowd.

"These are my people," he said holding his arms out and looking out over those assembled.

In unison, the crowd just seemed to know what to say: "The Lord is my God."

"I have work to do outside," He said. "You will all be safe here while I am away. There is plenty of good food, fresh air and cleansing water—the kind that will not only refresh your body but will take away your sin. Rest yourselves now, my people. You have had a trying time. I will see you all again soon."

Everyone knelt down as Jesus left.

There was still a lot of fighting around Jerusalem. Oh, it wasn't like the massive invasions of the Russians and Chinese, but there were still pockets of resistance to the vestiges of U.N. forces. One of the small armies still trying to storm the gates of Jerusalem was led by Ishmael Muhammad.

Hiding out in his cave in Lebanon, Muhammad and his small band of loyal followers had made periodic forays to collect weapons and ammunition left behind by the big armies. Over a period of nearly seven years, his arsenal had grown quite impressively. Since every Arab and Muslim capital had been destroyed along with the infrastructures of their nations, Muhammad was the closest thing the radical Muslims had to a leader.

He was admired in some quarters for launching the missile that started this great war. He took advantage of this position to assemble a force of several thousand fighters who were now threatening to enter Jerusalem with a force far superior to the remaining U.N. forces.

But just as they were about to enter the city—with

their infantry and armor—a lone figure wearing white robes stepped in front of them, his right hand raised. The sight of the lone figure defying this powerful army was enough to stop the Islamic Flame forces in their tracks. A hush fell over the troops.

"This is My holy city!' thundered Jesus in perfect Arabic. "How dare you attempt to defile it?"

Muhammad strode to the front of his column. He yelled out in defiance, "Who are you?"

"I am the Lord thy God," Jesus said. "Who are you?"

"I am sent here on a mission from Allah to reclaim this city," said Muhammad. "I recognize no God but Allah and Muhammad is his one true prophet."

"You are a blasphemer and a murderer," said Jesus. "Get on your knees and beg for forgiveness for all you have done to wreak havoc and death in this world."

Instead, Muhammad removed a sidearm from a holster and pointed the gun at Jesus. Just then, a bright light shone from heaven and a wave of heat swept through the attackers. Within seconds their flesh literally melted away while they still stood on their feet, their eyes burst in their sockets and their tongues rotted away in their mouths.

Like Lot's wife, their bodies resembled nothing so much as pillars of salt. All that was left of this imposing army was some now quiet machines, weapons on the ground and dust blowing in the light Mediterranean breeze.

Life in their new shelter was quite different from what Armstrong and company had experienced the last several years up north. For one thing, there was the light. They had become used to living without strong natural light for long periods of time. Some of them suffered from light deprivation. It made them tired and lethargic. They had to struggle with constant sleepiness.

That was no problem down here. At times they had to remind themselves that they were not outside in the sunlight. That's what it felt like. That's what it looked like—except there was no sun, no apparent source for this light. It just emanated from all around them. It was, as one rabbi explained it, the presence of God that illuminated this place.

They were not cramped down here either. Though there were apparently many thousands of people here, there was still plenty of room for more. There were comfortable places to sit, to sleep, to talk and pray in large groups or small. There was music, too. In different sections of the great room, they could hear different musical forms—piano, organ, string quartets. None of the music clashed. Even though there were so many present, the perfectly balanced acoustics kept the noise to a minimum.

Then there was the food—many, many variations from all over the world and some that no one recognized. The one thing it all had in common, though, was that it was delicious. People tasted food that they had never liked before and found that here it tasted good to them. Maybe it was because it had been so long since any of them had had well-prepared meals. Or maybe it was the preparer.

Interestingly, no one could find any chefs. No one could find any servers. The food just seemed to appear. Dirty dishes just seemed to disappear.

"Are we in heaven already?" asked Freeman.

"I think we're getting a taste of it, anyway." said Armstrong.

"I wonder how long we'll be here?" asked Barak.

"I don't think I will ever want to leave," said Oved.

Everyone was encouraged to shower or bathe in what was billed as the unique water in this facility. Jesus had alluded to it Himself. But there were people here who seemed to know more than others. There was speculation that they may actually have been angels. In any case, they passed along the word that the waters had tremendous healing and rejuvenative powers.

Of course, it wasn't difficult to persuade people who, in many cases, had not had a proper shower in years, to take one. There were plenty of individual rooms for this purpose—lots of privacy. There were no lines for any-thing—not for food, not for rest and not for cleaning up.

"It sure smells better down here than it did at our Metulla shelter," commented Armstrong.

"Yeah, even you smell better, Jeremy," joked Barak.

Something else occurred to Jeremy about this place. Since he had entered the cavern, his mind had been at perfect peace regarding Erin. This was incredible to him—given that he had spent the last seven years fretting about her. Why now, he wondered, did he just know that every-thing was going to work out?

"Hey," he asked Barak, Freeman and Oved, "do any of

you guys ever worry about anything anymore?"

They all looked at each other.

"No, really," Armstrong said, "since we came here, have any of you really worried?"

"As a matter of fact, I can't think of anything to worry about," said Oved.

"Neither can I," said Barak.

"Nope," said Freeman.

"Well, isn't that just a little peculiar, given the state of the world outside?" Armstrong asked. "I mean, it's not exactly heaven on earth upstairs yet."

"Yeah, but it looks like the world's in much better hands now than it was a few days ago," said Oved.

"Jeremy, don't tell me you're not worried about Erin anymore?" said Barak.

"That's the funny thing," he said. "I'm not. That's what made me ask the question. I really think that we are getting a little taste of heaven down here. We all just have a peace about us. It's not that I care any less about Erin. I just have an assurance that we're going to be together—that she's all right."

After disposing of Muhammad, Jesus walked into the Temple. Carlo was waiting for Him. There were no soldiers, no guards, even the pope had fled from this confrontation.

"You think you've won a great victory, don't you?" Carlo said.

"Why don't you come out of that man now and let him rest in peace?" asked Jesus. He was referring to the body of Gianfranco Carlo. He understood the entity He was speaking to was not Carlo, but the one called Lucifer, or Satan. He had inhabited Carlo's body long before the assassination. That's why he never feared death. Carlo's personality had simply been overtaken by one far more powerful than any human being.

"I will come out in due time, in due time," said a contemptuous Satan.

"I command you to come out now!" said the Lord. "I command you to come out in the name of My Father."

Instantly, Carlo's body dropped to the floor lifelessly and began to decompose rapidly.

"There, are you satisfied now?" asked Satan, appearing as himself. Once he had been the most beautiful created being in the universe. But now he resembled all those nightmarish depictions from collective human memory—horns, serpentine flesh, black, leathery wings, barbed tail.

"No, I am far from satisfied, Satan," said the Lord. "You know that. I will not be satisfied until you pay in pain and torment for the misery you have created on this planet and in heaven."

"Well, what's our next move, sonny boy?" asked Satan mockingly. Before the words were even out of his mouth, heavy arm and leg manacles and chains wrapped themselves around his appendages. Satan just laughed derisively. "You don't think these chains can hold me, do you?"

Jesus did not answer. But He grabbed Satan by the ear and pulled him outside.

"Say goodby to my Temple," said the Lord. "You won't be back here again."

Outside the Temple, a crowd of people had appeared. They were among those who had accepted Carlo's mark.

"Here is your god," Jesus said to them. "What do you think of him now?"

"We never believed him," shouted one woman.

"Kill him, Jesus! Crucify him!" shouted a man.

"We know you are the one true God," said another.

"Now, now, it's too late for that," the Lord said. "You have had more than one chance. You have made your choice. Now you must follow your lord and accept his fate as your own."

"No, Lord," the crowd cried. "Spare us! Forgive us!"

Instead, Jesus led them all to the edge of town—directly across from the Mount of Olives. There was another great crevice, apparently caused by the great quake. But this one did not lead to a fallout shelter. It did not lead to renewing springs of water or great banquets. It was simply a pit—a deep, deep crater that seemed to have no bottom.

"This is your new dominion," the Lord told Satan. "I'll see you in a thousand years." Jesus shoved the hapless Satan into the pit. He made not a sound on his descent. "Now the rest of you," Jesus said signaling the followers of Carlo toward the pit.

"No, I won't do it!" shouted one man.

"Run for it!" yelled another.

The crowd began to disperse in different directions. There was a flash of light, and a wave of heat. Every one of them met the same fate as Muhammad's army. Now it was time to find that false prophet, Pope John Paul III.

Jesus went back to the Temple. It was time to throw out all of the phony peacemakers. It was time to chase out the New Age Pharisees. It was time to redeem the structure itself—to cleanse it and purify it.

Jesus knew exactly where the pope was hiding. He was not in his office. He was not in the sanctuary. The Lord descended down into the lower floors and into Carlo's below-ground control bunker—the place from which he had directed World War III, safe from bombs and radiation. There the Lord found the pope, huddled alone and quivering in a corner.

"You know, Lord, I have devoted my whole life to your teachings," he said. "I have prophesied in Your holy name. I was misled by Carlo. I believed his power was Your power. Spare me, O Lord. I pledge my life to You."

"Even with your lord in the pit, you are still a liar and a coward," Jesus said. "In many ways you are worse than Carlo. He, at least, had the excuse of being possessed by Satan. There is no demon in you but your own lust for power. Who possesses you but yourself?"

"Lord I am heartily sorry for having offended you," said the pope. "I beg your forgiveness. Aren't you the God of forgiveness? What about my second chance?"

"You knew the truth but purposefully chose the lie," Jesus said. "Not only did you make this choice for yourself, but you used your position and power and the trappings of the church to deceive many. There is no forgiveness for you—only death. Come with me."

Jesus led the pope through the streets of Jerusalem to the pit.

"Go now," Jesus said.

"I can't," said the pope.

"Go now!" said Jesus in a commanding tone that frightened the pope, who lost his footing on the precipice and tumbled down into the pit, screaming like a banshee as he fell.

Jesus shook the dust off his feet, wiped his hands off and strode back to the Temple.

"Come out now all you sinners!" he commanded.

Slowly at first, the last vestiges of the U.N. forces, heretical priests and others began streaming out.

"Come out now!" Jesus shouted.

He knelt down and prayed quietly to the Father to cleanse the edifice. The ground beneath the Temple shook and rose several feet into the air. Cracks in the walls disappeared. The building was changing. The ground beneath it was rising. Every molecule that made up this once holy building that had become the center of unthinkable abominations was being renewed, remade, reshaped. Within minutes, the Temple was glorified. Gone were the worldly trappings. Gone were any reminders of Carlo's reign. Gone were all the unclean spirits that had made this place their home for the last seven years.

Now the reborn Temple stood above the rest of the world proudly. This would be Jesus' home and ruling place for the next thousand years.

"What will become of us?" asked one of the U.N. guards.

"Go and guard your master!" Jesus said pointing toward the pit.

Off in the distance, Jesus heard cannon fire. This war was not over. Even without their evil ruler, men still chose the path of rebellion. This force he knew to be a large one—the remnants of the Asian coalition, which had retreated across the Jordan River, escaping the worst of Carlo's nuclear wrath. Now they were coming back, thinking their regrouped force would be more than a match for Carlo's depleted army.

The Lord looked heavenward. As he did, the sky lit up and the temperature increased dramatically throughout the city. A mushroom cloud of immense magnitude, rising thousands of feet into the air, was seen off in the distance. The cannon fire was heard no more.

When Jesus came back, "clouds" of saints were seen with Him in the skies. They witnessed these final battles and confrontations on earth, but they did not participate in them. Instead, they waited—waited for instructions from their Lord.

Now, Jesus knew, it was time to take care of them. These were the believers swept off the face of the earth before this seven-year period of trial and tribulation. Jesus promised that they would return with him, and they had. But He wanted to prepare a special place in this new world for them, as had been promised by the prophet John in Revelation 21:9-27:

"And one of the seven angels who had the seven bowls full of the seven last plagues, came and spoke with me, saying, 'Come here, I shall show you the bride, the wife of the Lamb.'

"And he carried me away in the Spirit to a great and high mountain, and showed me the holy city, Jerusalem, coming down out of the heavens from God, having the glory of God. Her brilliance was like a very costly stone, as a stone of crystal clear jasper. It had a great and high wall, with twelve gates, and at the gates twelve angels; and names were written on them, which are those of the twelve tribes of the sons of Israel. There were three gates on the east and three gates on the north and three gates on the south and three gates on the west. And the wall of the city had twelve foundation stones, and on them were the twelve names of the twelve apostles of the Lamb. And the one who spoke with me had a gold measuring rod to measure the city, and its gates and its wall.

And the city is laid out as a square, and its length is as great as its width; and he measured the city with the rod, fifteen hundred miles; its length and width and height are equal. And he measured its wall, seventy-two yards, according to human measurements. And the material of the wall was jasper; and the city was pure gold, like clear glass. The foundation stones of the city wall were adorned with every kind of precious stone. The first foundation stone was jasper; the second sapphire; the third, chalcedony; the fourth, emerald; the fifth, sardonyx; the sixth, sardius; the seventh, chrysolite; the eighth, *beryl; the ninth, topaz; the tenth, chrysoprase; the eleventh, jacinth; the twelfth, amethyst. And the twelve gates were twelve pearls; each one of the gates was a single pearl. And the street of the city was pure gold, like transparent glass.*

And I saw no temple in it, for the Lord God, the Almighty, and the Lamb, are its temple. And the city has no need of the sun or the moon to shine upon it, for the glory of God has illumined it, and its lamp is the Lamb. And the nations shall walk by its light, and the kings of the earth shall bring their glory into it. And in the daytime (for there shall be no night there) its gates shall never be closed; and they shall bring the glory and the honor of the nations into it; and nothing unclean and no one who practices abomination and lying, shall ever come into it, but only those whose names are written in the Lamb's book of life."

Jesus looked up heavenward above Jerusalem, and with the wave of his hands created this "New Jerusalem"—a floating, airborne City so bright its glow would light the world both day and night for the next millennium. There his beloved "bride"—his resurrected church—would have great freedom and great powers. Living in glorified earthly bodies, these special raptured beings could visit earth or any other part of the universe, walk through walls, disappear and reappear at will and travel at the speed of their own thoughts and desires, just as Jesus did in His Resurrection body.

In a sense, this special class of beings had the best of both worlds. They could take part in earthly pleasures and also experience a supernatural existence. Like Jesus, in their spirit bodies they were able to be seen, to be touched, to partake of food and to co-mingle with the people of the Earth. And now they had a home of their own in a new Holy City that hovered over the old city of Jerusalem.

Now it was time for those people underground to come out and begin rebuilding this new world. Jesus walked back to the Mount of Olives and the ground opened up. He descended the stairs.

"It is time to come out," he said.

"I'm not sure I want to leave," said Armstrong.

"No, this has been wonderful," said Oved. "How long have we been here?

No one knew the answer to that question. They had lost all track of time. Their watches had stopped the moment they descended. It could have been hours, days, weeks or months, as far as they were concerned. All they knew was that they had never had a more enriching and purifying time in their lives.

But as soon as they reached the surface, some of their old human concerns began to reappear. Almost immediately, Armstrong began to worry about Erin again. No matter how hard he tried to convince himself it was going to be all right, he couldn't stop. No matter how many times he said to himself it did no good to worry, he only worried more.

The sight of the devastated planet did nothing to comfort them. Only Jesus' voice and words had a soothing effect. When they had all emerged from the safety of the cavern, they gathered quietly around Jesus.

"There is no one left on this planet except believers," explained Jesus. "Satan has been bound in chains and cast into the pit for the next thousand years. You have no more excuses to do evil things, and I know none of you desires to do so. But this remains a world of temptations. Even though you now walk with God, talk with God and fellowship directly with God, you are not immune to sin. Remember," he said, "Adam, too, walked in the garden with God. But that knowledge and fellowship did not keep him from sin. Your job is to rebuild this world for the glory of God. I will be here at the Temple to help you. Now go to work."

Armstrong, Oved and Barak looked at one another. Armstrong's men looked to him.

"Well," said Jeremy, "where do we start?"

"I know what I'm going to do," said Barak.

"What's that Isaac?" asked Armstrong.

"I'm going to see Jesus and ask Him what he would have me do with my life," he said. "I would like to work right here in Jerusalem if there is some way I could be of assistance to Him."

"Well," said Gen. Oved, "that's a pretty ambitious agenda. Don't you think everyone will have the same idea?"

"No," said Isaac, "I really don't. You didn't think of it, did you?"

"No," said the general, "to be honest, I didn't. But it sounds like a good idea. If you get an audience with our Lord and He has some use for an old soldier like me, let me know."

"I will," said Barak. "It will always be an honor working

with you, General. What about you, Jeremy? What are you going to do?"

"You know what I'm going to do, Isaac," he said. "I'm going to find Erin. Whatever it takes, I will track her down and marry that woman if she will have me."

"What about you, Ralph?" Armstrong asked Freeman.

"I'm going home to Nebraska," he said. "If there still is a Nebraska."

"Oh, there will always be a Nebraska," said Jeremy.

"I hope so," said Ralph.

Armstrong called the rest of his men together.

"Men, we've been through a lot together," said Jeremy. "You have all served your country and your God well. I want you to understand you're all free to go home, to make new lives for yourselves and to do as Jesus instructed—rebuild this world. I would suggest we set up a camp here in town and help each other out in any way we can. I don't think there are any flights home today, and there may not be any for some time. I know our Lord will provide us with whatever we need to live. But I want you all to know that I am eternally grateful to you for sticking with me. If there is anything I can do to help you—now or in the future—please don't hesitate to ask."

"I have a question for you, Colonel," said Cpl. Tom Johnston.

"Yes, Tom," said Jeremy.

"Where are the telephones?"

"That's just what I was wondering, son," said Armstrong. "That's just what I was wondering."

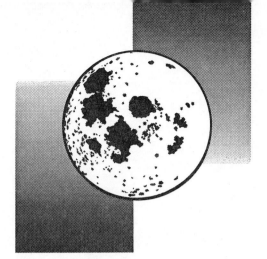

CHAPTER 10

The Promised
Golden Age:
At Last

The phones were working in Jerusalem within a few days. Most of Armstrong's men made arrangements to fly home to the States for reunions with their families. But Jeremy was beside himself. He didn't know what to do. He wasn't sure where Erin was and had no idea how to find her. He even tried calling Zeke at the U.N. in New York, but was told, rather brusquely, he was "no longer here."

Jeremy was tempted to jump on board the first plane back to America, but, not having any clue as to Erin's whereabouts, it didn't seem like a great plan. So, he waited...and waited...leaving messages at the U.S. Embassy in Jerusalem just in case Erin called there looking for information about his whereabouts. He also reported in with various branches of the U.S. military in case there were inquiries from anyone.

Finally, several days later, Jeremy decided he could wait around no longer. He went to the airport with the idea of purchasing a ticket on the next flight to New York. The airport was mobbed with people. In many ways, it resembled a refugee camp full of people wanting to go somewhere but having nowhere to go and no way of getting there. Very few flights were coming in or going out of the country. Carlo's international currency was no longer being accepted for the purchase of any goods or services, so barter or credit were the only forms of valid payment. Still, lots of people were trying to travel.

He fought his way through the crowds of crying babies, men and women sleeping on the floors and furniture, and the constant stream of people in movement. Just as he reached the ticket counter and was preparing to make a deal of some kind, his heart skipped a beat. There, walking toward him no more than 30 feet away, was the woman he was preparing to fly halfway around the world to search for. And she was with, of all people, his old pal-turned-nemesis, Zeke Charlton.

Jeremy was nearly frozen in excitement. He wasn't even sure if he was seeing things. Perhaps, he thought, his mind was playing tricks on him. His feet wouldn't move. Erin and Zeke had clearly not seen him yet. Suddenly, he became conscious of how he looked. He felt his face, forgetting, for the moment, whether or not he had shaved this morning. He had. Before he could convince his legs to move or his vocal chords to call out her name, Erin glanced his way.

She, too, was stunned—too stunned to say anything. Then, at exactly the same moment, they both dropped their bags and ran to each other. Erin literally leaped into

Jeremy's arms. He kissed her eyes, her nose, her lips—all in between long, ecstatic looks at her while he gently held her face in his hands. Not a word needed to be spoken.

"Good to see you, too," offered an uncomfortable Zeke Charlton after several minutes of quiet sobbing by both Jeremy and Erin. They continued to ignore him and everyone else around them, still searching for the words to express what they were feeling.

"Uh...how?" was all a suddenly stuttering Jeremy could muster.

"I don't know," offered Erin. "I don't really care, either. I just want to hold you."

"Oh, don't ever let me go again," said Jeremy.

"I don't plan to," she said. "As a matter of fact, my precious warrior, you are never going to get out of my sight again. So whatever you choose to do with our lives, I'm always going to be right at your side. Now are you going to marry me today and keep me an honest woman or what? I'm not leaving you, so you better marry me at once."

They could hardly stand up for all the exhilaration and joy they were experiencing. Tears flowed, as many from the eyes of the tough special forces guy as from Erin.

"Let's sit down for a minute," suggested Jeremy, whose legs were suddenly shaky.

"OK," said Erin. "By the way, Jeremy, this is Matthew and this is Denise. They helped me survive the last few years. Without them, I never would have made it. They're really special friends."

"Well, then, Matthew and Denise, what can I say? I am

glad to meet you, and I'm eternally grateful to you."

Erin closed her eyes and put her head on Jeremy's shoulder as they looked for a place to sit. There were no seats.

"Well, let's get out of this place," Jeremy suggested. "You guys must be exhausted. I know there are no direct flights. You must have been traveling for days. Are you guys hungry, thirsty, tired?"

"All of the above," said Zeke. "But I have a feeling we have so much to talk about that none of us will be sleeping for quite awhile."

"I think you're right about that," said Jeremy. "I wish I could take you all to some quiet little cafe for cappuccino or something, but there's nothing like that left in Jerusalem. For that matter, I don't know if there's anything like that left anywhere in the world. But we do have plenty of food and fresh water back at our little camp. It's a place to rest. And we've got a great view of the City in the sky."

"Let's go," said Erin.

The "City in the sky" was perhaps the most dramatic visual reminder that the world had fundamentally changed since Jesus came back. The Lord had made many personal appearances in the city and by His own miraculous ways to the whole world. He was beginning to explain how things would be different in this new world. But with a gleaming, illuminated, heavenly City hanging in space over the earthly city of Jerusalem, no one had any doubts that changes were in the offing—not just for Israel, but for the whole world.

This was the "New Jerusalem" spoken of in the Bible—a City so bright its glow lighted the world both day and night. This was the phenomenon recorded by the prophet Zechariah:

> *"And it will come about in that day that there will be no light; the luminaries will dwindle. For it will be a unique day which is known to the Lord, neither day nor night, but it will come about at evening time there will be light. And it will come about in that day that living waters will flow out of Jerusalem, half of them toward the eastern sea and the other half toward the western sea; it will be in summer as in winter. And the Lord will be king over all the earth; in that day the Lord will be the only one, and His name the only one"* (Zechariah 14:6-9).

Inside the transparent walls of this fantastic City lived the saints who had inexplicably disappeared from the face of the Earth before Carlo took over the reins of world power. They lived there, Jesus told the residents of the old city, in new spiritual bodies that allowed them to walk through walls, disappear and reappear at will and to travel at the speed of their own thoughts, just as the Lord Himself had done in His Resurrection body.

Though these saints had not yet visited the inhabitants of the earth, Jesus promised they would soon. Then, families and friends could be reunited. More importantly, these saints in glorified bodies, whom Jesus sometimes referred to as his "bride," would help the people of Earth restore the planet. The people down below—on Earth—living in their old human bodies under the rule of Jesus, would receive guidance and direction from those in the City in the sky. That's what Jeremy and the others were hearing, but it all still sounded a little surreal to them.

Jesus had told them a little of what to expect: "It will be a very different world. There will be real justice—true justice—from now on. Children will not die. War will be unknown. There will be no armies, no defense plants, no military camps. Globally, it will be a time of perfect peace. Hospitals will be shut down. There will be no poverty, violence or crime. There will be no wastelands, no storms, no droughts, no crop failures, no floods. Even the wild animals will be tame and harmless and will no longer devour each other, as Isaiah had promised hundreds of years before (Isaiah 65:17-25).

"This is the time," Jesus explained, "when the lion will truly lie down with the lamb, and they will eat straw together, as Isaiah predicted: *'The wolf and the lamb will feed together, and the lion will eat straw like the ox...'.*"

Evidently, there would be harsh penalties for those who reverted to the vices of the past. Jesus made it clear that He would simply not accept violent crimes, lying and thievery. He referred to Revelation 19:15, in which the Bible says the Lord would rule the world "with a rod of iron." Jesus taught all mankind that this meant he would be a truly benevolent dictator. The days of majority rule were over. The world will be operating under a true theocracy from now on. God will be in charge—and He will be keeping man on something of a short tether for the time being. No violence or taking advantage of each other will be tolerated.

"This is the time of which I spoke when I told My disciples to pray: 'Thy Kingdom come, Thy will be done, on Earth as it is in heaven,'" Jesus explained. "Death will occur only as discipline to the habitually criminal offenders. Life will be greatly extended. The vast majority of you will live for a thousand years."

"Though Satan will be bound in chains, mankind will not be entirely free of temptation, for the people of this time still have an old sinful nature," said Jesus.

"All of you have the Holy Spirit living in you, and a very high level of spirituality is now possible.

"Everything will not be perfect in this new world, but very nearly so. What I taught in the Sermon on the Mount will be lived out through you to a degree never before possible. After a thousand years of near-perfect environment, some of your children will not believe and rebel. This will be immediately judged, and time will be no more. I will then create a new heaven and a new earth, as depicted in Revelation 21:1. Then eternity begins with true 'perfection' realized at last."

Jesus explained to crowds in Jerusalem that this period on Earth would be one of "regeneration." He would be giving the people and the planet new life. He referred to Acts 3:21, in which the Bible calls this time a period of "restitution," or restoring of the Earth.

There was plenty to be restored, that's for sure. Simply

cleaning up the debris—weapons, armor, wreckage of every imaginable kind—would take years. Just burying the dead, especially those who had been killed by nuclear weapons, would require specially trained and equipped people, as Ezekiel had predicted (Ezk. 39:11-16). Jesus set aside a special quarantined burial ground on the east side of what was the Dead Sea. Two-thirds of the world's people were killed in the last seven years—most of them in the last three, He explained. The radioactive waste, the hazardous chemicals and biological warheads He had already cleaned up. Jesus said, "I have already completely renewed the ecological balance of nature to the pre-sin standards. All of the climate changes have been reset to ideal conditions. The whole earth will now have a mild climate, and almost all of the earth's surface will be suitable for agriculture."

But, Jesus explained, as horribly as the physical world had deteriorated in the last few years, man's mind and soul were more desperately in need of restoration and renewal. The environment and ecological balance were restored by a command from the Lord Jesus. Men's hearts are another matter. Everything that had occurred since the creation of Adam and Eve until now was a necessary lesson for the human race. A more lengthy period of retraining was what God had in mind.

It will take a thousand years for man's sinful nature to be finally removed. The people on Earth during the millennium are very much like those who preceded them. They had weaknesses, faults, vices, and were susceptible to the sin nature within. In addition, even though they had been through the most dramatic period of human history and witnessed the Second Coming first-hand, they will still have children. And children, no matter when they are born, can and will be rebellious. As hard as it was for people emerging from the great tribulation to believe, the Lord said there will again be an open rebellion by some of these children toward the end of this Millennium period. Satan will be unleashed once again before his final judgment, so that he will bring out the hidden unbelief and rebellion of the unbelievers at the end of this age. The wickedness of the human heart is a hard thing to comprehend. Even without the presence of Satan, people will go astray. They have no one to blame but themselves. They can't say, "The devil made me do it." All of humanity enters the Millennium righteous and repentant. But some people's faith will grow weak—even while witnessing God's greatness before their very eyes. And they will bear children who will turn away from God—even though they can see Him and have direct access to Him.

It was hard for people shortly after Jesus returned to imagine that there could still be rebellion in a society that literally lived in the presence of the Lord Jesus Christ. But, of course, Adam and Eve had this same relationship with God. Yet they disobeyed Him. They were deceived by pride. They fell. As long as people are born with a fallen human nature, there will always be those who doubt God, even though they can see Him living in and ruling their own world.

That is why Jesus told the people of the earth to continue to study their Bibles. Even though ninety-nine percent of the prophecies had been fulfilled, there were still vital lessons to be learned in order to avoid sin and the trap of a lazy faith.

Yes, the world was more orderly a week or two after the Lord had returned. But people were under control for one main reason—because Jesus had broken their stubborn natures and rebellious spirits with that "rod of iron" depicted in Revelation 19:15-16:

> *"And from His mouth comes a sharp sword, so that with it He may smite the nations; and He will rule them with a rod of iron; and He treads the wine press of the fierce wrath of God, the Almighty. And on His robe and on His thigh He has a name written, 'King of King, and Lord of Lords.'"*

The glow of the City in the sky did indeed provide light to the whole world. Erin and her friends had witnessed this new phenomenon in the States before they left. There was no longer any darkness at night in Montana or in South Dakota. But still, there was something different about seeing the City from Jerusalem. From here you could actually see activity within the City walls. You could almost make out the hustle and bustle of the saints going about their daily business. And the sight of the City itself—not just its glow—was, most people agreed, the single greatest sight human eyes had ever gazed upon.

The colorful gold and jewel-lined streets and passageways, the flow of the living waters, the brilliance of its crystal walls and the absolute peace it all represented, made for a breathtaking sight. Erin, Zeke, Denise and Matthew got their first opportunity to take all of this in as they left the airport and headed to Jeremy's encampment for some rest.

"This is all so fantastic," said Erin. "Somebody pinch me to make sure I'm not dreaming."

"Well, my darling," Jeremy said, "if you're dreaming, I'm having the same dream, so let's just not wake up for a while, OK?"

"I can assure you both this is no dream," said Zeke. "In all the years I've known you, Jeremy, I've never been asked to participate in one of your dreams before—nightmares, yes, dreams no. This is definitely a first."

The camp consisted of a series of U.S. Army tents pitched within a few hundred meters of the Temple in a clearing on the opposite side of where the Mount of Olives had split. Only three or four of Jeremy's men remained, still waiting for flights home. So there was plenty of room for company. Food and water were in abundance, too. There was no scarcity of such basics since Jesus returned. He made them available, but He also warned that this situation would not last. He did not want to create a dependency on free food. People had to work. People had to farm. The economy had to be recreated. In the meantime, he ensured that no one would starve.

Zeke plopped himself down on a cot outside Jeremy's large tent. Denise and Matthew said they were going to turn in and were directed to an empty tent. Jeremy and Erin had a lot of catching up to do, but, before they got started, there was something important on Zeke's mind.

"Listen, Jeremy," he began, "you've been my friend for a long time—through thick and thin. I just want to say how sorry I am for the way I behaved toward you in New York."

"Oh, now, Zeke, you don't have to do this," said Jeremy.

"No, no, I do," he said. "This is important and I had to wait years to say it. I'm just glad I finally have an opportunity to tell you this. I feel very blessed that God has given me this chance. I was out of line. I was lost. I was driven by my career and my desire for success. I sacrificed our friendship for those worldly things. And that's not right. Worse yet, I could have gotten you killed."

"Actually, Zeke, if you meant the things you said back then, you would have ordered me killed," Jeremy said. "That's why I always knew that our friendship—however strained it might have been under those circumstances— had not really ended. You let me go—you let me get out of there with my life. That wasn't what your boss would have had you do. You protected me."

"Yeah, I protected you by getting you sent to the hottest war zone in the history of the world," Zeke said. "Some kind of protection that is. Some friend..."

"Well, you knew how resourceful I was in those situations," Jeremy said. "That's what I was trained to do—survive. And that's all we really had to figure out here for the last seven years. You must have known I would make it after all we've been through together."

"Yeah, I kind of had a feeling that you would pull through," Zeke said. "But...my point is that I'm sorry. I want your forgiveness, Jeremy. I already owed you my life before this. Now I can't even calculate what I owe you."

"Zeke, just having you here—alive—and hearing you say these things, that's all I could ever ask," Jeremy said.

"Well, then, if we're all right, I think I'm going to get some sleep. I know you two have a lot to talk about," said Zeke.

"Zeke, having some time alone with Jeremy would be much appreciated," Erin said.

"Yeah, Zeke," said Jeremy, "I love you and I've missed you, but I think we'll have plenty of time to get reacquainted. Erin and I do have some important business to discuss."

"OK, guys, good night," said Zeke.

"Good night, Zeke," said Erin. Without even waiting for Zeke to clear out of earshot, Erin smiled and asked," So, what's this important business we have to discuss?"

"Well, before we even attempt to tell each other all the things that have been going on in our lives for the last seven years, I have a question that I've been waiting to ask you that entire time," said Jeremy.

"You do?" she said.

"Yes, I do," he said.

"Well, what is it?" she asked.

Jeremy gallantly knelt down before her, looked into her eyes and said:"Will you marry me?"

"Oh Jeremy," she said, I've already said I want to marry you tonight. Please find someone who can give us a Christian wedding."

Then, to their utter amazement, they heard the most

wonderful voice behind them say, "Will I do?" They turned to see the Lord Jesus standing there in all His glory. And standing next to Him were both their parents and families in radiant, glorious, resurrected bodies. The Lord said, "I watched you long for each other with such a pure love during those last horrible days of the Tribulation. It was I who brought you together and kept you both alive for the joy of this hour."

The Lord Jesus Himself performed their wedding, with their parents as witnesses. It can safely be said there has never been another wedding quite like it. They promised their families there would be a great reception and dinner later.

Then the Lord sent the ecstatic newlyweds off to a beautiful villa which he had prepared in a garden. When they came together at last, it was like the melting together of two souls in a fire of passion. All of their pent-up passions and fantasies were expressed in a rapturous union that made their two bodies as one.

As they made love, they experienced the complete fulfillment that can come only from the God-given, self-sacrificing love that cares more about the other's needs than one's own.

Jeremy looked into his adoring bride's eyes as a new day dawned and whispered, "Darling, I think God must have created sex with our total happiness in mind. This is what the world kept seeking but never found."

Jeremy and Erin truly were the happiest of all the happy people on earth. Even in their wedding they had experienced the immeasurable grace of the Lord Jesus

Christ, which can never be earned, merited, or even completely understood...but only received as a gift.

●

Jesus proclaimed an important announcement the next day. Hundreds of thousands gathered around Jerusalem to hear it delivered in person. All over the world, people heard the the Lord's message via His special miraculous powers which made him appear in the sky. His deep, melodious voice resonated all over the earth and was understood by everyone.

"I introduce to you today some very special people," Jesus began. "I refer you to Revelation 20:4-6:

"And I saw thrones, and they sat upon them, and judgment was given to them. And I saw the souls of those who had been beheaded because of the testimony of Jesus and because of the word of God, and those who had not worshipped the beast or his image, and had not received the mark upon their forehead and upon their hand; and they came to life and reigned with Christ for a thousand years. The rest of the dead did not come to life until the thousand years were completed. This is the first resurrection. Blessed and holy is the one who has a part in the first resurrection; over these the second death has no power, but they will be priests of God and of Christ and will reign with Him for a thousand years."

"These special people—my good and faithful servants—are returning to earth today. They are your friends and family members who chose martyrdom over submission to the Anti-Christ and his false prophet. They are legion. And they are coming to help me rule over this new world. They have great insight and a keen sense of justice. I ask you all to welcome them into your communities and look to them as you look to me for answers to your problems."

Jesus was explaining that millions of people who had been persecuted and killed by Carlo during the last seven years were being resurrected to help Him administer His new kingdom. These people would hold special rank and authority in the new society. Jesus introduced some of them in Jerusalem. But they would be reappearing literally all over the world in the next few hours, He said.

This was a tough one for Zeke. He had personally seen that some of these people were put to death. He had been, for a short time anyway, the key architect of Carlo's execution plan. Tears were streaming from his eyes as Jesus explained what was happening.

"I don't deserve forgiveness," he babbled. "I killed those people. How can I be forgiven for that?"

"Zeke, you've already been forgiven," said Jeremy. "We've all committed sins for which we're not worthy of forgiveness. That's why Jesus came to earth. That's why you survived. He loves you and has given you what you could never earn or deserve. Now don't blow it by not accepting that gift."

"Yes, Zeke," said Erin, "remember—the Apostle Paul was a persecutor of believers too, before his conversion."

"Yeah, well, I'm not Paul," Zeke said. "I don't know if I

can take this." He wandered off, choking back his emotions.

But Jesus had more news and more surprises for those gathered in Jerusalem and watching around the world. Not only were those killed during the tribulation period coming back, but so were millions who had disappeared in a moment, in the twinkling of an eye, almost a decade earlier.

Jeremy and Erin looked at each other with excitement in their faces. They had already seen their beloved parents and families.

Unlike the martyrs of the Tribulation period, who would actually live on earth and assume key positions of responsibility under Jesus' authority, these others would continue to live in the celestial Jerusalem. But they could and would make regular appearances on the surface of the planet. They would visit loved ones and offer assistance as needed in the earth's reclamation project.

"Hey, look who's coming this way," said Jeremy. "This is the man I've been telling you so much about. Erin, I want you to meet Major Isaac Barak. Isaac, this is Erin, my favorite wife," he said with a chuckle.

"Erin, you made it! It is such a pleasure to meet you," said Isaac. "I've been hearing about you every day for the last seven years. I've prayed for you with Jeremy a thousand times. There were times when I thought my good friend here was going to lose his mind because he couldn't talk with you."

"Thank you, Isaac," Erin said. "Jeremy has been telling me all about you in the last few days, too. I'm so glad you were there for each other during those terrible days. He says he would not have made it without you."

"Well, to be honest, Erin, none of us would have made it without Jeremy," Isaac said. "His military talents kept us alive. He kept us focused on the Lord. This is a very special man," Isaac offered, putting his hand on Jeremy's shoulder.

"Isaac," Jeremy interrupted, "I need to talk to you about something very important."

"Yes, my brother, what is it?"

"Erin became my wife last night," he said.

"Well, congratulations!" Isaac said, throwing his arms around Jeremy first and then warmly embracing Erin and planting a kiss on both her cheeks. "That's wonderful!"

"Now," Jeremy continued, "I would like you to stand as my best man at our wedding reception and dinner."

"Jeremy, you honor me," Isaac said. "Of course I would be thrilled to be part of that celebration. You know, I have some good news to report, too. It's not nearly as big as your news, but..."

"Oh really, what's that?" asked Jeremy.

"I got a job," said Isaac.

"A job? What kind of job?" asked Jeremy.

"A job on the personal staff of the Lord Messiah," said Isaac. "I'm going to be a priest working right here in the Temple."

"Wow," said Jeremy. "How did that come about?"

"Well, it was easy," said Isaac. "An old friend hired me. You see, I'm going to be working under my old boss, General Ariel Oved. He has been named as one of the chief priests, and I will be a priest with him. The Lord revealed to us both that we are from the priestly tribe of Levi."

"That is wonderful," said Jeremy.

"It's too bad you have to leave, Jeremy," said Isaac.

"Who says I'm going to leave?" asked Jeremy.

"You mean you're not going back to the States?" asked Isaac. "I just assumed you and Erin would want to return to what used to be America."

"No, we decided there's nothing for us there," said Jeremy. "We just want to be close to the Temple and our Lord Jesus. We want to try to make a new home here."

"Well, that's great," said Isaac. "The Lord is going to need all kinds of strong believers to help Him with the hundreds of thousands of pilgrims who will be coming to Jerusalem."

"I'll apply," said Jeremy, "though I don't know exactly what to do."

"Are you kidding?" said Isaac. "You're a great teacher and leader. Millions of people are going to be making pilgrimages to Jerusalem from every country in the world. Virtually everyone must come here at least once a year. This will be the biggest and most important city in the world. People like you will be needed. Just think of how many people from the other hemisphere will be coming—all needing a shepherd to teach and guide them into the presence of the living God. That's a different kind of mission than we were used to in the old days. It's not a political job anymore—it's really spiritual and personal."

"That sounds exciting," said Jeremy, "but I am still as much in awe as anyone just to be within half a mile of the

Lord when He makes an appearance. Do you really think I could be of help?"

"There's no question about it," said Isaac. "The Lord is equipping all of us with the necessary spiritual gifts."

"Stop being so self-critical, Jeremy," added Erin. "You would be perfect for that kind of a mission."

"What about you, Erin?" asked Isaac. "Are you interested in getting back to work, too?"

"Not at all. I'm only interested in having my man's babies," she said clutching Jeremy by the arm.

Jeremy was hanging out in camp with Zeke a few days later, trying to cheer him up. He was in deep mourning, and Jeremy was concerned about him. In all the years he had known Zeke, he had never seen him like this.

"Zeke, you've got to see this thing more clearly," said Jeremy. "Whether you feel it or not, you're forgiven for what you did in your old life. You're a new creature now. He has paid for all your sins. You only have to accept your forgiveness and receive what the Lord has done for you. We were all hopelessly lost and didn't deserve anything but His wrath."

"The words sound good, Jeremy," Zeke said. "I've read them. I've heard them. I've wrestled with them. But it's just not real to me. I still feel every bit as responsible for the horrible deaths of those martyrs as I ever did. I just can't seem to forgive myself."

The two of them were sitting on some old rusted patio

furniture that they had salvaged. There was more hustle and bustle around camp today. In fact, every day, Jerusalem seemed to be coming to life more. There were more flights coming into the city. And the planes were much more crowded coming in then leaving. People were deciding to stay here. It seemed as good a place as any to make a new start for people from all over the world, just as Isaac had predicted.

Furthermore, this was where the action was. The Lord ruled from this city—personally, in the flesh. He appeared daily. Occasionally he would just walk through the city with His entourage. He needed no military escorts, no armed guards. He was God. He could handle any situation that might occur—whether it was an overzealous follower or someone, like Zeke, in need of a special blessing because of an emotional or spiritual problem. Who would want to be anywhere else? There was always excitement here. There was always hope so close to the God of hope and new beginnings. There was always anticipation here. There was always something happening. And today was no exception.

Jeremy sat there concerned about his inability to artic- ulate exactly what Zeke needed to hear. Zeke curled up in his seat, head in hands in a virtual fetal position. Jeremy noticed a woman walking up from behind Zeke. She seemed to be looking at him. Jeremy could tell she was one of those who resided in the heavenly Jerusalem— slightly ethereal, though nevertheless human appearing in almost every way. She walked up to Zeke and put her hands on his shoulders.

"Don't despair, my son," the woman said. "God loves you as much as He did when you were just an innocent little boy in my arms."

Zeke looked up. He knew the voice. But how could it be?

"Mother!" he exclaimed, otherwise speechless.

"Yes, Zeke," she said. "It's me."

"How?" he mustered.

"I'm living up there, Zeke," she said, pointing to the City in the sky. "But it's been so long since I've seen you. And I heard you were troubled."

"Is it really you, Mom?" he asked, holding his mother in disbelief of his own eyes and ears.

"Of course it is, Zeke," she said. "I want you to know that you are forgiven, son. I know what you have been through. I know why you are hurting. I understand your pain and your sadness. I know you are grieving for all those people you persecuted and delivered over to death. But that's over now, Zeke. Jesus died in your place for all of those transgressions. He has put them out of His memory and will never bring them up again. All who are forgiven have also forgiven you. Now shouldn't you forgive yourself?"

Zeke was weeping openly because he finally understood grace. It wasn't the words she spoke, so much as who was speaking them. Zeke just held his mother and cried—big sobbing, man-sized tears that wouldn't stop. Jeremy walked over and held his friend, too. He knew Zeke was going to be all right now.

Several days later, Erin was searching for an apartment. It was an exciting time to be looking. Much of the old city of Jerusalem had been destroyed by the earthquake. As promised by the prophet Zechariah, the city's terrain had been completely changed. It was leveled and greatly enlarged. The new city rested on a high plateau that rose above all the surrounding mountains. The Lord Himself had created beautiful, perfectly coordinated housing with the timeless look of age. The stones of Jerusalem appeared a golden color.

Erin had not find the right condo on this first trip. She decided she would take a break and see what was new in the restaurant district, with its coffee shops and bistros. The new Ben Yahuda Street was hopping with excited visitors. Foreigners were everywhere. She heard Spanish, English, Dutch and Japanese being spoken. "Japanese," she thought, "I sure do miss sushi. I haven't had sushi in at least five years."

She looked around the street for any signs of a sushi bar. There was a French restaurant. Down the street was an Italian place. A Chinese restaurant was right next door. What was that? About a block away, a sign caught her eye. Could it be? It was Mikuni! She walked faster and faster. As the storefront came into view, she was stunned to see what appeared to be an exact replica of her favorite restaurant in Manhattan.

Before she walked in, she stared at the outside—just

soaking in every detail. How did they do it? she wondered. Who did it? She must find out.

"Kinitchiwa," said a familiar voice as she walked in tentatively. It was a bright sunny day outside and her eyes had not fully adjusted to the indoor light. Could it be? "Erin, so good to see you!"

It was him. It was Tony Suzuki—the Christian restaurateur she had feared was dead. In fact, she was sure he had been killed. Tony was a devoted believer who, like so many others, just disappeared one day during Carlo's days of rage and was never seen again. Where could he have been? Had he been hiding like her?

"Tony!" she cried.

"Yes, Erin, it's really me," he said. "What's the matter? You look like you've seen a ghost."

'Well, I was sure you were killed in the great persecution," she said.

"I was," he said. "But by the grace of God, I am back."

"You mean...?" she began

"That's right," said Tony, "I'm one of those people," he joked. "I'm one of the walking dead."

"Oh, Tony, you don't know how glad I am to see you," she said. "I felt so awful that day I came by the restaurant and it was shut down."

"Oh, you just love me for my sushi, that's all," he said with a laugh. "You missed your spicy tuna roll."

"Well, that's true, Tony," she smiled, tears streaming down her face. "But you know it was much more than that. I admired you so much for the church services you conducted in your restaurant on Sundays and for your fearless stand for the Lord even in the worst of times."

"Look, why don't you stop crying and come have some sushi," he said. "You can't believe how good the fish is since the Lord Jesus cleaned and purified all the oceans, lakes and rivers.

"You know, there's nothing I would rather do right now" she said. "I'm absolutely starving. I'm craving sushi like I never have before. But I simply have to get Jeremy. It just wouldn't be right to eat here without him. What time do you close?"

"Erin, just tell me what time you'll be back and we'll be here," Tony said. "I want to see Jeremy too."

Jeremy was very excited about the public wedding reception and dinner. He helped Erin plan it so that families from the celestial Jerusalem would be with their friends on the new earth.

There was no telephone service established between the two worlds. There didn't need to be. Erin found that whenever they prayed, the ones addressed would answer.

Erin and Jeremy prayed and requested their families to come down and help plan the reception-dinner.

In the twinkling of an eye, two women appeared at Erin's side. "Sweetheart," the older woman started, "you didn't think we would miss something like your wedding reception and dinner, do you?"

"Mom!" Erin screamed. "Jackie!" she said, hugging them both, first one, then the other, then both at once. "I've prayed every night you would come back. I didn't really know if you'd be back after being allowed to attend our special wedding."

"I heard your prayers and we came," her mother replied. "We are allowed to come to Earth anytime we wish."

"Oh Mom and Jackie, Jeremy is even more of an angel than I thought," Erin exclaimed. She brought her husband out to them with such adoration in her eyes.

"I'm so happy to know you are here," said Jeremy shyly to both his mother-in-law and sister-in-law. "Have you seen my mom, dad and sister up there?"

Mrs. O'Hara and Jackie looked at each other.

"Why, yes, we have," said Mrs. O'Hara with a smile. "As a matter of fact, they are right behind you."

At that very moment, Jeremy felt hands on his shoulders. He got weak in the knees as he turned slowly and saw his mother, dad and sister, both looking radiant—more alive and beautiful than he ever remembered them. They seemed to have been frozen in time in their most flattering age. Mom appeared older than his sister, as he would expect. Yet, in a way, she was not nearly as old as he remembered her when they had last visited almost a decade ago. But that was to take nothing away from the way his sister looked. While she was always quite attractive, she now seemed to glow with beauty.

"Mom! Carolyn!" he said. "I still can't get used to this miracle."

"Jeremy," his mother said, "I adore your wife. Let me help her now and get more acquainted."

Jeremy and Erin had been married on the evening of June 1 in the year One. (Jesus wanted to start the calendar again from the time of His second coming.) Their reception dinner was planned for June 30th. It seemed like the perfect time to Erin. And Jesus Himself showed up for the dinner on June 30th at 6:30 p.m. and gave His special blessings. The words had such special meaning being spoken by the Creator of the universe.

Jesus had special words for both Erin and Jeremy.

"My son," He said, "I watched you and heard you during those dark days. You walked in faith admirably. I was very proud of your strength and your faith. You are most welcome in my Father's house and you will be given a special mission."

To Erin, He said: "You also have a unique place and role in this new world, Erin. I will bless you with some very special children—some of whom will hold leadership roles in this kingdom for the next thousand years."

Gen. Oved and Isaac had helped make some of the arrangements for this special occasion. Not everyone could expect to be received inside the Temple, let alone by the Lord Himself. But Gen. Oved was happy to do it for his new priestly assistant, Jeremy. And Isaac was happy to do what he could for his best friend. They had become like brothers by battling adversity, cheating death and clinging to life together.

Of course, Zeke was there too, beaming for joy at what

he knew was the happiest days in his good friends' sometimes harried and challenging life. Both moms were there, too. They had stayed around for weeks getting reacquainted with their children. After the celebration days, they, along with Jackie, Carolyn and the dads, would be headed home to the City in the sky. They promised to visit frequently—to just drop in unexpectedly, as it were.

Jeremy and Erin had seven beautiful children—four sons and three daughters. They became great in the service of the Lord, turning many to righteousness.

Jeremy became one of the wise counselors of the Lord's personal staff. He helped train and oversee many of the rulers of the new countries and cities.

Erin became more beautiful as the centuries went by. Her love for Jeremy only grew, and her chief delight was to help Jeremy in all his work for the Lord.

Ariel Oved and Isaac Barak became the most godly and distinguished of the Lord's Temple priests. And the Lord provided Isaac with a beautiful wife from the daughters of the tribe of Levi.

At last the world saw a near perfect environment for the thousand years of the golden age.